PON

The Heart Remembers

Also by Al and JoAnna Lacy in Large Print:

A Prince Among Them
Undying Love
A Measure of Grace
Let Freedom Ring
So Little Time
The Secret Place
The Little Sparrows
Ransom of Love
Sincerely Yours
Until the Daybreak
Blessed Are the Merciful
Secrets of the Heart
The Tender Flame
A Time to Love
One More Sunrise
Beloved Physician

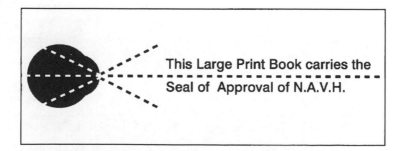

This Large Print Book carries the
Seal of Approval of N.A.V.H.

Frontier Doctor Trilogy
Book Three

The Heart

Remembers

Al & JoAnna Lacy

Thorndike Press • Waterville, Maine

Published in 2006 by arrangement with Multnomah Publishers, Inc.

Thorndike Press® Large Print Christian Historical Fiction.

The tree indicium is a trademark of Thorndike Press.

The text of this Large Print edition is unabridged. Other aspects of the book may vary from the original edition.

Set in 16 pt. Plantin by Elena Picard.

Printed in the United States on permanent paper.

Library of Congress Cataloging-in-Publication Data

Lacy, Al.
   The heart remembers / by Al & JoAnna Lacy.
      p. cm.
   Originally published: Sisters, Or. : Multnomah, c2004.
(Frontier doctor trilogy ; bk. 3).
   ISBN 0-7862-8356-4 (lg. print : hc : alk. paper)
   1. Physicians — Fiction. 2. Colorado — Fiction.
3. Large type books. I. Lacy, JoAnna. II. Title.
PS3562.A256H43 2006
813'.54—dc22   2005031434

This book is lovingly dedicated to
Emily Grace Custer, our "adopted" niece
and a dedicated fan of our novels.
We love you, Emily,
with all of our hearts.

Psalm 33:2

National Association for Visually Handicapped
serving the partially seeing

As the Founder/CEO of NAVH, the only national health agency solely devoted to those who, although not totally blind, have an eye disease which could lead to serious visual impairment, I am pleased to recognize Thorndike Press* as one of the leading publishers in the large print field.

Founded in 1954 in San Francisco to prepare large print textbooks for partially seeing children, NAVH became the pioneer and standard setting agency in the preparation of large type.

Today, those publishers who meet our standards carry the prestigious "Seal of Approval" indicating high quality large print. We are delighted that Thorndike Press is one of the publishers whose titles meet these standards. We are also pleased to recognize the significant contribution Thorndike Press is making in this important and growing field.

Lorraine H. Marchi, L.H.D.
Founder/CEO
NAVH

* Thorndike Press encompasses the following imprints: Thorndike, Wheeler, Walker and Large Print Press.

Prologue

When the challenge of the Western frontier began luring men and women westward in the middle of the nineteenth century, they found a land that was beyond what they had imagined. From the wide Missouri River to the white-foamed shore of the Pacific Ocean, wherever they settled, they clung to the hope of a bright new beginning for their lives.

Often their hopes were dashed by fierce opposition from the Indians who had inhabited the land long before them. At times there was also struggle for survival against the hard winters and the loneliness of the vast frontier.

Those determined pioneers who braved the elements, the loneliness, and the attacks of the Indians proved themselves to be a hardy lot and were unknowingly entering upon a struggle that would ultimately give their descendants control of half a continent.

In his book *The Winning of the West,*

Theodore Roosevelt said, "The borderers who thronged across the mountains, the restless hunters, the hard, dogged frontier ranchers and farmers, were led by no one commander. They were not carrying out the plans of any far-sighted leader. In obedience to the instincts working half-blindly within their hearts, they made in the wilderness homes for their children."

These commendable accomplishments, however, were not without tremendous cost of life. Of all the perils confronting the settlers of the Wild West, serious illness, injuries from mishaps of countless number, and wounds from battles with Indians and outlaws were the most dreaded. The lack of proper medical care resulted in thousands of deaths.

The scarcity of medical doctors on the frontier in those early years made life extremely difficult and sometimes unbearable.

As towns were being established in the West, little by little, medical practitioners east of the Missouri River caught the challenge of the frontier and headed that direction.

Communities that grew around army posts and forts had the military doctors to care for them. But many towns had no doctors at all. However, as time passed, this improved. By the mid-1870s, towns of any size at all had at least one doctor. The larger towns had clinics, and a few even had hospitals.

Often the frontier doctor had to travel long distances at any hour — by day or night — in all kinds of weather. Time and again the doctor's own life was in jeopardy. He might ride on horseback or drive his buggy thirty miles or more to a distant home in the mountains, to a home in a small settlement on the prairie, or to a ranch or farm where he would care for a patient.

He would perform surgery when needed, set broken bones, deliver a baby, or administer necessary medicines. Most of the time, he would sit with his patient for hours before leaving his or her side, then sleep on the return trip while his horse found the way home.

Quite often the frontier doctor's only remuneration consisted of fresh vegetables from a garden, maybe a jar or two of canned corn or beans, a plucked chicken, or a chunk of beef cut from a recently-slaughtered steer. Not everyone had sufficient funds with which to pay him.

The successful frontier doctor was not

only a hardy man, but was obviously dedicated to his profession.

In this Frontier Doctor trilogy, we will tell our readers three stories involving just such a physician.

Introduction

In our third book of the Orphan Train trilogy, *Whispers in the Wind*, we introduced teenagers Dane Weston and Tharyn Myers, who were orphans living on the streets of New York City in the spring of 1871. Dane, who had just turned fifteen, had endeared himself to thirteen-year-old Tharyn by risking his own life to save hers, and soon they became very close, calling each other brother and sister.

After a lengthy period of separation — during which they both realized their feelings for each other went deeper than a brother-sister relationship — they eventually found each other, and Tharyn accepted when Dane proposed marriage. The story of the extraordinary events leading up to their marriage was told in *One More Sunrise*, book one of the Frontier Doctor trilogy.

In the second book, *Beloved Physician*, Dane and Tharyn were married in June 1881.

At the same time, there was an Indian uprising in the area, led by a few renegade Ute chiefs. One of these renegades was Chief Tando, whose village was in the Colorado Rocky Mountains, not far from Central City.

In the third week of July, Melinda Kenyon — Tharyn's close friend from the orphan train days, who now lived in Denver — was riding alone along the South Platte River. She was captured by Chief Tando and a band of his warriors, who happened to be riding nearby. Leaving evidence that made it appear Melinda had fallen from her horse and drowned in the river, the Utes took her to their village near Central City to make her a servant to the chief's squaw and other women in the village.

In Denver, Melinda's fiancé, Dr. Tim Braden, her family, and friends, were all stunned at what they believed was her death. When word reached Tharyn and Dane in Central City, they were equally stunned.

One day in mid-September, Dr. Dane Logan had just delivered a baby on a mountain ranch owned by a family named Drummond a few miles southwest of Central City when a band of Utes led by subchief Nandano were seen stealing cattle from the ranch. A gun battle ensued, and Chief Tando's son, Latawga, was wounded in his left thigh. The others in the band galloped away, but were soon pursued by an army patrol from nearby Fort Junction. Dr. Dane Logan saved the young warrior's life by keeping the ranchers from murdering him and by removing the slug and bandaging the wound lest he bleed to death.

Carrying Latawga on his horse with him, Dr. Logan took him to the Ute village. Latawga was laid on a blanket on the ground, and in the presence of the other Indians, he told his father and mother how Dr. Dane Logan had saved his life.

As Chief Tando was thanking him, Dr. Logan looked up to see a young blond woman running toward him from among the tepees and calling out, "Dane! Dane!"

Suddenly he recognized her and gasped, "Melinda! You're alive!"

Thy word have I hid in mine heart.
Psalm 119:11

For with the heart man
believeth unto righteousness.
Romans 10:10

That Christ may dwell
in your hearts by faith.
Ephesians 3:17

One

The late-morning sun was shining brightly out of the Colorado sky as Melinda Scott Kenyon wove her way speedily through the throng of Ute people toward the tall, stalwart Dr. Dane Logan. She hardly dared to believe her eyes. Was she dreaming once again of making an escape from this village? Or could this really be Dane?

She held her skirt ankle-high and ran for all she was worth, calling out his name. Her eyes widened in pleasant surprise as he called back to her.

Chief Tando, his squaw, Leela, their son, Latawga, and all the others in the village looked on in amazement as their captive dashed toward Dr. Dane Logan.

Dane's words of astonishment, "Melinda! You're alive!" seemed to hover in the air.

Tears streamed down Melinda's cheeks as she skidded to a halt in front of Dane. He extended his hands toward her. She grasped them with trembling hands and cried, "Dane, help me! Help me!"

His dark eyes glinted with elation as he put an arm around her shoulder, then looked at the Ute leader, his brow furrowed. "Chief Tando, is Melinda being held captive?"

Suddenly the warriors in the crowd who had their rifles in hand cocked the hammers, put fierce eyes on the young doctor, and pointed the black muzzles at him.

Melinda stiffened and uttered a tiny cry, staring in numb, open-mouthed horror. Her body began trembling like a leaf in a cold autumn wind, and new fear lanced her heart.

Dane tightened his grasp on her shoulder. "It's okay, Melinda," he whispered. "Stay calm. The Lord will work this out."

Melinda looked up at Dane and took a shaky breath, trying to trust his words. He gently patted her shoulder, then looked straight into the chief's eyes.

Tando gave his warriors a hand signal and said, "Lower your weapons."

As the hostile-eyed warriors were doing so, Tando stepped closer to Dane, meeting his gaze. "We have held Melinda captive since Tando and his warriors found her at the South Platte River many moons ago. We brought her to village to serve Tando's squaw and other women in village."

Dane wondered what Tando and his warriors were doing so far from their village, but he decided not to ask. He said, "Chief Tando, as you can see, Melinda and I are friends. I am asking you to release her to me."

At these words, the warriors once again raised their rifles.

Melinda grabbed Dane's arm and put her free hand over her mouth to stifle the cry that was begging for release.

Tando shook his head at the warriors and grunted, "Lower your weapons!"

While the warriors reluctantly obeyed, Tando gave Melinda a slight smile, then turned to the doctor and said in a pleasant voice, "Dr. Dane Logan, because you saved Latawga's life, I will grant your request. Melinda is free to go with you."

Melinda's eyes brightened as she looked up at Dane.

Leela smiled and nodded, showing her agreement with her husband's compliance to the doctor's request.

From where he lay on the blanket a few feet to the doctor's left, Latawga spoke to the chief. "Father, I am pleased that you are allowing Melinda to go with Dr. Dane Logan. Thank you."

Tando smiled down at his son, nodded, then asked, "Does Latawga know what has happened to Nandano and the other warriors?"

A blank look came over Latawga's dark features.

Dane said, "Chief, your son was down and bleeding as the rest of your warriors were riding away. He did not see that shortly after they were off the farm property, an army patrol from Fort Junction — apparently having heard the gunfire — went after them. We heard no gunfire from that direction, so I am assuming that since the band hasn't returned here to the village, the patrol captured them. No doubt they are being held as prisoners at the fort by now."

Tando's dark eyes dilated as he squared his jaw. He glanced around at the taut faces of his people, then looked at Dane and said, "I have been wrong, Dr. Dane Logan. I thought all white men were enemies of Ute and hated us. You have shown me this is not true. You saved Latawga's life and brought him home to the village, not knowing what we might do to you. Certainly you are not our enemy."

Dane smiled. "There are many more white people just like me, Chief. We are not your enemies. We want to live in peace with you."

Leela and some of the women standing close to her were smiling and nodding.

Tando cleared his throat slightly. "Dr. Dane Logan, I am asking for your help."

Dane smiled again. "In what way can I help you, Chief?"

"Will you go with Tando to the chief soldier coat at Fort Junction so I can make peace with the whites and beg for the release of my warriors? I will gladly sign peace treaty."

Dane ran a palm over his mouth. "It is my understanding that this is what the noble Chief Ouray had attempted to get you to do many grasses ago."

Tando's head dipped for a brief moment, then he lifted it, met Dane's gaze, and said, "This is true."

"I am acquainted with the chief soldier coat at Fort Junction, Chief Tando. His name is Colonel Perry Smith. I will go with you to the fort, but may I make a suggestion?"

Tando nodded.

"I feel it would be wise if we had Chief Ouray with us when we go to talk to Colonel Smith. Chief Ouray is very much respected by our army and our government officials. Colonel Smith will be much more likely to release your warriors if Chief Ouray is present."

"Um. Tando will send a messenger to Chief Ouray immediately with my request to accompany us to Fort Junction. Chief Ouray's village is many miles away in southwest Colorado, near town of Durango. It will take two moons for messenger to arrive there, and two moons for him and Chief Ouray to return."

"All right, Chief. This will give me time to take Melinda to Central City and see that her future husband and her parents are advised by telegraph that she is alive, and that they can come and get her. I will also wire Colonel Perry Smith from Central City, let him know the situation, and advise him that I am bringing you and Chief Ouray to the fort to talk to him."

Tando let a slight smile curve his lips. "Um."

"I will come back here to the village in four days, Chief, so we can travel together to Fort Junction."

Tando smiled once more. "Um."

"Right now I need to put Melinda on my horse and take her to Central City. She and my wife, Tharyn, are very close friends, and Tharyn will be very happy to see her. All of us thought she was dead."

The chief nodded.

"Dr. Dane Logan," came Latawga's warm voice from where he lay on the ground. "Once again, I wish to thank you for saving my life. And I want to thank you for being willing to go with my father and Chief Ouray to Fort Junction."

Dane grinned down at him. "Be sure to keep that bandage clean. I'll take a look at the wound when I return."

The doctor then turned to Melinda. "Ready to go?"

Her face a bit pale, Melinda was still in shock from the events of the morning. "Yes. I sure am."

Dane took her by the hand and led her to his faithful gelding, Pal. He hoisted her into the saddle, then turned to Tando. "Chief, I notice a cool breeze has come up. Could one of the women spare a shawl for her to wear?"

Leela removed her own shawl and handed it to Dane. He thanked her and handed Melinda the shawl. When it was around her shoulders, he swung up behind her.

Melinda smiled down at Leela. "Thank you."

Leela nodded. "You are welcome."

Dane looked down at the chief. "See you in four days."

Tando let another smile curve his lips. "Yes. Four days."

As Dane put Pal into motion and headed northward out of the village, Melinda felt as though she were in a dream.

"You all right?" queried the doctor.

"Yes. It's just that after being a captive in this village for so long, what's happening now doesn't seem real."

Dane chuckled. "It's real, all right. I guarantee it."

Melinda twisted around in the saddle and looked past Dane's shoulder at the Indian people standing quietly, watching them ride away. "It's actually true, isn't it? I'm really free! I'm going home!"

"You sure are."

She took a deep breath. "Oh, Dane, it sounds wonderful! *Home*. Truly, there's no place like home! It will be so good to see my darling Tim again . . . and my precious parents!" She took a sharp breath. "Ah, Dane . . ."

"Hmm?"

"Is — is Tim, ah . . . seeing some other woman by now?"

"No. He's still clinging to your memory."

She let out a pent-up breath. "Bless his heart."

Soon they were out of sight from the Ute village. As they rode, Melinda filled Dane in on how she had fallen from her horse into the South Platte River, and was hauled out of the swift current by Latawga. She added that even though Latawga's motive was wrong, she would have drowned if he had not dived in after her.

"Did they hurt you in any way, Melinda?" Dane asked.

"No. They were surprisingly kind to me. Chief Tando did warn me when they got me to the village that if I tried to escape, they would catch me and kill me. Even though I never tried to escape, I was always very much afraid. Living in the village, I never knew what might or could happen. They live a very primitive life."

"Mm-hmm. Quite different than what you were used to."

"True, Dane, but I did learn some things."

"Like what?"

"Well, they have the highest regard for all of nature. Even though they wouldn't let me tell them about my Jesus, they at least believe in creation by the hand of their god, whom they call the Great Spirit. Chief Tando has learned somewhere about

23

Charles Darwin's evolution theory, and rejects it, saying that all of nature coming into existence was not an accident."

"Good for him. If he only knew who the true God is . . ."

Melinda sighed. "Yes. I will say, though, that there is a certain beauty in the simplicity of the way they live, and in the customs they hold dear to their hearts. In many ways, their culture taught me a great deal, and gave me a new love and respect for the land. I know we, as white people, call them savage, but to them their lifestyle makes perfect sense. They are so close to the earth. And there most certainly is great love within their families. Their children are special treasures to them — much like it is with us, but they are more careful to train their children in Ute ways than most white people are to train their children in our ways."

"I think I understand what you mean. They hover more carefully over their children than most white people do."

"Yes. But I'm very grateful to be going back to what we call *civilization*. What I had was a valuable experience, most definitely allowed by God, and now that I'm free, I don't regret it. And neither will I forget it."

Dane chuckled. "I'm sure you won't."

Pal was carrying them through a forest of tall pine trees. After a few minutes, Melinda said over her shoulder, "Dane, I spoke a few minutes ago about the love the Utes have for their children . . ."

"Mm-hmm."

"It was that very love that Chief Tando has for his son that caused him to be so grateful to you for saving Latawga's life, and to agree to let me go with you. I'm no longer a captive because of your kindness and compassion in saving the life of a young Indian man."

"I took an oath when I became a doctor, Melinda. In the Hippocratic oath, there are no racial distinctions when it comes to a physician saving lives. The human race is just that . . . *human.* I swore to always do everything possible to save human lives."

"Of course."

"I'll say this, though . . . I'm glad the Lord let it be my care for Latawga that brought about the change in Chief Tando's heart attitude toward white people."

"Yes. Praise Him for that."

Dane guided Pal around a fallen tree in their path, and said, "Melinda, I can hardly wait to see the look on Tharyn's face when she sees you."

She giggled. "Oh, yes! There are some precious moments coming up, aren't there?"

"There sure are." Dane then told her about the memorial service that had been held for her in Denver by her pastor, and of the flood of tears that were shed by her family, her fiancé, and all of her friends who attended the service.

Melinda swallowed hard. "Oh, it will be so good to see all of them again. What a surprise they are going to have."

"It certainly was a jolt to me when I heard your voice and saw you running toward me. A *pleasant* jolt. But still a jolt."

They were coming out of the forest and heading down a steep path in open country. They saw a herd of deer collected near a large patch of trees below them. The deer looked up at them and bolted into the trees.

They were surrounded by jagged mountain peaks that still carried snow from last winter, and the cold wind that was blowing was becoming stronger and colder.

Melinda tugged the shawl up tighter around her neck and let her eyes stray to the scenery around her. The restful green of the pine and fir patches were there, and the cool gray of the crags along the edges of the various canyons. Bold and rugged indeed were the rocky peaks around them, some with fleecy clouds resting on them. She saw a sailing eagle in the blue sky. The cold wind carried with it the incense of pine.

"Melinda," said Dane, "when we get to Central City, I'll take you to our house so you can rest. I'll go wire your parents and Tim, then, and let them know you're still alive."

She nodded without looking back at him. "Thank you." A tired sigh escaped her lips, and she felt herself finally relaxing. *I'm going home!* she thought. *I'm really going home!*

She closed her eyes and offered a silent prayer of thanksgiving to her Lord.

At the doctor's office in Central City, it was almost three in the afternoon. Tharyn Logan had several patients sitting in the waiting area. As a certified medical nurse, she had taken care of those patients who had come in during the day that she could, but at the moment, everyone in the office needed a doctor's attention, and Dr. Robert Fraser was out of town for the day.

Tharyn was concerned that Dane had not yet returned from the Drummond ranch. She wondered if there had been un-expected complications in the delivery of Sherrie Drummond's baby.

At three o'clock, Tharyn left her desk and moved to the waiting area. Three mothers were holding small children who were crying and fussing. All others were adults.

"Folks," said Tharyn, "I feel sure that Dr. Logan will be here very soon. I've done everything I know to do to make you and these hurting children as comfortable as possible."

"We know that, dear," said an elderly woman, who was suffering from a problem in her abdomen.

"We realize your husband would be here now if he could, Mrs. Logan," said a young mother. "Thank you for your kindness."

"I appreciate your patience," Tharyn said softly. "It sure helps to have patient patients."

There were smiles and a few chuckles.

The sunny September day had turned quite cold by the time Dane and Melinda topped a rise and the town of Central City spread out below them. The wind off the mountains was stronger yet.

Dane saw Melinda shiver and rub her

arms beneath the shawl. "We're finally here," he said. "I'll have you at the house shortly."

He took the pocket watch out of his vest pocket and saw that it was almost three-thirty. "Tharyn may have left a fire burning at the house when she was home for lunch. If not, I'll build one. You can rest comfortably while I go send those telegrams to your parents and Tim."

"Thank you for being so kind to me, Dane."

He patted her arm. "My pleasure. It's just so good to know you're alive. I'll go directly to the office after I send the telegrams, but I'm not going to tell Tharyn about you. I'll let it be a surprise when we come home after closing the office at five o'clock."

"Oh, Dane, you're sneaky!" Melinda felt goose bumps cover her skin. She turned her head and spoke over her shoulder. "I'm thrilled about seeing Tharyn. And I'm so glad that Tim and my parents will soon learn that I'm alive and safe."

Soon they entered the town, with some of the people on the street waving at the young doctor. Dane waved back each time, and soon he turned off of Main Street. Moments later, he guided Pal into the yard

29

of their home and hauled up at the back porch.

Dane slid off the horse's back, then raised his arms and said, "Okay, Melinda. Let me help you down."

When Dane eased her down and her feet touched ground, her knees threatened to give way. He grasped her arms and said, "Let me help you up the steps."

Melinda's breathing was coming in short spurts as he helped her up the porch steps and into the bright kitchen. It was warm, and a sweet aroma filled the air.

"Oh my," said Melinda. "Something sure smells good."

Dane guided her toward the kitchen table. "Tharyn must have put supper in the oven to cook when she was home for lunch." He pulled a chair from the table. "Here, little gal. You seem pretty shaky. Sit down, and I'll make you a cup of tea. Won't take long, since the stove is already hot."

"Sounds good to me," she said as she eased onto the chair. "Maybe some nice hot tea will help to drive the chill out of my bones." Still wearing the shawl, she ran her hands briskly up and down her cold arms.

Again she sniffed the air. "Whatever's

cooking sure smells good."

Dane grinned. "Smells like roast chicken and sage dressing to me. We'll enjoy it this evening, I'll tell you that much. That sweet little spouse of mine is an excellent cook."

Dane picked up the teakettle, already full of water, and set it on the stove. Then he opened the stove top and tossed in another log. Next, he opened the cupboard and took out a blue and white teapot, dropping in tea leaves from a metal can. He took from the cupboard a cup and saucer the same color and design as the teapot, and set them on the table in front of his guest.

Melinda was still shaking from the chill that the wind had driven into her bones. Dane pulled one of Tharyn's shawls from a peg by the back door and draped it around her shoulders. "There. That should help."

"Thank you," she said, smiling up at him.

While Melinda was warming up under both shawls, Dane went to the water bucket, used the dipper to pour some water into a pan, and washed his face and hands. By the time he had dried himself, the teakettle began to whistle. Picking it up, he poured the steaming water over the tea leaves in the teapot. While she kept her eyes on the steaming pot, Dane poured the tea into her cup.

She smiled at her host. "Mm-mm. This will surely hit the spot."

As she began sipping the hot tea, Dane reached again into the cupboard and brought out a brown sack and a small dish of butter. Taking bread from the sack, he placed it on a small plate, took a table knife from a drawer, and set them in front of her. "I'm sure you're hungry, so help yourself. I've got to go now. The guest room is the first door on the right at the top of the stairs. Please make yourself at home. There are plenty of covers on the bed. Try to take yourself a little nap. Tharyn and I should be home shortly after five, barring some unforeseen emergency, and we'll see you then. Boy, is she ever going to be surprised!"

Tears misted Melinda's eyes as she looked up at him. "Dane, how can I ever thank you for what you did today?"

Dane chuckled and said, "All in a day's work. Now please drink your tea and eat the bread and butter. Get that nap, too, and you'll feel better real soon. I need to go now. I'm sure Tharyn must be wondering what's keeping me."

The doctor hurried out the door, and

Melinda soon heard him put Pal to a trot.

Melinda sat quietly sipping her tea and nibbling at a piece of brown bread she had spread with butter. Soon her head began to droop and her eyelids became very heavy. She drained the cup, carried the dishes to the cupboard, then went into the hall and toward the front of the house. When she reached the staircase, she let her eyes run up to the top. Her knees still felt a bit shaky, and the distance to the top of the staircase just seemed too far.

She turned and looked into the beautiful parlor. There was a soft-looking sofa near the fireplace, which had no fire. But on a chair near the sofa two folded blankets lay. There was a pillow at each end of the sofa. Using both shawls to help keep her warm, she lay down on the sofa, spread the blankets over her, and soon she was fast asleep.

Two

Just before four that afternoon at Denver's Mile High Hospital, young Dr. Tim Braden walked out of the surgical ward washroom, having just finished assisting the hospital's superintendent, Dr. Matthew Carroll, with a difficult lung operation.

Two nurses were passing along the hall, and stopped, asking how the surgery went.

Tim smiled. "Dr. Carroll says we did a good job. Mrs. Lankenshire will live."

"That's wonderful," said one of the nurses. "I have an idea that when you finish your internship next May, Dr. Carroll and the other doctors around here are going to miss you."

"No doubt about that," put in the other nurse. "Every time you work with one of the other doctors in surgery, they always say how good you are."

Tim blushed. "Well, I'm glad they feel that way."

As the nurses walked away, Tim's attention was drawn to one of the hospital's orderlies, who was waving a yellow envelope while hurrying up the hall toward him.

Tim moved in that direction, and as the orderly drew up, he said, "Dr. Braden, this telegram just came in for you down at the receptionist's desk, and Rosie O'Brien said I should run it up to you, since the Western Union agent said it was very important."

"Thanks, Bernie." Tim stepped into a shallow alcove out of the way of people moving up and down the hall, and opened the envelope.

As his eyes fell on the printed words, his throat went dry. His breath was coming in gasps as he stared at the telegram, his mouth working silently.

Dr. Matt Carroll — having spent a little longer in the surgical washroom — came up behind him, stepped around in front of him, and with a frown, asked, "Dr. Braden, are you all right?"

"Dr. Carroll! I just got this telegram from Dr. Dane Logan in Central City, and — and —"

"Yes?"

"Melin— Melinda is alive! Dr. Logan found her in a Ute village being held as a captive. He has her at his home right now! She's alive! She's alive!"

By this time, other hospital doctors, nurses, and employees were collecting at the spot. All of them, of course, were aware that Dr. Tim Braden's fiancée had presumably drowned in the South Platte River, though her body had never been found. Tim's loud words of elation had them all rejoicing, and he had to repeat the message of the telegram over and over as new people gathered.

Wiping tears, Tim said, "Dr. Carroll, I need to go to Melinda's parents. In the telegram, Dr. Logan said he had wired them, too. I need to be with them."

"Sure," said Carroll. "You go ahead. I'm sure all three of you will be heading for Central City tomorrow morning."

"Without a doubt, sir!"

"Keep me posted, okay?"

"Sure will, sir," said Tim, and hurried down the hall. Seconds later, he ran past the receptionist's desk in the lobby, telling her that Melinda was alive, and bolted out the door.

Rosie O'Brien smiled and started to call out her joy at the news to him, but he was through the door before she could do so.

As Tim ran toward his horse and buggy, he spotted a buggy pulling into the lot. In the buggy were George and Hattie

36

Kenyon, Melinda's adoptive parents. Their faces were bright with elation as George waved a yellow envelope at him.

It was just after four o'clock in Central City as Tharyn Logan was sitting at her desk, trying to keep the remaining three patients calm while waiting for her husband to return. The rest of them had gone home, saying they would return tomorrow morning. One middle-aged woman was complaining about the pain she was experiencing from a broken bone in her right hand. Tharyn's attention was drawn to the large window as she saw Dane ride up to the hitch rail outside.

She jumped out of her chair and cried, "He's here! It's okay, folks. He's here!" With that, she bolted out the door to meet him.

Dane was on the ground, lifting his medical bag from the pommel of the saddle when he saw the young woman with the long auburn hair dashing across the boardwalk. He smiled as she threw her arms around him.

Holding him tight, Tharyn asked, "Honey, were there complications in Sherrie's giving birth to her baby?"

"No complications," he breathed into

her ear. "Sherrie and her baby boy are doing just fine."

Tharyn eased back and set her quizzical blue eyes on him.

"But, honey, I expected you back long before now. Most of the patients gave up and left for home, saying they would be back tomorrow morning. We've still got three in there who very much need your attention. What kept you?"

"Well, for now let me say that what kept me longer than expected was that a band of Utes came onto the Drummond ranch while I was there, and bullets were flying."

Tharyn's eyes widened and her jaw slacked. "Oh no! You seem all right. Were any of the Drummonds hit?"

"No. I'll tell you all about it later. Right now let's get in there to those patients."

Dane began with the woman with the broken hand, and had taken care of the other two patients by the usual closing time — five o'clock. They closed the office and stepped up to Pal, who whinnied a greeting to Tharyn. Dane hoisted her up into the saddle, then swung up behind her and put Pal into motion.

"Tell me now, darling, about the Indians at the Drummond ranch," Tharyn said.

While they rode toward home, Dane told her of Chief Tando's son being shot; of the rest of the Ute band being chased by the patrol from Fort Junction, of his caring for Latawga's wound, and of taking him home to the Ute village.

Dane went on to tell Tharyn of Chief Tando's change of heart about white people because of the compassion he had shown to Latawga; of Chief Ouray coming to Tando's village in four days and that he was going with Chief Tando and Chief Ouray to Fort Junction so Tando could make peace with Colonel Perry Smith, sign a peace treaty, and try to get his captured warriors released.

Tharyn hipped around in the saddle, smiled at her husband, and said, "Oh, Dane, I'm so happy to hear this! I hope this will cause the rest of the renegade Ute chiefs to make peace, too!"

"Wouldn't that be great?" he said with a wide smile.

As they turned off Main Street, Tharyn said over her shoulder, "Dane . . . ?"

"What, honey?"

"Something really strange."

"What?"

"Well, today, I've had Melinda on my mind so much in spite of trying to keep all those patients comfortable while waiting for you to arrive."

"Well, sweetie, that doesn't surprise me. You've told me all along that she is still in your thoughts every day."

"Yes, but today, it's been so much more." She was quiet a few seconds, then said, "Maybe it's because of Pastor Shane's sermon last Sunday night about that great cloud of witnesses in Hebrews 12:1. It seemed to bring Melinda closer to me."

Dane nodded. "Well, Pastor made it very clear that those people in heaven are looking down at us, and they know a great deal of what we're doing down here."

"I like the way Pastor put it when he said that great cloud of saints in glory are gathered in God's heavenly amphitheater, looking down at us as we run the race down here in the arena right now. While he was preaching, I was picturing Melinda up there, cheering us on."

Dane pictured the reunion that was about to take place between Tharyn and Melinda, and his heart pounded his ribs.

Tharyn choked a little as she said, "Dane, do you suppose up there in heaven, Melinda knows how very much I miss her?"

They were turning into the yard. Dane

was trying to think of a way to answer, when Tharyn noted the smoke coming from the kitchen chimney at the rear of the house. "I didn't expect the logs in the kitchen stove to last this long."

"Oh. Well, I haven't mentioned it, but I stopped by the house before coming to the office earlier. I put another log on the fire."

"Wanted to make sure your supper was hot when we both got home, eh?"

Dane hauled Pal to a halt at the front porch and slid to the ground. As he raised his hands up to help her from the saddle, he said, "Well, for sure after this hectic day, I want my supper hot at suppertime, yes. But . . . ah . . . sweetheart, I came by the house before going to the office for another reason, too."

"What was that?" she asked as he was lowering her to the ground.

"Oh, I . . . have a little surprise for you."

"A surprise? What is it?"

Dane laughed and hugged her, then looked down into her soft blue eyes. "If I told you, it wouldn't be a surprise, now, would it? Let's go in and you can see it for yourself."

As they were moving up the porch steps, Dane caught a glimpse of Melinda peeking at them from the edge of the parlor window from behind a drape.

He took out a key, unlocked the door, and pushed it open, allowing Tharyn to enter ahead of him.

Melinda was standing in the foyer, smiling at Tharyn.

Tharyn stopped dead in her tracks, gasped, choked, and stared at her, eyes bulging, jaw working. The jolt of seeing Melinda standing there lifted her up on the balls of her feet and stripped away her breath. Her voice came out strangled as she cried, "Melinda! Y-you're alive!"

Melinda rushed to her friend, and the two young women were instantly in each other's arms, tears flowing.

Dane looked on, wiping his own tears.

Tharyn and Melinda stood there for several minutes, sobbing happily, and clinging to each other. When their emotions had settled some, Dane gestured toward the sofa. "You two gals sit down here and talk for a while. I'll go upstairs and build a fire in the guest room and the master bedroom."

Tharyn nodded excitedly. "Yes! Tell me what happened!"

As Melinda took hold of Tharyn's hand and started the story, Dane rushed up the stairs.

Some twenty minutes later, when Dane returned to the parlor, Melinda was just finishing the story.

"Oh, praise God!" exclaimed Tharyn. "Praise His name!"

Dane stood over them and said, "I wired Tim, and I wired Melinda's parents, letting them know that she's alive and with us. I also wired Colonel Perry Smith at Fort Junction about next Monday's meeting with the Ute chiefs. I should be getting replies pretty soon."

At that instant, there was a knock at the front door of the house.

Dane raised his eyebrows. "Hey, that may be a reply or two right now."

Tharyn and Melinda followed Dane as he hurried to the front door and opened it. He smiled at the sight of Central City's Western Union agent and said, "Howdy, Charlie! Did you get a reply already to one of the telegrams you sent for me a while ago?"

"Yes, sir," replied Charlie Holmes, extending a yellow envelope to him. "Dr. Braden and the Kenyons sent this reply together."

"Thanks for getting it right to me," said Dane.

"You're more than welcome, Dr. Logan.

43

I'll bring the reply from Colonel Smith as soon as it arrives."

Charlie looked past the doctor, touched his hat brim, spoke to the ladies, then hurried off the porch and made his way toward the street.

Dane hastily opened the envelope, took out the telegram, read it quickly, then turned to the women. "Melinda, Tim and both your parents will be leaving Denver together at dawn tomorrow. They said to tell you they love you, and are so happy that you're alive. They will come to the office, expecting you to be there with Tharyn and me, since they will arrive in Central City in late morning."

Melinda popped her hands together. "Oh, praise God! It will be so wonderful to see them!"

Dane frowned.

Tharyn saw it. "What's the matter, darling?"

He shook his head, running splayed fingers through his thick hair. "Tim and the Kenyons shouldn't have to have their reunion at the office with several patients looking on."

Melinda shook her own head. "Dane, don't worry about it. Just seeing them is all that matters. I don't care if all of Central City is watching!"

Dane grinned. "Okay, Melinda. We'll do our best to give you at least a measure of privacy."

Melinda and Tharyn embraced each other again.

Dane said, "Ladies, right now, I want us to go back into the parlor and kneel down at the sofa. I want us to thank the Lord together for protecting Melinda, sparing her life, and bringing her back to us!"

The trio entered the parlor together, dropped to their knees at the sofa, and joyful tears were shed as Dane led them in prayer. When he said his amen, Melinda raised her eyes toward heaven and said aloud, "Dear Lord, thank You also for sending Dane to Chief Tando's village so he could find me and take me away from there."

Tharyn hugged her friend with one arm and her husband with the other, squeezing them hard. When they rose to their feet, Tharyn said, "I'll hurry and prepare supper."

Melinda sniffed the air. "It sure has smelled good since I first got here."

"Tell you what, Melinda," said Tharyn, "since the guest room is getting warm, why don't you go up there, and I'll have Dane bring up some hot water so you can have a nice bath. I'm sure you would love to soak and feel clean again."

Melinda smiled at her. "Tharyn, that sounds like a little bit of heaven to me. Like I told you, I could only bathe in the creek nearby the village with two squaws watching me. I haven't had a *hot* bath since they captured me. And I could only wash this dress in creek water once a week."

Tharyn patted her cheek. "Tell you what. Since you and I are the same size, we'll toss these worn-out clothes of yours away, and I'll give you some of mine. Okay, now. Up the stairs you go. I'll be right there with soap, towels, and clean clothes. Dane will be there ahead of me with the hot water. The guest room has its own tub."

Melinda patted Tharyn's cheek in return. "I'm so glad the Lord brought us together way back there on the streets of New York before we rode the orphan train together."

"Me, too, sweetie. Now go on up to your room. First door on the right at the top of the stairs."

Melinda giggled and looked at Dane. "Yes, your husband told me where it is. I just got so sleepy down here in the parlor, I couldn't make it up the stairs. I can make it now."

Melinda slowly climbed the stairs and entered the guest room, which was already toasty warm. The first thing she saw was the bathtub in one corner, near a closet. She looked around the lovely room, which was all decorated with white furniture. She noted the beautiful spread of dusty-pink roses covering the bed, and the curtains at the windows that matched the spread. As she moved to the nearest window and looked outside, she heard Dane's heavy footsteps on the stairs. When he entered the room carrying a bucket of steaming water and a pail of cool water, she said, "This is a lovely room, Dane. I know I'll sleep good here tonight."

He set the bucket and pail beside the bathtub and smiled. "I'm sure you will. I'll let you and Tharyn mix the water so you'll be comfortable."

She thanked him, and he hurried away.

Just as Dane exited the room, Tharyn came in, her arms loaded with sweet-smelling soap, fluffy towels, and a most welcome change of clothes.

Together they poured the water into the tub, mixing it so the temperature was just right. Carrying the bucket and the pail, Tharyn headed for the door. "Okay, sweetie, you just take your time and soak as long as you want. Supper will keep. Enjoy yourself, and come down to the kitchen whenever you're ready. We'll be waiting for you."

"Thank you so much for your kindness, Tharyn," Melinda said with tears misting her eyes. "All that time at the Ute village was like a nightmare. This is like a dream."

Tharyn smiled and stepped into the hall, closing the door behind her. She entered the kitchen and found Dane sitting at the table. As she set the bucket and pail down on the cupboard by the water pump, she sighed and said, "That poor girl. What a horrific experience. I can't even begin to imagine what she's been through."

Dane reached up, took hold of Tharyn's hand, pulled her onto his lap, and nuzzled her neck. "I know, sweetheart. She seems to be getting over it already, though. And she told me she has learned a lot from the Indians about their love for the earth, and all. But I'm so thankful to the Lord that she doesn't have to be there any longer. I know she'll be so happy to see Tim and her parents . . . and to go home."

"Home will look mighty good to her, I'm

sure, my love. Truly, there is no place like home. Be it a palace or a humble shanty, home is truly where the heart is."

Dane kissed her soundly. When he released her, he said, "This home is sure where *my* heart is — because *you* are here."

The next morning, Dane, Tharyn, and Melinda arrived at the office half an hour before time to open, and Melinda took a seat in the waiting area while doctor and nurse prepared for the day.

Ten minutes later, there was a knock at the door. Tharyn was at her desk. She looked through the window and saw that it was Western Union agent Charlie Holmes. She hurried to open the door and said, "Good morning, Charlie."

Charlie touched his hat brim and smiled. "Good morning, Mrs. Logan. I have the telegram here for Dr. Logan that he has been expecting from Colonel Perry Smith at Fort Junction."

Dr. Dane came into the office from the back room and saw Charlie. "Hey! Is that my telegram from Colonel Smith?"

"Sure is," said Charlie.

Dane rushed up and took the envelope from Holmes. "Thank you, Charlie."

As Charlie turned and walked down the boardwalk, Tharyn closed the door while her husband tore the envelope open. Melinda left her chair and stepped up beside Tharyn.

The women waited for Dane to read the message. When he had finished, he smiled and said, "Colonel Smith says he is very happy to hear that Chief Tando wants to sign a peace treaty with the United States government. He is glad that Tando is willing to come to Fort Junction to do the signing, and that Chief Ouray is coming with him."

"That will make a lot of people happy," said Melinda. "I know it will make Chief Tando's squaw happy. Leela shared with me many times that she feared if her husband didn't cease his war against the whites, the tribe would one day be wiped out by the army."

"This is so good," put in Tharyn. "What else does the colonel say, darling?"

"He says he has advised General Joseph G. Dayton by wire, who is presently at Fort Laramie, Wyoming. General Dayton is coming to Fort Junction to be there for the signing of the peace treaty." Dane looked at Melinda. "General Dayton is the top army official over the forts in

Colorado, Wyoming, and Montana."

Melinda nodded. "It's good that he will be able to be there."

"Yes. Very good. It was General Dayton who led in the signing of the peace treaty several years ago when Chief Ouray made peace with the majority of the Ute chiefs. Colonel Smith also says that he is sending a twelve-man cavalry unit to escort the two chiefs and myself to the fort. The unit will be led by Captain Darrell Redmond, and will arrive late Sunday afternoon at Tando's village. They will camp at the village for the night, and be ready to move out when I get there Monday morning."

Tharyn sighed. "I feel much better about you going to Fort Junction with the two chiefs, accompanied by the cavalry unit, darling."

Dane nodded. "Yes. Me, too."

Melinda returned to her chair in the waiting room, which was positioned so she could see through the large window whenever Tim and her parents pulled up to the hitch rail.

Dane returned to the back room, and Tharyn sat back down at her desk.

The first patients to appear were those who had been there to see the doctor the day before.

Time passed slowly for Melinda as patients came and went while she kept an eye on the hitch rail out front. While sitting there, Melinda observed the patients, listening as they stepped up to the desk and talked to Tharyn. She marveled at how far people came from mountain towns and ranches all around to be treated by Dr. Logan. She was especially surprised when she heard one family who came in say they were from a small town fifty miles to the northwest. They added that two towns they passed through to get to Central City had doctors, but they liked Dr. Logan best.

Melinda smiled to herself and thought, *Dane probably has a lot of patients who pass up other doctors to come to him.*

Three

It was almost eleven o'clock, and Melinda Kenyon was still sitting in the waiting area of the doctor's office anticipating the arrival of Tim Braden and her parents. She had watched patients come and go, while keeping an eye on the hitch rail outside. At the moment, she was the only person in the waiting area.

Tharyn Logan was at her desk, doing some paperwork while her husband was with a patient in the back room, when she heard voices outside the door and looked up to see a young couple enter with the husband carrying their daughter, who was very pale and in a great deal of pain.

Melinda watched as Tharyn rose to her feet and said, "Good morning. I'm Dr. Logan's wife and nurse, Tharyn. It appears we have a sick little girl here."

"Yes," said the father. "Is Dr. Logan in?"

"Yes. He's with a patient at the moment. Please sit down and let me get some information from you."

The couple eased onto the two wooden chairs in front of the desk, with the father still holding the child. When Tharyn sat down, he said, "Mrs. Logan, I'm Ben McDonald. This is my wife, Clara, and our daughter's name is Robin. She's ten years old. We live in Nederland, which you may know is a town some fifteen miles north of here."

Tharyn was writing as Ben spoke. She paused and looked up at him. "Yes. I haven't been to Nederland yet, but they tell me it is a nice town. I'll get your address and other pertinent information from you later. Right now, tell me about Robin's illness."

"Her stomach's been hurting for about twenty-four hours," said Clara. "Her pain has gotten worse this morning, and her stomach is quite distended. Our neighbors in Nederland recommended we bring her to Dr. Logan."

Tharyn laid the pencil down and rose to her feet. "Let's take Robin to the back room."

The McDonaldses followed Tharyn into the back room, where they saw four sections, each surrounded by curtains. They could hear male voices in section number one as Tharyn led them to number four.

When they stepped in, Tharyn moved up to the examining table and said, "Lay her down here, please, Mr. McDonald. I want to check her over."

Ben carefully placed his little girl on the table. Robin winced, bit her lower lip, but did not cry out. Tharyn laid a palm on the child's brow. "She definitely has a fever."

Robin watched as her parents stood by and the nurse examined her swollen midsection.

Going over the child's stomach with tender, experienced hands twice, Tharyn looked at the anxious parents and said softly, "Robin must have peritoneal surgery immediately."

Clara frowned. "What does that mean?"

"The abdominal cavity is lined with a thin membrane, which is called the peritoneum. It encloses the stomach, intestines, liver, and gallbladder. Peritonitis is the acute or chronic inflammation of the peritoneum. I assume she hasn't had this before."

Clara shook her head. "No."

"Then it's acute. Peritonitis is caused by invasion of bacteria or some kind of foreign matter from elsewhere in the body, which has caused infection. This is why her stomach is distended. There is obviously a localized abscess in the peritoneum which must be incised. Dr. Logan will have to open her up, assess the damage, and locate the source of the infection. Don't worry about it. He will know what to do, and will take care of it. The treatment, once he has established the source, will include antibiotic therapy."

The parents looked at each other, concern showing in their eyes.

"Wait here," said Tharyn. "I'll go alert the doctor and see how soon he can get to Robin."

Tharyn hurried out of the curtained section. The parents each took hold of one of their daughter's hands and tried to calm her fears.

Tharyn stepped up to section number one and said in a low voice, "Doctor, we have a ten-year-old female patient with peritonitis. She's in a great deal of pain. She's had it for some twenty-four hours."

"Come in," came Dr. Dane's invitation.

Tharyn stepped in and saw that her husband was wrapping a bandage on the hand of the elderly man who had come in about half an hour earlier.

Dane said, "I'm almost through. Is the child's midsection distended?"

"Yes."

Still wrapping the bandage, Dane said, "All right. I'm almost finished. Go ahead and prepare her for surgery. I'll be there in less than five minutes."

Seconds later, Tharyn entered section number four. Running her gaze between the anxious mother and father, she said, "I must prepare Robin immediately for the surgery. Doctor will be ready in a few minutes. I'll need both of you to go sit in the waiting area. She'll be fine, believe me."

Both parents leaned down, and each kissed one of their daughter's cheeks. Clara said, "Don't be afraid, sweetheart. You heard the nurse say you will be fine. Mama and Papa will be right out there in the office."

Tears were in Robin's eyes, but she managed to nod and give them a brief smile.

"If other patients come in while you're waiting," Tharyn said, "will you tell them that I'm assisting the doctor with the surgery on your daughter, and that I'll return to the office as soon as possible?"

Both parents nodded and walked away slowly.

While Tharyn was with Robin and her parents in the back room, Melinda was doing her best to be patient as she sat in the waiting area. But to her, time seemed to drag.

She kept glancing out the window for any sign of Tim and her parents, then at the clock on the wall above Tharyn's desk. She wondered if the clock was in need of repair. The hands seemed to move so slowly.

Unable to sit still another minute, she rose to her feet, stretched her back, then circled the empty room several times, always stopping at the large window to peer anxiously at the street and hitch rail. Each time she surveyed the street, there was no sign of her loved ones — and she took another slow walk around the tidy room.

She was just sitting back down on her chair when she saw Ben and Clara emerge from the back room, and she heard them talking about the impending surgery on their little girl. She could see that they were on edge. The elderly gentleman with the bandage on his hand moved on past them and out the door.

As Ben and Clara sat down near her, Melinda said, "Mr. and Mrs. McDonald, my name is Melinda Kenyon. I was here when you brought your little Robin in. Do I understand correctly that she's about to undergo surgery?"

"Yes," said Ben. "Mrs. Logan called it peritoneal surgery. But she assured us that Robin will be all right. Dr. Logan is about to do the surgery right now."

Melinda pressed a smile on her lips. "Well, let me assure both of you that Robin is in the best of hands. Dr. Dane Logan is an excellent surgeon."

Clara took hold of Ben's hand. "Thank you, Miss Kenyon. It is *Miss* Kenyon, isn't it?"

"Yes, ma'am. I'm waiting right now for my fiancé and my parents to arrive."

Even as she spoke, Melinda's attention was drawn out the large window as she saw a buggy pull up to the hitch rail. Her heart leaped in her chest as she jumped to her feet and bolted for the door. "There they are now! They're here! They're here!"

Outside, George Kenyon was helping Hattie out of the buggy while Dr. Tim Braden was tying the reins to the hitch rail when they saw Melinda burst through the door, tears flowing.

Tim vaulted the rail, gasping, "Oh, thank God! Thank God! Melinda, sweetheart, I love you!"

"I love you, too, darling!" she cried as he wrapped her in his arms and kissed her soundly.

59

They clung to each other, both weeping for joy.

When George and Hattie drew up, tears flowing from their eyes, Tim let go of Melinda and stepped back so they could embrace her. People on the street were looking on, as were Ben and Clara McDonald from the office window as both George and Hattie took Melinda into their arms.

Tim waited a minute or so, then joined them, making it a four-way embrace.

Melinda caught her breath, and anxious to tell Tim and her parents all about her experiences, found her words tumbling on top of each other. She stopped, took a breath, and said, "I'm sorry. Let me start again."

"Whoa, now, honey," said George with a lilt in his voice, "let's find a quiet place, and you can tell us where you've been, and all about what happened to you."

"Oh Papa, of course. I'm sorry to run on so, but I'm so very eager to tell you all about it. Let's go inside the doctor's office. I'll slow down and start at the beginning."

"Good girl," exclaimed George, giving his daughter another quick hug.

Taking Tim's arm, Melinda retraced her steps back inside the office while her parents followed.

Ben and Clara were seated once again, but smiled as the group came in. Melinda introduced Tim and her parents to the McDonaldses, explaining that Dr. Logan and Tharyn were doing surgery on their ten-year-old daughter at the moment. She then said to Ben and Clara, "You can tell that we're having a reunion here. You'll understand it all when you hear me tell my story to Tim and my parents."

Ben said, "Maybe we could go elsewhere, so —"

"Oh, no," Melinda said. "You need to be right here when Dr. Logan comes out to tell you about Robin's surgery. We'll just go over here in the corner."

The foursome sat down together with Melinda facing them, and George, Hattie, and Tim each touching her as she slowly related her story, starting with her fall into the South Platte River. Ben and Clara listened intently.

As Melinda told the story in detail, every eye was glued to her, and they hung on every word.

When Melinda finished the account, tears streamed down Hattie's face and a small sob broke the silence. "Oh, Melinda, how courageous of Dr. Logan to tell Chief Tando he wanted to take you with him!

And how grateful we are for our heavenly Father's faithful care of you all of this time! We — we thought you had drowned . . . that the river had claimed your life. What a marvelous miracle to find you alive and well! I — I guess in one sense we owe Latawga a debt of gratitude. He did save you from drowning."

Melinda drew a shuddering breath and wiped tears. "Yes, he did, Mama. And I thanked him for that. But I have no desire to ever see that village again."

George wiped a palm over his mouth. "Well, those Indians made a servant of you, honey, but they did feed you, and they never harmed you. I'd at least like to tell them that I appreciate this. And I'm sure Tim does, too. Maybe Dr. Dane would accompany Tim and me to the village, and we could express our appreciation to them."

Tim was holding Melinda's hand. "I'd be happy to ride with you and Dr. Dane to the village, Mr. Kenyon. The chief's son saved Melinda from drowning, and in that sense, also gave *me* my life back. Or if Dr. Dane would tell us that our going to the village would not be good . . . . maybe next time he sees Chief Tando and his son, he could convey our appreciation for us."

Just then the back room door came open, and Dr. Dane appeared with a smile on his face. He glanced toward Melinda and her small group, and his smile broadened as he nodded at them, then said to the anxious parents, "The surgery went well, and Robin will be fine. I found the source of the infection, and it's taken care of."

Clara's eyes misted. "Oh, thank God!"

Dr. Dane looked at Clara. "I'll give you some medicine to ease Robin's pain for the next few days, and I'll give you instructions on how to keep the incision from getting infected. She's coming out from under the ether now. I suggest that you find a way to cushion the ride home for her. I'll come to Nederland in a couple of weeks and remove the stitches."

Tharyn came from the back room carrying Robin, and soon the couple drove away with their drowsy daughter in Clara's arms on the back seat of the buggy.

The Logans, the Kenyons, and Dr. Tim Braden then had a good time rejoicing in Melinda's return. The Logans closed the office and led the rest of them as they walked to a nearby café.

When they first began eating, George brought up the gratitude he felt toward

63

Latawga and Chief Tando. When he asked Dr. Dane if he would accompany them to the village so both he and Tim could express their gratitude, Dr. Dane said, "I really don't think it would be wise for Melinda's father and her husband-to-be to present themselves at the village, though your intentions are good. Tell you what, I'll be seeing Latawga and the chief on Monday. I'll express your appreciation to them for you."

George and Tim accepted this, and thanked Dr. Dane for doing this for them.

As lunch went on, Dr. Dane said, "When we're done here, I'd like to take all of you to the parsonage so you can meet Pastor Mark Shane and his wife, Peggy. Pastor Shane has had the church praying for you all as you've carried the grief of Melinda's death."

"Bless his heart," said George. "I'd love to meet him and his wife."

"We'd have let the Shanes know Melinda was alive yesterday, but they've been out of town and were to arrive back this morning. They'll sure rejoice when they get to meet the living Melinda and her loved ones!"

"This will be good," said Hattie. "We certainly want to thank Pastor Shane for having the church pray for us."

"Then we'd best head back for Denver," George said. "You want to ride to the parsonage in our buggy?"

"That'll be fine," said Dr. Dane. "The church is several blocks from the office."

When lunch was over, they left the café and walked toward the doctor's office. They were almost there when Tharyn pointed to a buggy moving along the street and said, "Look, Dane. There's Pastor and Peggy now. They must just be getting back to town."

"Sure enough," said Dane, and stepped into the street, waving his arms at the Shanes. Tharyn moved off the boardwalk and stood beside her husband.

The pastor guided the buggy to a halt where Dr. Dane and Tharyn stood. He smiled and said, "If you're looking for a good doctor, mister, I can recommend one."

Dr. Dane laughed. "Really?"

"Mm-hmm. Dr. Robert Fraser. He used to own the practice that Dr. Dane Logan owns now. Dr. Logan's office is right over there, but Dr. Fraser is presently semi-retired. He just works for Dr. Logan when he needs him. But Dr. Fraser is really very good. I highly recommend him."

By this time, both Tharyn and Peggy were laughing.

Dr. Dane motioned for Melinda to come to him. When she drew up, he said, "Pastor Shane, I'd like to introduce you to this fine Christian young lady."

The preacher nodded with a smile, and stepped down from the buggy.

"All right. And just who is she?"

The doctor grinned. "Melinda Kenyon."

Peggy Shane sucked in a quick, sharp breath, her eyes bulging as she looked at Melinda from the buggy seat.

Mark Shane's eyelids fluttered and his shoulders twitched with an involuntary shiver. "Mel— Melinda Kenyon? Tharyn's friend who was drowned — I . . . I mean —"

"Who was presumed drowned, Pastor," cut in Dr. Dane. "But as you can see, she's very much alive!"

Peggy bounded out of the buggy and hurried up to Tharyn and Melinda. "Tell us about it!"

"Yes!" said the pastor. "This is wonderful! Tell us!"

Dr. Dane said, "Let me introduce you to these people, first, then I'll tell you the story." He called for Dr. Tim and the Kenyons to step up, and made the introductions, then told them Melinda's story.

The Shanes marveled at how the Lord

had used Dr. Dane to free Melinda and to bring Chief Tando to the place where he was willing to sign the peace treaty.

The pastor said, "I'm sure going to tell the story to my people at church on Sunday morning!"

Good-byes were said, and when the Shanes drove away, George said, "Well, we'd better head for Denver."

Tharyn and Melinda clung to each other for a long moment, tears flowing. Tharyn wiped tears and said, "Melinda, we can work out the details by mail, but let's agree to get together again real soon."

"I'm all for that!"

Melinda then turned to Dr. Dane with tears still flowing and embraced him. The Kenyons and Dr. Tim Braden also thanked him, and Dane and Tharyn stood in front of the office, waving as the Kenyon buggy drove away.

The next day was Saturday, and the Logans were kept very busy at the office all day.

On Sunday morning, the people of the church indeed rejoiced when Pastor Mark Shane told them that Melinda Kenyon was alive, and explained the story in brief, including the upcoming signing of the peace treaty. There was much rejoicing.

After the service, Dr. Robert Fraser and his wife, Esther, approached Dr. Dane and Tharyn in the foyer as they were about to leave. "Hey, you two!" Dr. Fraser said. "Not so fast! Esther and I are so thrilled at the good news. We want to hear the details of Melinda's story."

Dr. Dane smiled. "Well, that will take a little while."

"No matter," said Esther. "I've got a nice big roast in the oven at home. Come and eat dinner with us, and Robert and I will get to hear every detail. Okay?"

Dane and Tharyn looked at each other.

She said, "Sounds good to me, darling."

Dane chuckled and set his dark eyes on Esther. "Sounds good to me, too!"

At the dinner table, Dane was asked to pray over the food, and as soon as they started eating, Dr. Fraser said, "Okay, we're all ears."

The Frasers rejoiced over and over as Dane told the whole story. They also rejoiced when they were told the details of how Chief Tando had shown a change of heart toward white people, and was willing to sign the peace treaty with the United States government.

Dr. Fraser then said, "Well, my boy, since you'll be leaving early in the morning for the Ute village, it seems to me that your assistant here should plan to be at the office all day."

Dane grinned. "I was going to get to that in another minute or so. Will you take over for me tomorrow?"

The elderly physician's eyes were beaming. "I sure will!"

Early on Monday morning, Tharyn waited for her husband at the back porch of their house while he saddled Pal, then led him from the small barn to where she was standing.

Dane took her into his arms, kissed her soundly, and said, "I love you so much, sweetheart."

She smiled up at him. "I love you so much, too. You be careful, won't you?"

"I sure will." He kissed her again, then mounted up and rode toward the street.

Tharyn hurried alongside the house, stopped at the front porch, and watched him trot Pal along the street. When he was about to pass from view, he pulled rein, hipped around in the saddle, and threw her a kiss.

She threw one back, then as he rode

from sight, she said, "Thank You, Lord, for the way You used Dane to help Chief Tando see the error of his ways. And, please, Lord. Keep Your mighty hand of protection on my wonderful husband."

Four

As Dr. Dane Logan trotted Pal out of
Central City, he thanked the Lord again
for bringing Melinda Kenyon back to her
parents and to Dr. Tim Braden. He
smiled to himself as he thought of next
May when Tim would finish his internship at Mile High Hospital. He recalled
hearing Tim and Melinda talking together on Friday and renewing their plan
to marry as soon as Tim was through at
the hospital.

Soon horse and rider were in high
country. Dane studied the mountains directly ahead of him as he headed due
south. He loved the sight of the towering
Rockies boldly cutting their bite into the
blue sky.

Dane thought about the one time in his
life when his parents took him, as a ten-
year-old boy, to northeast New York into
the forested mountain wilderness of the
Adirondacks. He recalled the many scenic
gorges, waterfalls, and lakes. He thought of

how high the New Yorkers thought their mountains were with peaks at just over five thousand feet above sea level, then once again let his gaze roam over the towering Rockies all around him. There stood the vast long chains of mountains, all clad with pines and firs, some speckled with birch and aspens, with peaks ranging from eleven to fourteen thousand feet above sea level, many already capped with snow.

Just as Dane topped the crest of a rise, he caught sight of two riders coming toward him. They were close enough that he quickly recognized one of them as Central City's chief lawman, Marshal Jake Merrell.

Dane then recalled that at church yesterday, Merrell's deputy, Len Kurtz, had told him that the marshal wasn't at church because he was on the trail of a Central City man named Earl Dubose who had slapped around his invalid wife, Dora, in a fit of anger for defending their five-year-old son, whom Earl had whipped far too hard for a minor disobedience.

As Dane drew nearer the riders, he saw that Earl Dubose was in handcuffs and had black and blue marks on his face and his right eye was almost swollen shut. The marshal was leading Dubose's horse.

Marshal Merrell lifted a hand to signal the doctor to stop.

" 'Mornin', Marshal." Dr. Dane squinted at Dubose, then said to Merrell, "Len told me at church yesterday why you were on Earl's trail. What happened to him?"

Dubose glared at the marshal as Merrell said, "Well, since you know why I was chasing Earl, it'll suffice to say that he resisted arrest, and knowing what he did to his wife, I wasn't too gentle in beating down his resistance. I have a hard time with a man who beats on a woman. Especially when she's an invalid."

Dubose glowered at the lawman. "Okay, okay, so I had it comin'. But I don't think I ought to do jail time for it."

"Well, you and I think differently. If you give me any lip, it'll be longer than I'm planning on right now." Then to Logan, "Doc, you got anything in your medical bag that could help take down the swelling in Earl's eye?"

"I do, but I'm on a very important mission right now. Dr. Fraser is filling in for me today. After you lock Earl up, go to the office and tell him to come over to the jail and tend to the eye. Explain that we met here on the road and that's what I suggested you do."

Dubose showed his teeth. "You shouldn't be too busy to tend to a man who's hurtin', Doc."

Dane met his gaze with hard eyes. "Like I said, I'm on a very important mission right now, and I have to keep moving. But I'll say it real plain. I have the same feelings Marshal Merrell has about men who beat up on women. So you'll just have to hurt a little till Dr. Fraser can see to the swelling around that eye.

"Marshal, I'll detain you no longer, but as soon as you have a few minutes to talk to your deputy, ask him about yesterday at church, and the announcement Pastor Shane gave about Melinda Kenyon and the Ute Chief Tando."

Jake looked perplexed. "Melinda Kenyon? She's dead. And what's that got to do with Chief Tando?"

The doctor chuckled. "Well, I'll tell you this much. Melinda's not dead. And Chief Tando is no longer the enemy of white men."

Jake's eyes widened. "What?"

"Like I said, talk to Len as soon as you can."

With that, the doctor put Pal to a gallop and rode away, leaving the two men to stare after him.

★ ★ ★

Some two hours later, Dr. Dane Logan left the dense forest and trotted Pal across the open land toward the Ute village. As he drew near, he saw the dozen army horses gathered inside a makeshift rope corral, and the men in uniform standing among the Indians. All were watching him as he rode toward them.

When Dane drew up and dismounted, Tando shook hands with him Indian-style. The doctor then shook hands with Captain Darrell Redmond, and Redmond introduced his men collectively to the doctor.

Chief Tando then took the doctor to a stately-looking, gray-haired Ute in a chief's headdress, and said, "Dr. Dane Logan, I want you to meet Chief Ouray."

Dane greeted the venerable Ute chief warmly as he shook hands with him — Indian-style, of course.

Chief Ouray said in his deep bass voice, "Dr. Dane Logan, it is a pleasure to meet you, and I want to thank you for the influence you have had on Chief Tando. I am very pleased that Chief Tando and his warriors are now ready to cease warring against the white men, and that he has agreed to sign the peace treaty."

"I'm very pleased at this, too, Chief Ouray."

Ouray nodded. "And I am also very pleased that Colonel Perry Smith has sent Captain Darrell Redmond to escort us to the fort."

"And did Captain Redmond tell you that your friend General Joseph G. Dayton will be there for the signing?"

A broad smile captured Chief Ouray's thin lips. "He did! It will be nice to see him again."

Dr. Dane looked at Chief Tando. "How is Latawga doing, Chief?"

Tando's face went grim. "Our medicine man, Rimago, asked that before we leave for the fort, Dr. Dane Logan come and examine Latawga's wound. There seems to be some infection."

Dane nodded, then looked at Captain Redmond. "I need to take a look at Latawga's wounded leg before we leave."

Redmond touched the brim of his hat. "Sure. We'll go ahead and prepare to pull out."

Dr. Dane hurried to Pal, took his medicine bag from the pommel, and returned to Tando, who led him amid the crowd toward the medicine man's tepee. As they neared it, Dane saw Leela standing at the opening, smiling at him. The long shower of her black hair fell glistening over her shoulders, down her back, almost to her hips.

"I will feel better about Latawga's wound when you examine him, Dr. Dane Logan," Leela said.

Dr. Dane nodded, then followed Tando inside the tepee, where Rimago was standing over Latawga, who lay on a blanket on the dirt floor, covered with another blanket.

Latawga smiled at the doctor as he knelt down beside him. "It is good to see you again, Dr. Dane Logan."

Dane smiled warmly while removing the blanket so he could examine the wounded leg. As he removed the bandage, he saw that infection had set in. Looking up at Tando, he said, "It is infected, all right, but I can treat it."

While the chief and the medicine man looked on, Dr. Dane took a bottle of carbolic acid from his medicine bag and said to Latawga, "This is going to burn a little, but it will kill the germs that are causing the infection."

Latawga steeled himself for the burning, and winced when the liquid touched the wound.

Dr. Dane capped the bottle and handed it to Rimago. "You saw how much I poured on the wound."

Rimago nodded.

"I'll put a new bandage on the wound, but I want you to pour the same amount on the wound two times a day until the bottle is empty. That should completely clear up the infection."

"Rimago will do."

Almost the entire village looked on as their chief, the young doctor, and Chief Ouray rode northward with the cavalry unit toward Fort Junction.

Soon the riders were making their way through the rugged mountain country. The leaves of the aspen and birch trees were a brilliant gold in the bright sunlight.

Dr. Dane was filling Captain Redmond in on how he happened to be in Chief Tando's village — which resulted in the chief's change of heart toward white men — when a sergeant rode up beside him, smiling.

Dane stopped his story as the sergeant said, "Excuse me, Dr. Logan — Captain, sir. I just wanted to ask Dr. Logan a question."

"Go ahead," said Redmond.

"Thank you, sir." Then to the doctor: "My name is Jim Thatcher, Dr. Logan. Are you still the only surgeon in this part of the country who does hip replacements?"

"I am. How do you know about me?"

"You did a hip replacement for my Aunt Frances Benton in Casper, Wyoming, a couple of months ago. She's my father's sister."

Dr. Dane grinned. "I sure did. How's she doing?"

"According to Mom's letters, Aunt Frances is doing fine, and she is still talking about what a wonderful surgeon you are."

"Well, I'm glad she feels that way."

The sergeant reached toward the doctor from his saddle and shook his hand. "It's a pleasure to meet you, sir." With that, he pulled rein and rode back to his place in line.

Dr. Dane finished telling the captain his story.

Redmond then said, "Dr. Logan, I sure hope Chief Tando's change of heart will cause the other renegade Ute chiefs to quit making war on the white people, and live in peace with us, too."

Twilight was on the rigorous mountain

land as the cavalry unit, the two Ute chiefs, and Dr. Dane Logan drew near Fort Junction, situated at the junction of the Boulder and St. Vrain Rivers. A beautiful light showed upon that mountain country — the afterglow of sunset. The surrounding peaks wore crowns of gold. All the lower ranges were purpling in shadow.

The light magnified the rocks, the upper portions of the canyon walls, the winding ranges, and the bold peaks until all seemed almost unreal.

Soon they rode up to the fort, with its long stockade fence, punctuated by gates at the front and halfway back on one side. There was a lookout tower beside the front gate, manned by four armed guards. Two of the guards had descended the steps from the tower and were opening the gate.

One of the guards on the ground saluted and said, "We're glad you're back, Captain Redmond."

"Glad to be back, corporal. Do you know if Colonel Smith is in his office?"

"He's not, sir. He said to tell you when you arrived to take Dr. Logan and the two chiefs to his office, then come and get him at his house. He has General Dayton there, too."

As the riders entered the military compound, the shadowed figures of spectators appeared at the stable, the smithy shed, the barracks doors, the quartermaster's porch, and the side door of the mess hall.

The men of the army unit guided their horses toward the stable while Captain Redmond led Dr. Dane and the two chiefs to Colonel Perry Smith's office. They dismounted, and Redmond led them inside, where lanterns were already burning.

Redmond ran his gaze over their faces. "You men heard what the corporal said. Please sit down in these chairs facing the desk, and I'll go get the colonel and General Dayton."

The chiefs chose to sit beside each other, leaving the third chair for the doctor.

Moments later, Colonel Smith entered the office, followed by General Joseph G. Dayton and Captain Redmond.

Chief Ouray rose to his feet, smiled, and did a half-bow. "General Joseph Dayton, it is very good to see you again, my friend."

"Good to see you again, Chief," said the silver-haired general as they shook hands Indian-style.

Chief Ouray then turned to his Ute brother, who was now on his feet, and introduced him to the general. Dayton and Chief Tando shook hands in the same manner, then Dayton said, "Chief Tando, I am so glad that you are wanting to make peace."

Tando took a deep breath, gathering his dignity about him like a robe, and said, "The gates of the heart of Chief Tando were opened by Dr. Dane Logan. I am sorry that it has taken me so long to learn that for the sake of my people and myself, it was the only thing to do. I had mistakenly believed that all white people hated Indians."

"Well, I'm glad you know the truth about that now."

Tando nodded.

The general then turned to Chief Tando and said, "Chief, I learned from Colonel Smith that he is holding your subchief, Nandano, and four other warriors, who were captured recently by a cavalry patrol when they were caught stealing cattle from a rancher."

Tando bit down hard. "Yes."

"Well, the colonel and I have agreed that since you have come here to sign a peace treaty, we will release your subchief and the other warriors to you."

Chief Tando's dark face showed the relief he felt as he said, "This chief cannot express his gratitude sufficiently, but please know it from the language of his heart."

The general's eyes twinkled. He looked at Colonel Smith. "I believe we both know it from the language of Chief Tando's heart, don't we, Colonel?"

"We sure do."

Tando smiled. "I am glad."

Colonel Smith said, "Chief, we will have the signing of the peace treaty after breakfast in the morning. We will do it outside in front of my office. I want all the people in the fort to witness it, and we'll have Nandano and his band there, too."

Tando nodded. "That will be good."

"And tell you what. After we feed you some supper, I will take you over to the guardhouse so you can see Nandano and the others. Chief Ouray and Dr. Logan will accompany us."

"You are very kind, Colonel Perry Smith."

"I just want you to know that we whites mean business when we say we want no more war with the Indians. We want to be your friends."

"You have made this clear."

Smith then said, "After the signing of the treaty in the morning, Captain Redmond and his cavalry unit will escort the group — including Nandano and his band — back to your village."

Dr. Dane Logan spoke up. "Colonel, I'll only be riding with the cavalry unit about twenty miles, then I'll veer off and take a direct route to Central City."

As Smith was nodding, Captain Redmond, who stood near, asked, "Where will you veer off, Doctor?"

"Best place will be right where you and the others make a westward turn at the first of the Rainbow Lakes. I'll go east around the lakes, then straight south to Central City."

Redmond nodded. "Makes sense."

The colonel said, "Well, gentlemen, it's time we go to the mess hall for supper."

When they entered the mess hall, they saw about thirty men just finishing their supper. Smith stepped to a sergeant at one of the tables and told him to alert the guards at the guardhouse that after supper, he would be bringing Chief Tando there to see his five warriors. The sergeant nodded, then Smith led his guests to the serving line, where the cooks were ready to dish up their food. With their plates and cups full, Smith led them to a long table.

During supper, Colonel Smith explained to Chief Tando that after he took him to

84

the guardhouse to see Nandano and the others, they would go to his office, where he and General Dayton would discuss the terms of the peace treaty with him.

General Dayton said, "Colonel, I'll just go on over to your office and wait for you there."

When supper was over, Smith led the chiefs and Dr. Logan across the compound toward the guardhouse. A cold wind howled through the fort, causing the Indians to pull their blankets tighter around their bodies and the white men to tug their hats firmly on their heads and pull up their coat collars around their ears.

When they entered the guardhouse, Nandano and the other four warriors were in two adjacent cells, and were standing at the barred doors, waiting for their chief to appear. Two armed guards stood in the circle of light from a pair of kerosene lanterns that hung from the ceiling in the open area outside the cells.

The Ute prisoners smiled at their chief as he stepped up to the bars with Chief Ouray beside him. Chief Tando said, "I am here to sign a peace treaty with white man's government."

The smiles turned to frowns, and Chief Tando asked Chief Ouray to speak to them. Ouray reminded Nandano and the others that for years, he had been trying to convince Chief Tando to make peace with the whites, but Chief Tando had refused. Ouray brought to mind the many warriors of Chief Tando's village who had been killed in battle with the white man's army over these years, saying those men would still be alive if Chief Tando had listened to him when he first implored him to cease his warfare against the whites.

Chief Tando reminded the warriors of the day they were captured by the Fort Junction patrol. He pointed out Dr. Dane Logan, who stood a few feet behind him, then told them how the doctor had saved Latawga's life, showing that all white men did not hate the Indians. Tando explained how this truth came home to his heart, and because it did, he was at the fort to sign a peace treaty with the United States government.

Nandano and the other four smiled broadly when Chief Tando told them that because he was going to sign the peace treaty, Colonel Perry Smith would be releasing them to return home with him.

The colonel then took the chiefs and Dr. Dane back to his office, where General Dayton was waiting. They sat down together, and the general and the colonel discussed the terms of the peace treaty with Chief Tando as Chief Ouray and Dr. Logan listened.

When the army officers found Tando so agreeable to the terms laid down, General Dayton said, "It won't take long in the morning to wrap this up, Chief Tando."

The chief smiled. "That is good."

Dayton leaned toward the chief. "Colonel Smith has told me about Dr. Logan saving your son Latawga's life."

Tando nodded.

"Chief, I would like to hear in your own words how Dr. Logan's act of kindness brought about this change in your thinking."

Chief Tando gladly related to Dayton the details of how Dr. Dane Logan saved his son's life because of his compassion for all human beings, and explained how this made him see that all white men do not hate Indians.

The chief then said, "I want no more bloodshed between Indian and white man. The people of my village are completely in agreement. They, too, want to live in peace."

The general smiled. "Wonderful! This is going to make a lot of people happy." He set appreciative eyes on the young doctor. "I am impressed, Dr. Logan, with the story of your having saved Latawga's life, and how you took him to the village, knowing you could very well be in danger from the chief and his warriors. I'm going to see that the story gets to every newspaper in Colorado and Wyoming, and I guarantee you, it'll spread all over the country when it does."

Dane shook his head. "General, I don't want any glory."

"Listen to me. The people of these two territories are going to rejoice at another Ute chief signing a peace treaty, and they need to know what brought on Chief Tando's change of heart. This chief was especially known to harbor a hatred for whites. Your compassion and courage made the change, and the people of Colorado and Wyoming have a right to know it. And it sure won't hurt for the rest of the country to know about it, too."

Colonel Smith chuckled and looked at Dane. "So there, Dr. Logan. You're going to get some glory whether you want it or not."

Dane laughed and shrugged. "Okay, okay. Whatever you say." He paused, then added, "If it weren't for the Lord Jesus in heaven, I would be nothing. He is the one who deserves the glory."

The Indians looked on quietly as the army officers smiled and Smith said, "I very much appreciate your attitude, Doctor. Well, this meeting is over. I have had a special private room prepared in one end of the barracks for you and our Ute friends, Doctor. I'm sure all three of you could use a good night's sleep."

Dr. Dane smiled at the Indians. "I'm sure we could."

The colonel led them to their room, and as the three men were preparing to retire for the night on their bunk beds, Chief Tando said, "Dr. Dane Logan, I would like to know how life is going for Melinda."

Dane grinned. "Melinda is doing fine, Chief. She's back in Denver with her parents and is planning to marry Dr. Tim Braden next spring. I'm sure she told you about him."

"Yes. Many times. I am happy for her."

"And by the way, Chief. I'm supposed to ask you to express thanks to Latawga from Melinda's parents and from Dr. Braden for saving her from drowning. And they want me to thank you that even though she was made a servant in your village, that she was treated well."

89

The next morning, the gray gloom in the eastern sky was lightening as breakfast was being served in the mess hall. The fort's physician and the chaplain had made a special point to sit with Dr. Dane Logan at breakfast.

Less than an hour later, long lines of pink fire appeared over the mountain peaks to the east. Just above them, a bank of fleecy clouds was turning rose-colored as the day brightened.

Everyone in the fort gathered in front of the colonel's office, where a table had been placed on the ground so all could view the signing of the treaty.

Seated at the table were General Joseph G. Dayton, Colonel Perry Smith, and Chief Tando. Chief Ouray and Dr. Dane Logan stood close by. Nandano and his warriors stood next to them.

In the crowd were the uniformed men, the officers' wives and children, the fort's physician, and the chaplain.

General Dayton rose from his chair and ran his gaze over the crowd. Speaking loud enough for all to hear, he told them in brief how Dr. Logan's compassion and courage were the reason Chief Tando was there to sign the peace treaty.

Dr. Dane's features flushed as the general lauded him.

General Dayton explained the terms of the treaty, then sat down. When Chief Tando had signed the peace treaty, everyone applauded.

Moments later, Captain Darrell Redmond and his cavalry unit mounted up, as well as the doctor, the two chiefs, the subchief and the other Ute warriors. Everyone in the fort walked to the front gate and waved as they rode away.

After some twenty miles had been covered, the traveling party came upon the Rainbow Lakes, where Dr. Logan bid them farewell and took the straight path toward Central City.

Five

Dr. Dane Logan found himself riding down a steep path toward a wide valley. There were several ranches in the valley, and he enjoyed the peaceful setting of the cattle grazing in the pastures.

On two of the ranches, he saw the ranchers busy putting up their last cutting of alfalfa hay for the season and stacking it in their fields close to the barns and corrals.

Moments later, Dane looked up ahead and saw a large herd of cattle, with at least a half-dozen cowboys riding in a wide circle on the edges of the herd. The herd seemed to be eddying like a whirlpool, and Dane could hear the bawling and bellowing, along with the crackling of horns and pounding of hooves.

As Dane drew nearer, he saw a few small fires and two or three ranch hands at each fire, holding branding irons in the flames. The motion of the cattle slowed from the inside of the herd to the outside, and gradually ceased. The pounding of hooves, the crack of horns, and the thump of heads also ceased, but the bawling and bellowing continued.

While Dane looked on, a few stragglers in the herd appeared about to bolt through the line of mounted cowboys. When one of the bulls tried it, he was quickly driven back into the herd, and the others gave it up.

The young doctor drew rein so he could get a good look at the branding, and saw one cowboy on a black horse was chasing a steer. He whirled a lasso above his head, then gave it a toss.

The rope shot out, and the loop caught the right rear leg of the steer. The black horse stopped with adept suddenness, and the steer slid in the dust.

With lightning speed, the cowboy was out of the saddle and winding the rope around the rear legs of the steer before it could rise.

Quickly, one of the men with a smoking branding iron left the nearby fire and applied the iron to the flank of the steer. The steer ejected a loud yowl, quickly rose to its feet when the rope was removed from its hind legs, and ran away, bawling.

Dane saw a young heifer on the ground

in the grasp of two other cowboys, and when the red-hot branding iron seared her side, she bawled lustily. The sight of the smoke rising from the touch of the iron made Dane wince. He had never been able to bear the sight of any living being suffering, be it human or animal. He knew the branding was necessary, but wished there was a way to do it without inflicting pain.

As he moved on past the branding spot, the odor of burning hide and hair assaulted his nostrils.

Time passed, and when Dane was within ten miles of Central City, he was riding Pal at a steady trot.

Suddenly he heard a wagon coming up behind him with the team at a full gallop. He hipped around in the saddle and saw a young man on the wagon seat, snapping the reins and loudly shouting at the team.

Dr. Dane guided Pal off the edge of the road to give the wagon plenty of space to pass.

As it raced past him, he saw a middle-aged woman sitting in the wagon bed, leaning over a man lying on a mattress. The man was definitely injured or very sick.

Dane put Pal to a gallop and soon drew up beside the bounding wagon. He called out, "Hey! Stop!"

The young driver shouted back, "There isn't time to stop! I'm taking my father to Dr. Dane Logan in Central City."

Dane shouted back, "I *am* Dr. Logan! Stop!"

The young man's eyes widened, and at the same time, the woman shouted, "Barry! Stop!"

The young man pulled hard on the reins, shouting, "Whoa! Whoa!"

The team skidded to a halt, as did Pal.

Dane leaped from the saddle and hurried up to the side of the wagon. "What's wrong?"

"You said you're Dr. Dane Logan, sir?"

"Yes, ma'am."

"We're ranchers, Doctor. My husband was gored by a bull about half an hour ago."

Dr. Dane quickly tied Pal's reins to the tailgate, took his medical bag from the saddle, and hopped in beside the woman and her husband. "Let's go, Barry! We need to get him to my office as soon as possible! Avoid all the bumps you can."

"Yes, sir!"

As the youthful driver put the team back to a gallop with Pal following, the woman said, "Doctor, I'm Shirley Chandler. My husband's name is Michael."

Dr. Dane nodded, then said to the injured man as he pulled the blanket down, "Mr. Chandler, I've got to take a look at the damage the bull did."

Michael ran a dry tongue over equally dry lips and closed his eyes. "Sure, Doctor."

Dr. Dane gritted his teeth when he saw the bloody shirt where the bull's horn had punctured Michael's chest. The blood was flowing freely from the wound. He looked up at Barry and shouted, "Keep the team at a full gallop!"

Barry looked over his shoulder, "Yes, sir!"

Dr. Dane took a roll of bandage from his medical bag as Shirley looked on, her features gray and drawn.

The doctor saw the dismay on Shirley's face, then looked down at the rancher and said, "Mr. Chandler, I'll do everything I can to stay the flow of blood as much as possible with this wagon bouncing as it is. When I get you to the office, I'll fix you up right."

Michael Chandler licked his lips again and said, weakly, "Thank you, Doctor."

Dr. Dane rolled off a length of bandage, wadded it up, and pressed it on the wound. The blood continued to flow. He rolled off more bandage and added it to what was already there. Still the blood flowed.

"Mrs. Chandler, I'm running short of bandage material," Dr. Dane said, lifting his voice above the noise of the wagon wheels and the thunder of the horses' hooves. "Could you tear off a strip of your petticoat for me? I need to get a sufficient pressure bandage on this wound."

"Oh, of course, Doctor." She turned her back to the doctor, lifted her dress a few inches, and ripped a long piece of white cloth from her petticoat. Turning back around, she held it up so he could see it. "Will this be enough?"

"I think so."

Shirley's hands were shaking as she placed the material into the doctor's grasp, and stark fear showed in her eyes.

Dr. Dane gently patted her hand. "We'll get him taken care of, ma'am. Try not to worry. We'll be at the office in a few minutes."

Shirley watched as he carefully folded the cotton cloth into a thick pad, placed it over the bloody bandages, and applied as much pressure as he dared. In his heart, he prayed, *Dear Lord, please make this bandage slow down the bleeding.*

Central City came into view in the distance. Watching the wound intently, Dr.

Dane was pleased to see that the rush of blood was slowing. He looked at his patient, who now had his eyes open. "Mr. Chandler, lie very still. We're almost there. You're doing fine now."

As they approached the edge of town, Dr. Dane said to Shirley, "How did you know about my office being here?"

"We're patients of Dr. Fraser, but haven't been to him in a year or so. We heard about his retiring, and that a Dr. Dane Logan was taking over the practice. I'm so glad we found you back there on the road."

At the doctor's office, Tharyn Logan was helping Dr. Robert Fraser in the examining room as he removed a long splinter from a teenage boy's hand. When the job was done, and the boy and his parents left the office with the promise of payment in about two weeks, Tharyn began cleaning up the examining table.

Dr. Fraser washed his hands at the basin on the nearby counter, and as he was drying his hands on a towel, he smiled at the lovely redhead. "Thank you, Tharyn. You did a good job helping me get that splinter out."

She smiled. "Oh, you could have gotten it out without me."

"Maybe so, but the way you talked to that frightened boy and kept him calm while I extracted that splinter sure made it a lot easier and a lot faster."

She smiled again. "That's what I'm here for, doctor."

"Well, you're good at what you do, Tharyn. You have tremendous medical knowledge for as young as you are, and you have a way with people that is marvelous."

As the aging physician headed for the office door, Tharyn said, "Thank you for your kind words, sir." She noted that he was holding a hand to his lower back as he walked. "Dr. Fraser, your back is hurting again, isn't it?"

He turned, looked at her, and grinned. "Mm-hmm. I need to see a good doctor."

"Well, I know a real good one, and he ought to be here pretty soon."

Fraser chuckled and passed through the door.

Tharyn went back to cleaning up the examining table. "Lord," she whispered, "please take care of Dane, and please help him to get back here real soon."

Suddenly the door to the office came open, and Dr. Fraser said, "You were right, Tharyn. Your husband is back. He just arrived, riding in a ranch wagon with a family named Chandler, who are longtime patients of mine. Michael — the husband — is hurt, and Dane is carrying him toward the office."

Tharyn hurried with Dr. Fraser into the office, and Barry was just opening the outside door, with Dr. Dane's medical bag in one hand. Dr. Dane came through the door with Michael in his arms, and Shirley following. Barry closed the door.

Tharyn gave her husband a loving glance as she moved toward him. "What happened?"

"Mr. Chandler was gored by a bull earlier this morning. He's hurt pretty bad. This is Mrs. Chandler, and their son, Barry."

Tharyn smiled at Shirley and Barry. "Glad to meet you."

Dr. Fraser hurried ahead of Dane and opened the door to the back room. While Dane was carrying Michael through the door and toward curtained section number one, he said to Tharyn and Fraser, "I met up with the Chandlers on the road, on my way home from Fort Junction."

"I'm so glad we met him on the road, Mrs. Logan," said Shirley. "Michael may have bled to death by now if we hadn't."

100

Tharyn met her glance. "Thank the Lord."

"That's for sure."

Dr. Dane carefully laid Michael on the examining and surgical table. To Tharyn, he said, "We need to prepare for surgery. I've got to work on the internal damage before I can suture him up and stop the bleeding completely. His rib cage and the left lung are both damaged. I'll have to examine him completely and make sure I haven't missed something now that we're out of that bouncing wagon."

"I'll hurry," she said, and dashed to the medical cabinet across the room.

As Tharyn began placing chloroform, scalpels, needles, thread, and other necessary items on a small cart, Dr. Dane turned to Shirley and Barry. "You can wait just outside the curtain, there, while I do a thorough examination. Once I'm able to determine the extent of the damage, I'll step out and tell you. Then you can go sit in the waiting room out front while I do the surgery. When I'm done, I'll come out and let you know how it went. Okay?"

Shirley nodded. "Yes, Doctor. Thank you."

Barry took his mother by the hand and led her to the table. Michael looked up at them with dull eyes.

Shirley patted her husband's cheek. "Darling, Dr. Logan is going to do surgery on you. Understand?"

Michael nodded.

"Barry and I will be in the waiting room once the surgery is started." With that, Shirley bent down and kissed his cheek. "I love you."

With dry tongue, Michael said, "I love you, too."

Barry bent down and looked into his father's hazy eyes. "I love you, Papa. And I'll be taking care of Mama."

Michael tried to smile, but it was very faint. With that, mother and son stepped out of the curtained section.

By this time, Tharyn had arrived with the cart and wheeled it up beside the table, placing it at the head.

Dr. Fraser stood by, silently looking on. Dr. Dane hurried to the wash basin, scrubbed his hands, and returned to begin his examination.

Some five or six minutes later, the young doctor stepped between the curtains, leaving Tharyn holding the pressure bandage in place, and Dr. Fraser looking on. They could hear him as he said to Shirley and Barry, "It's as I thought. Michael will be all right. The bull's horn only punc-

102

tured the left lung and broke two ribs. It didn't touch his heart or any other vital organ."

Shirley sighed. "Well, that's good news, Doctor. We'll go to the waiting room now."

"I'll be glad to help you with the surgery, my boy," Dr. Fraser said.

Dr. Dane smiled. "Thank you, Dr. Fraser, but I can handle it all right." He frowned and squinted at the elderly man. "You don't look like you feel well."

Still holding the pressure bandage, Tharyn looked at her husband. "Dr. Fraser has been having some pain in his lower back, honey."

The frown still intact, Dr. Dane squinted at the elderly physician again. "Do you know what's causing the pain?"

Fraser got a crooked grin on his face. "Yes."

"And what is it?"

"Old age."

Dane smiled. "You go on home and get some rest. That'll help you a whole lot."

Fraser scrubbed a hand across his mouth. "Yes, Doctor, I'm sure you're right. Is there any charge for your expert opinion?"

Dr. Dane chuckled. "Not this time."

"Good. See you later."

"Tharyn and I will come by your house on our way home this evening. I'll check on you then."

Dr. Fraser thanked him and left the building from a side door.

"Are you ready, darling?" Tharyn asked her husband.

"Yes. Administer the anesthetic."

While Tharyn was picking up the bottle of chloroform from the cart, Dr. Dane leaned over Michael, who was almost asleep already. "You're going to be all right. Just relax now, and this will soon be over."

Michael closed his eyes, opened them again, and said, "Thank you, Doctor."

Tharyn poured chloroform into a soft cloth and placed it over Michael's nose and mouth. "Don't fight the anesthetic, Mr. Chandler. Like Doctor said, just relax. Breathe deeply for me, will you?"

Michael closed his eyes again and nodded.

A few minutes later, when Michael was almost under, Tharyn said to Dane, "I'm going to make a quick check just to see if anyone else has come into the office."

"Okay."

When Tharyn entered the office, she saw that Shirley and Barry were the only ones there. Barry was seated in the waiting area, staring at the floor. Shirley was standing at the large window, looking out onto the street, while wringing her hands into tight knots.

Tharyn stepped up and placed her hands on Shirley's shoulders with a gentle squeeze. "Dr. Dane is young, but he has plenty of experience, Mrs. Chandler. He'll do a good job on your husband. You and Barry did the right thing getting him here as quickly as possible. There's coffee over there on the stove. You and Barry feel free to help yourselves to it."

Stepping back from Shirley, Tharyn looked at the young man as he raised his line of sight and placed it on her. "Barry, take care of your mother, won't you?"

Barry nodded and gave his mother a slight smile. "Yes, ma'am. I sure will."

Barry left his chair, moved up to his mother, and put his arm around her shoulders.

"The surgery may take longer than you might expect, but with the Lord's help, everything will be all right," Tharyn said.

"I'm sure it will," said Shirley.

"I need to ask a favor of you," Tharyn said softly.

Shirley nodded. "Of course."

"There are no appointments scheduled at this time, but if anyone comes in wanting to see the doctor, please tell them that we won't be available until about two hours from now. But if there's some kind of emergency, please come and knock on the back room door and let us know."

Barry nodded. "I'll do it, ma'am."

Tharyn thanked them, then hurried to the back room door and disappeared.

Six

Almost two hours had passed since Tharyn Logan had gone to the back room to assist her husband with the surgery on Michael Chandler.

Shirley and her son were pacing around the waiting area, and glancing out the large window that faced the street each time they passed it. Shirley looked up at the clock on the wall above Tharyn's desk, then stopped at the window. She noted the breeze that had picked up in the last few minutes, and watched as the breeze scattered the colorful leaves that had fallen to the ground from the trees on Main Street, making a pattern on the broad street like a patchwork quilt.

Barry stepped up beside her and took hold of her hand. She looked at him, then put her gaze back outside the window. "It's my favorite time of the year."

Barry grinned. "I know, Mama."

She sighed, then said, "All too soon a white blanket of snow will cover this scene."

"Yes, Mama, but wintertime is easier at the ranch, and this season, it will give Papa some time to recuperate before the hard work of spring and summer begin."

Shirley nodded. "You're right about that, son."

At that moment, they heard footsteps in the back room, then the door opened, and Dr. Dane Logan appeared. They started toward him, and he hastened his pace. As they drew up to face each other, Dr. Dane said, "Michael came through the surgery just fine."

Barry put an arm around his mother as she said, "Wonderful! Thank you, Dr. Logan."

Dr. Dane sat them down and explained the details of the damage and what he had to do to repair it. When he was sure that mother and son clearly understood, he said, "It'll be at least a couple of months before Michael can begin doing any work on the ranch. Even then, he'll have to go at it slowly until spring. And he mustn't do any lifting at all until I say so."

"Did you explain this to him?" queried Shirley.

"No, but I will. He's still under the chloroform right now."

"Oh. Of course."

"Did anyone come in while we were doing the surgery?"

"There were three women and one man, but none was an emergency. Each time Barry and I explained what was going on in the back room, they said they would come back tomorrow."

"Good. Thank you for helping us in that way."

"Glad to."

They noticed Tharyn come out of the back room and head toward them as Dr. Dane said, "I want to keep Michael here at the office overnight. I'll spend the night with him, and sleep on a cot close by. If he's doing all right by morning, you can take him home."

Tharyn drew up. "Michael's resting peacefully under the anesthetic."

Shirley smiled at her, then worry lines furrowed her brow as she said to the doctor, "Barry has chores to do at home, including cows to milk. But I don't think I can go home and leave my husband. I'll be glad to stay and look after him through the night."

Dr. Dane met her worried gaze. "I appreciate the offer, Mrs. Chandler, but it would be best if I stay close to Michael tonight, just in case there should be a

109

problem. Please trust me in this. It's important that you go on home with Barry, get some food in your system, and have a good night's rest. Michael is going to need a great deal of care when you get him home. Right now you need to lay some extra strength in store for the task ahead of you."

Shirley looked at her son, then back at the doctor. "Well, I — I —"

"I promise I'll be right here with him all night. He'll sleep for a few more hours, and when he does start to come out of it, he's going to experience quite a bit of pain. I'll administer whatever is needed to alleviate the pain, and he will no doubt go right back to sleep again."

Worry still was evident in Shirley's eyes. Dr. Dane patted her arm. "I promise I'll take real good care of him. Really, you need to go home and get some rest yourself."

Shirley bit her lower lip and nodded. "I understand, Doctor. You're right. Barry and I will go on home and prepare the house for Michael."

Dr. Dane smiled. "Good. I need to emphasize to you as I will to him — it's important that he get plenty of rest. And he's to do absolutely no lifting until I say so. I'll keep an eye on him by coming often to check on him."

"I'll see that Michael obeys your orders, Dr. Logan. He is one energetic man, and will want to help Barry with the work around the ranch. But maybe between you, Barry, and myself, he'll listen to reason."

"I'm sure you and Barry will have the proper influence on him, ma'am, and at least for the first couple of weeks, I'll be there every day to check on him."

The doctor's calming voice relieved Shirley's apprehensions about her husband. "All right, Doctor. Barry and I will head for home as soon as we go in and look at Michael. It *is* all right if we just slip in and take a look at him, isn't it?"

"Certainly. Tharyn and I will take you in. Ah . . . one other thing."

"Yes, Doctor?"

"You need to do something about that bull. He could have killed Michael."

Barry grinned. "We're needing some more beef to salt away for winter, Dr. Logan. I'll take care of the bull."

Dr. Dane nodded. "Let's take you in to see Michael."

The four of them made their way to the back room, and into a corner where Michael Chandler lay on a single bed under

111

the influence of the chloroform.

Mother and son moved up to the bed and gazed down at Michael's pale face while doctor and nurse looked on. Shirley took his inert hand in her own, and brought it up to her cheek. The patient did not move. Shirley kissed the hand and laid it back on the bed, gently caressing it. Leaning down, she placed a soft kiss on his forehead and whispered, "Sleep well, my love. Barry and I will see you tomorrow."

Tears dimmed Shirley's eyes as she turned away from the bed.

Tharyn put an arm around her and said, "He will have the best of care, Mrs. Chandler. Of that, I can guarantee you. We'll see to his every need."

This small gesture of kindness was enough to start the tears rolling down Shirley's cheeks. She quickly covered her eyes with her hands.

Tharyn squeezed her tight. "It's all right to cry, Mrs. Chandler. You've been through a tremendous ordeal today. Let the tears heal your distress. God gives us tears sometimes to relieve the stress we're feeling."

Shirley took a handkerchief from the cuff of one of her sleeves and mopped at the tears. "Thank you, dear, for understanding."

"We're here to help in any way we can," Tharyn replied softly.

Shirley saw that Barry was looking down at his father, with a hand on his arm. "Well, son. Let's go home."

The Logans followed Shirley and her son to the office, and when Barry opened the door, Shirley said, "Dr. and Mrs. Logan, I want to thank both of you for the way you have taken care of my husband, and are continuing to take care of him. It means more than I could ever tell you."

Dr. Dane smiled. "That's what we're here for, ma'am."

When Barry and his mother pulled away in the wagon, Dane closed the door and turned to Tharyn. She smiled and said, "Well, honey, I'll go home, cook supper, and bring some to you."

He took her in his arms, kissed her tenderly, and said, "Thank you, sweetheart. I am sort of feeling a little hungry."

"So tell me. How did the peace treaty signing go?"

"Couldn't have been better. Chief Tando was fully cooperative. He was definitely ready to make peace."

"I'm so glad. And it is a blessing to me to know that it wouldn't have happened if my husband hadn't saved Latawga's life

113

and taken him back to the village."

Dane shook his head. "Give the glory to the Lord, honey. I've already had plenty of glory showered on me for the deed."

Tharyn reached up, tweaked his nose, and giggled. "You needn't be afraid of a little praise."

He laughed. "By the time we got the treaty signed, I'd been given more than a *little* praise. I just did what any doctor would have done."

The next morning, Marshal Jake Merrell and his deputy, Len Kurtz, were sitting at their desks when they looked up to see Dr. Robert Fraser coming through the door.

Fraser entered, holding his medical bag, and said, "Good morning, Marshal . . . Len."

"Good morning, Doc," chorused the lawmen.

Merrell frowned. "Doc, you don't look like you feel well."

"Just some trouble with my back," Fraser said as he approached the marshal's desk. "How's the swelling around Earl's eye?"

"It's almost gone. You want to see him?"

"Best that I do. I'll check on him, then go back home."

★ ★ ★

At the same time Dr. Robert Fraser was checking on Earl Dubose at the jail, Tharyn Logan was at her desk at the doctor's office. She smiled when she saw a wagon pull up to the hitch rail out front. It was Shirley Chandler and her son.

When Shirley and Barry entered the office, Tharyn greeted them and said, "You'll be glad to know that Michael had a good night, and no complications have set in. Doctor is with him right now."

"So we'll be able to take him home. Right, ma'am?" said Barry.

"Mm-hmm," replied Tharyn as she rose to her feet. "Take a seat in the waiting area. I'll go tell Doctor you're here."

When Tharyn entered the curtained section where Dr. Dane had Michael stretched out on the examining table, she said, "Shirley and Barry are here."

A thin smile curved Michael's lips.

Dr. Dane nodded. "I'm almost finished, honey. Would you bring them in here, please, so I can talk to them?"

"Be right back."

Less than two minutes later, Michael's eyes brightened when he saw his wife and son step up to the table.

Barry smiled. "Good morning, Papa."

115

Shirley bent down and kissed his cheek. "Mrs. Logan told us you had a good night, without any complications."

"That's right."

"So, how are you feeling?"

"Well, I'm experiencing some pain in my chest, but Dr. Logan said this is normal. He expected it."

"I did," said the doctor. "I just gave him some powders to help relieve the pain. I'm sending some of the same powders home with you, Shirley. You'll need to mix them periodically with water and administer it to Michael as per my written instructions. It will keep the pain from getting too bad."

"All right."

Dr. Dane glanced at Tharyn, then looked back at Shirley. "I wish we had a clinic here so there would be several beds to care for patients on a long-term basis, and the medical staff to go with it. I'm hoping that someday we can do just that."

Shirley smiled. "Well, I hope so, too, Doctor."

Dr. Dane looked down at Michael, then ran his gaze between mother and son. "As I told you yesterday, for the next couple of weeks, I'll come to your home every day and check on him."

"I'd better draw you a small map so you

116

can easily find the place, Dr. Logan," said Barry.

Tharyn moved toward the medical cabinet. "There's paper and pencil right over here, Barry."

Barry followed her, and made a sketch on a slip of paper. He carried it to the doctor, explained a couple of things in the sketch, and Dr. Dane assured him he would find the Chandler ranch with no problem.

Barry looked at his mother. "Well, I guess we'd better get Papa in the wagon so we can head for home."

Dr. Dane said, "I want to caution you, Barry. Drive the wagon very slow on the way home. Even though your father has the mattress to lie on, he must not be bounced hard. It could tear the sutures loose."

"I assure you, Doctor, I will drive very, very slow."

Together, Dr. Dane and Barry carried Michael out to the wagon with Shirley and Tharyn following, and carefully placed him on the mattress in the wagon bed.

All three Chandlers thanked the Logans for their good work and kindness toward them, then Barry helped his mother into the wagon bed and climbed up onto the wagon seat.

The Logans watched the wagon pull

away, then stepped back into the office.

Since they were alone for the moment, Dane folded Tharyn into his arms, kissed her, and said, "Sweetheart, I hope except for the house calls I have to make, I can stay home for a while, now, and spend some time with you. I miss you very much when I'm away. Of course, I even miss you when I'm making those house calls many miles away."

Tharyn looked up into his eyes and smiled. "I miss you, too, when you're away from me, darling. But your having to make house calls sometimes many miles away is just part of being a country doctor."

Dane chuckled. "Well, at least I won't be having to leave town to help the government make peace with the Indians anymore. I was glad to have a hand in the Chief Tando situation, but as for me, my part is done."

A serious look captured Tharyn's features. "Darling . . . what you said to Shirley about wishing we had a clinic and the medical staff to go with it . . ."

"Mm-hmm?"

"I hope someday we can realize that dream."

"Well, with more people moving into the area, and the way the practice is growing, a clinic with several beds for long-term care

118

will become absolutely necessary. It will mean far fewer trips to Denver for surgery. There will, of course, have to be some surgeries still done at Mile High Hospital, because it's far better equipped than even our clinic will be, but at least half of the surgeries that would usually have to be done at Mile High can be done right here."

"That will be a real blessing."

"It sure will. Of course, in order to have the clinic, we'll have to build a new building to house it. So it will probably be a year or two, at least, before we can afford to do it."

Tharyn nodded.

Dane chuckled. "Of course by the time we have the clinic, you and I will be getting our family started, and you'll be staying home to take care of our baby . . . and then *babies*."

Tharyn smiled. "I'll miss the nurse's work, but I know I'll enjoy taking care of little Dane Junior and little Tharyn Juniorette even more."

Dane laughed and raised his eyebrows. *"Dane Junior,* eh? And I never heard of a *juniorette."*

"Well, you have now!" Then in a serious tone: "I'm just kidding, of course, but as that time grows closer, we need to talk about names for our children."

There was a twinkle in Dane's eyes. "Well, I have a good Bible name for our first-born son."

"You do?"

"Uh-huh. Tiglath-pileser."

Her eyes bulged. "T-Tiglath-pileser? Tiglath-pileser!"

"Yeah. Wouldn't you just love little Tiglath-pileser Logan?"

Tharyn clipped his chin playfully. "Well, of course I would. And how about you? When our first daughter is born, will you love little Secacah Logan? Secacah is a Bible name, you know."

He made a mock frown. "*Secacah?* I don't recall any female in the Bible named Secacah."

"There isn't. But there was a village in the wilderness of Judah by that name. It's in the book of Joshua."

"But at least the name I suggested was the name of a *person* in the Bible. A *man.*"

She snickered. "Well, you're going to come as close to naming any son of ours Tiglath-pileser as I am of naming a daughter of ours *Secacah!*"

They laughed together, then as a buggy pulled up in front of the office, Dane said, "I agree, though, we do need to talk about names for our children sometime soon."

They both looked at the couple in the buggy outside and saw that it was Jack and Sally Miller, who were members of their church. The Millers lived just a few blocks away, and Sally was due to give birth to their first child any day.

As Jack hopped out of the buggy and was helping Sally down, Tharyn said, "Speaking of having babies, it looks like Sally is about to have hers."

"I'd say so," said Dane, and hurried out to help Jack assist Sally into the office.

As they came through the door, Tharyn looked at Sally with concern. "How far apart are the contractions, honey?"

Sally winced and bent low. "Ab-about three minutes."

Tharyn closed the door behind them, then hurried ahead and opened the door to the back room.

Minutes later, Sally was on a table in one of the curtained sections, and Dr. Dane said to her nervous husband, "Jack, you can go out to the waiting room. We'll let you know when the baby is born, and you can come back in and see him or her and Sally."

"Okay," said Jack, glancing at his wife, who was in the grip of another contraction. "She's all right, isn't she?"

"Sure. What she's experiencing is only natural."

When the fidgety Jack Miller was gone, Dr. Dane hurried to the counter where the wash basin was positioned.

Sally was experiencing increased pain as the contractions were now coming no more than a minute apart. While Tharyn was collecting the necessary items to have on hand during and after childbirth, Dr. Dane was hurriedly making his own preparations.

When he returned from the wash basin, he stood over Sally, who was just getting over another contraction. "Sally," he said, "you'll recall that in the last two or three months, you and I talked about administering chloroform if your pain became extreme. What do you think?"

Though Sally was hurting a great deal, she said, "I want to bring my baby into the world without anesthetic if possible, Doctor. I'll let you know if I need it."

Tharyn came in, wheeling the supply cart.

Suddenly another contraction came on, and Sally gritted her teeth and let out a tiny wail.

Tharyn grasped Sally's hand and squeezed it tight. "Sally, take deep breaths and let them out slowly."

Sally looked up, and between breaths said, "You and . . . Dr. Logan have been married . . . three months, Tharyn. Any plans . . . for a baby yet?"

While Sally was taking another deep breath, Tharyn said, "Not yet. Dr. Dane and I have agreed that we'll give it a couple of years before we start our family."

As Sally was once again taking a deep breath, Tharyn glanced at her husband, who was positioned to deliver the baby when it started to come, then looked back at Sally. "Of course, the motherly instincts within me have aroused my desire every time I've assisted in childbirth since I first became a nurse. My desire is even stronger now that I'm married. I can hardly wait to be a mommy."

Dane smiled at Tharyn, then Sally jerked, jumped, and let out a tiny cry.

The doctor went to work.

Some twenty minutes later, a slap against soft skin was heard, followed by the cry of a newborn baby.

Tharyn still had a grip on Sally's hand. Both of them looked at Dr. Dane, who smiled and said, "You've got a new baby girl, Sally!"

Sally gasped and cried in a half-whisper, "Oh, praise God!"

Seven

Tharyn Logan took the wailing baby from her husband, saying, "I'll clean her up, honey." She looked back at the joyful mother. "I'll have her in your arms shortly, Sally."

Sally smiled and nodded.

Tharyn rushed away with the baby, and Dr. Dane went to work on his usual postnatal duties.

Across the room at a counter where she was gently laid on a small, folded blanket, the newborn infant continued to cry as Tharyn dipped a soft cloth into a basin of warm water and ever so gently washed mucus and blood from her tiny body.

With extreme care, Tharyn bathed the baby's eyes, clearing away any matter left there. Then, picking up a fluffy towel, she dried the tiny one off and pinned a diaper on her.

The baby's cries diminished to whimpers, and soon she went silent.

Dr. Dane drew up and said, "I'll check her over now, honey."

Tharyn nodded. "I estimate her at pretty close to six pounds."

The doctor picked the baby up in his hands and did a slight bouncing motion thoughtfully. "I agree. Just about six pounds."

Tharyn looked on as her husband carefully examined the baby and listened to her heart and lungs with his stethoscope. Smiling, he took the earphones from his ears, let the stethoscope dangle around his neck, and said, "She's perfect."

Tharyn smiled. "Praise the Lord. I'll take her to her mommy now."

Dr. Dane said, "I'll wash my hands, then go tell Jack that he has a fine baby girl." With that, he hurried to the wash basin.

Tharyn wrapped the tiny one in a small pink flannel blanket, then picked her up, held her close, and crooned in a half-whisper, "Welcome to the world, precious little girl. Someday soon I hope I'll have a sweet little girl just like you." A faraway look stole across her face as she stood there for a long moment, gazing at the newborn babe.

The sound of Dane going through the office door met Tharyn's ears.

Mentally shaking herself, she thought, *What am I doing, dreaming of my own fu-*

ture child while this baby's mother is waiting eagerly to hold her!

She turned and walked briskly back to the curtained section where Sally lay, covered by a sheet with her head propped up on two pillows, a look of anticipation on her happy face.

Tears instantly filled the new mother's eyes as she took the baby into her arms from a smiling Tharyn, who said, "Dr. Dane checked her over, Sally, even her heart and lungs. She's just fine, and in perfect health."

Sally raised her eyes heavenward. "Thank You, Lord Jesus!" Then gazing at the tiny face, she said, "Hello, Lydia Marie Miller. I'm your mommy." She kissed the chubby little cheeks and cuddled the infant close to her heart.

Tharyn smiled down at Sally. "Doctor and I estimate she weighs just about six pounds."

Sally kissed the top of the baby's fuzzy little head. "Why, that's just right for a little girl."

Then unwrapping the blanket, the joyful mother examined her precious baby. Caressing Lydia Marie's dark hair and her rosy cheeks, Sally took one of the tiny hands into her own hand, and the baby curled her tiny fingers around her mother's thumb.

"Aw-w-w, isn't that sweet?" said Tharyn.

"It sure is." Sally kissed all ten fingers and all ten toes, then did a thorough check of her daughter.

When the inspection was completed and Sally was satisfied that everything about her firstborn baby was in working order, she rewrapped the blanket closely around her and cuddled her in loving arms. Little Lydia snuggled her head close to her mommy, stuck her thumb into her rosebud mouth, and closed her eyes.

At that moment, a smiling Jack Miller came through the office door with Dr. Dane on his heels. Quickly, Jack moved into the curtained section and stepped up beside the table. Dr. Dane eased up close to Tharyn, and took her hand in his.

Still smiling, Jack gazed at his little daughter for a moment, then bent down and kissed a chubby cheek. He then kissed Sally's forehead and said, "Isn't she just beautiful?"

"She sure is!" agreed Sally.

"She looks like her mommy."

"You really think so?"

"Oh, yes. And Dr. Logan says she's perfect."

"Yes. Praise the Lord."

Jack's voice was soft and slightly hushed as he added, "Thank you, sweetheart, for our wonderful little girl. She's a precious, awesome miracle from God, and a priceless gift from Him, too."

Sally smiled. "Well, *Daddy,* you're welcome. And, yes, she is a precious, awesome miracle and a priceless gift. I don't understand how anyone could look at a newborn baby and say there is no God."

"That's for sure." Jack tenderly ran his rough, calloused fingers over his little daughter's soft, round cheeks. Tears glistened in his eyes. "Little Lydia Marie will be raised with much love and care, and we'll teach her that the Lord loves her, too."

"Yes we will. And every day when I feed her and bathe her, I'll tell her the story of Jesus and the cross."

Jack nodded and wiped tears from his cheeks as he took in the wonder and responsibility of it all.

Sally and Jack continued making over their little gift from God.

As Dane and Tharyn held hands and observed the beautiful scene before them, Dane felt Tharyn's hand trembling, and looked down at her.

He whispered, "Honey, are you all right?"

Tharyn looked up at him through a wall of tears. "I'm all right," she whispered back. "I'm fine. I'm just happy for Sally and Jack."

Dane thought there was more to it than she was telling him, but accepted it for the moment. He looked at the happy father. "Jack, I'd like to keep Sally and Lydia Marie here for another three hours, just to observe both of them and make absolutely sure they're all right."

Jack nodded. "Sure, Doctor. I'll be back after my lunch break at work, and if all is well, I'll take them home then."

Patients came and went all morning. In between, either Dr. Dane or Tharyn checked on Sally and little Lydia Marie.

When Dr. Dane and his wife were finally alone just before noon, he stood over her as she sat at her desk and said, "Sweet stuff, I believe I know you well enough to figure out when you're not being totally honest with me."

Tharyn raised her gaze to him with a look of mock astonishment in her sky-blue eyes. "Why, Dr. Logan, sir, what are you talking about? *Me* not be totally honest

129

with my precious husband? How silly!"

He leaned down, putting the palms of his hands on the desktop, and looked her square in the eye. "Earlier this morning, when we were observing the Millers as they were making over little Lydia Marie, I saw those big tears in your eyes and asked if you were all right. You said you were. That you were just happy for Sally and Jack. Remember?"

Tharyn nodded, her eyes filling up with a sheen of tears. "Well, I was telling you the truth. I *was* happy for Sally and Jack."

Dane stood erect again. "I'm not doubting that, honey, but there was more to it than just being happy for the new parents. There was something else."

"Oh, Dane, there's something I've been meaning to talk to you about. We've just been so busy, I haven't had a moment to bring it up. Dr. Fraser —"

"I'll let you tell me about the Dr. Fraser thing later. Right now I want to know what else you were crying about when I asked if you were all right."

Tharyn took a handkerchief out of a desk drawer and wiped the tears from her eyes. "Darling, what makes you think I was crying about something else?"

He gave her a mock frown. "Like I just

said, sweetheart. I know you well enough to figure out when you're not being totally honest with me." He bent down and put the palms of his hands on the desktop again. "Come on. Out with it."

Tharyn cleared her throat gently and smiled at him. "Think you're pretty smart, don't you?"

Dane grinned. "Smart has nothing to do with it. I just know my wife. Come on. What is it?"

Tharyn cleared her throat again. "Well, I . . . ah . . . was simply thinking about — about the wonderful day in the future when I would give birth to our first child." She choked up and swallowed hard. "Darling, helping Sally give birth to little Lydia Marie just — well, just made the motherly instincts work feverishly in me."

Dane leaned farther over the desk and met her gaze head-on. "Do you want to advance our previous plan to wait for a couple of years before we start our family? Do you want to start sooner?"

Tharyn swallowed with difficulty again. "The prospective mother part of me wants to hold my own child in my arms right now . . . but the wife part of me, which includes the nurse-receptionist part, is saying that we should wait the two years

131

that we agreed upon before we got married. If I gave in to the motherly instincts, I'd say let's have a baby as soon as possible. But if we followed my motherly instincts, you'd have to hire another nurse-receptionist sooner than we have planned."

Dane moved around the desk, bent down and kissed her tenderly, then said, "Honey, that's no problem. How about we pray about this in the days ahead and ask the Lord to guide us as to when we should start our family?"

"Okay. I only want God's will in the matter. I'm twenty-three years old, and most married women my age already have at least two children. But if the Lord makes it clear that He wants me to wait a couple of years, I can accept that and be perfectly happy."

Dane chuckled. "I'll have to tell you that it has passed through my mind several times lately. I'm two years older than you. And most twenty-five-year-old married men are the fathers of at least two, if not three children. I guess it's the fatherly instinct talking to me. Let's really pray hard about it and see how the Lord leads us."

"All right, darling. That's exactly what we'll do. Well, we'd better eat lunch before we have to miss it because those patients with appointments start coming through that door."

They sat at a small table in the waiting area. After Dane prayed over the food and spent two or three minutes seeking the Lord's guidance as to when they should start their family, they ate the box lunch Tharyn had prepared before coming to the office that morning.

Just as they were finishing, the front door opened, and Jack Miller came in with a bright beam on his face. "Well, how's my wife and my new little daughter?"

Dr. Dane rose from the table, smacking his lips, and said with a wide smile, "They're doing just fine, Jack."

Tharyn also rose to her feet. "We gave Sally some lunch before we came in here to eat lunch, ourselves. Your little Lydia Marie was getting *her* lunch when we left them."

Jack's eyebrows arched. "She's nursing already?"

Tharyn laughed. "You men! Don't you understand that it doesn't take a baby long to know he or she is hungry? When their mother offers nourishment, they know exactly how to take it."

Jack looked at the doctor. "Would you know that if you weren't a physician?"

"Probably not."

Tharyn headed for the door to the back room, saying, "I'll check on Sally and the baby. I'll let you know if they're ready to go home."

When Tharyn entered the small curtained section, she found Sally holding little Lydia Marie in her arms. The baby was asleep.

Sally smiled. "She seems satisfied with the woman the Lord chose to be her mother."

"Well, that's good. Jack's here, wanting to take his family home. You feeling okay?"

"Yes. A bit weary, of course, but I'm sure that goes with the territory."

"That's what they tell me. You sit tight. Doctor will want to check on both of you one more time. If he's convinced that both of you are all right, he'll let Jack take you home."

Tharyn returned to the office and found the two men standing near the door, talking. When they turned and looked at her, she said, "Lydia Marie is now sleeping on a full tummy. Sally says other than being a bit weary, she's fine."

Dr. Dane looked at Jack. "I want to check both of them one more time, and if all is still well, you can take them home. Sit

134

down here in the waiting area, and I'll be back shortly."

Jack watched doctor and nurse hurry through the door to the back room and sighed. "Thank You again, Lord, for my precious little Lydia Marie."

Less than fifteen minutes had passed when Dr. Dane appeared at the door and said, "Okay, Jack. Mother and child are ready to go home."

Jack and the doctor made their way to the curtained section. When Jack stepped into the small area, he found Sally sitting up on the examining table in her maternity dress. The baby was wrapped in a small blanket, and was in Tharyn's arms.

Tharyn cuddled the baby and said, "Jack, you'll need to carry Sally out to the wagon. She's too weak to walk yet. I'll carry Lydia Marie."

Dr. Dane smiled to himself while he observed the look in Tharyn's eyes as she held the baby.

"Sure, I'll carry Sally," said Jack as he smiled at his wife, then moved up to his little daughter, whose eyes were still drowsy. He kissed her chubby cheek. "Daddy loves you, sweetheart."

Then he turned to Sally, kissed her cheek also, and said, "I love you, too.

Thank you for giving me such a beautiful little girl. And she looks even more like you than she did the first time I saw her."

Sally chuckled. "That makes me proud."

Jack lifted her in his arms. "It should. Well, Lydia Marie's mommy, let's take our precious little girl home."

Dr. Dane walked ahead of Jack as he carried Sally toward the door, and Tharyn followed with the newborn baby in her arms. They passed through the office, and when they moved outside, two couples who were members of their church came walking along the boardwalk together.

One of the women said excitedly, "Look! Sally's had her baby!"

All four moved up close as Dr. Dane was helping Jack place Sally on the buggy seat.

One of the husbands said, "Looks like mother and baby are going home. What have we got here, Mrs. Logan? A little girl?"

"Yes," said Tharyn, smiling. "Her name is Lydia Marie."

The two women crowded up close to Tharyn, both of them saying how beautiful the baby was.

"Does Pastor Shane know your baby's been born?" asked the man who had not yet spoken.

"Not yet," said Jack. "I was going to go to the parsonage and let him know after I got home from work this evening. Right now, I have to get Sally and the baby home so I can go back to work. Rosemary Campbell has already volunteered to help Sally for the first few days after the baby is born."

"Would you like for us to let Pastor and Peggy know for you?" asked one of the men.

"Sure. I'd appreciate it," said Jack.

"We'll go to the parsonage right now."

Jack thanked them and climbed onto the buggy seat beside Sally.

Dr. Dane looked on as Tharyn moved up to the side of the buggy in order to place the baby in Sally's arms. Before she did so, Tharyn looked down at the tiny face, kissed Lydia Marie's forehead, and said, "The Lord has been very good to you, sweet baby. He's given you parents who know Him as their Saviour, and will raise you in church and by the Word of God." With that, she kissed the baby again, then handed her to Sally.

Jack looked at the Logans with appreciative eyes. "I want to thank both of you for a job well done. I'll see you in church on Sunday."

Sally smiled at them. "Yes. Thank you for taking such good care of Lydia Marie and me. It . . . ah . . . will be a few weeks before mother and baby can come to church."

Dr. Dane said, "Well, just take your time and don't overdo it. I'll be by the house in a couple of days to check on both of you. In the meantime, if you need me . . ."

"We'll sure let you know," said Sally.

While the Millers were driving away, Dane put an arm around Tharyn's shoulders and smiled. "You're so cute, honey. You've got *MOTHER* written all over you."

As they were walking back toward the office, Tharyn smiled up at him. "Oh, I do, eh?"

"You sure do."

"Well, let's just pray about it in the days ahead — even as you did at lunch — and ask the Lord to guide us as to when we should start our family."

"Oh, yes!" Dane replied. "I can't wait to see little Tiglath-pileser Logan!"

"What do you mean? Don't you know we're going to have a girl first? Get ready to see little Secacah Marie Logan!"

Dane raised his eyebrows, a grin curling his lips. "Oh, Secacah *Marie,* huh?"

"Sure, then she and little Lydia Marie

can have fun together, each having the same middle name!"

Dane shook his head. "Now, look here, Mrs. Logan, I —"

"Hey, Dr. Logan!" came a voice well-known to both. "Glad to see you back from Fort Junction."

Dane and Tharyn turned around to see Marshal Jake Merrell and Deputy Len Kurtz coming toward them on the boardwalk.

"Well, if it isn't Central City's finest!" Dr. Dane said. "Hello, Marshal. Hello, Deputy."

Merrell said, "Doctor, when I ran into you up there in the high country, you told me to talk to Len about the announcement Pastor Shane had given to the whole church on Sunday concerning Melinda Kenyon and Chief Tando. You really jolted me when you said Melinda wasn't dead, and that Chief Tando was no longer the enemy of white men. Well, Len told me what Pastor had said. Praise the Lord that Melinda is alive! And praise the Lord that Chief Tando has had a change of heart! So tell us . . . how did it go at the signing of the peace treaty at Fort Junction?"

"It went very well."

"Great!" said Len. "I'd like to hear all the details."

Dr. Dane grinned. "Well, as soon as we can get some time together, I'll tell you the whole story."

"I know you're a busy man," said Merrell, "but you feel free to come by my office anytime you can."

"I'll do it. Oh, and how's it going with Earl? I assume you got Dr. Fraser over to the jail to look at his eye."

"That's what I was going to say to you a little while ago about Dr. Fraser, honey," Tharyn said. "I was going to tell you that he had treated Earl's eye, and said there was no permanent damage."

Merrell said, "Doc Fraser came to check on Earl this morning, and confirmed that there is no permanent damage to his eye. He told Len and me that you got back from Fort Junction yesterday. Said he was having some trouble with his back, so after he checked Earl, he was going home."

Dr. Dane nodded. "So how long are you going to keep Earl in jail?"

"A month. I think that'll teach him never to smack Dora around again. She has neighbors taking care of her and their little boy."

Dr. Dane grinned. "Seems to me the beating you gave him will help him to think it over, too."

"I hope so, because if he ever does it again, he's gonna wish he'd never been born."

Tharyn's brow furrowed. "Dora hasn't come to the office, Marshal. Is she all right?"

"Mm-hmm. She wasn't hurt bad enough to need a doctor's attention."

"That's good."

Merrell nodded. "Well, Len and I have to keep moving. Stop by whenever you can, Doctor, and tell us the whole story. We'll be looking forward to it."

Both lawmen tipped their hats to Tharyn and moved on down the street.

As Dane and Tharyn entered the office, she looked at the clock on the wall. "It's almost one-thirty, darling. Mrs. Southard has an appointment at one-thirty."

"All right. And what other appointments do we have this afternoon?"

Tharyn named five other people who had appointments just as Mrs. Southard came through the door.

Eight

Captain Darrell Redmond was leading a cavalry unit of thirty men in the high country south and a bit west of Fort Junction as the sun in the Colorado sky passed its apex and began its normal slant downward. They were following tracks made in the soft ground by a band of Indians, whose horses wore no horseshoes.

Riding at Redmond's side was Lieutenant Rex Farley, and just behind them were Sergeants Jim Thatcher and Grant Connors. At the rear of the column were two wagons. Each one carried a .58-caliber Gatling machine gun, and a trooper to man it.

All around them lay a vast sweep of sunken gorges, above which stood towering timber-clad mountains.

As they entered a dense forest, Captain Redmond turned to Lieutenant Rex Farley and said, "Even though some of the men at the fort have said they think these latest acts of violence against the ranchers here in the mountains are being led by Chief Tando, I insist they are wrong. Tando meant business when he signed that peace treaty. When we run these bloody savages down, we'll find they're renegades, led by either Chief Yukana or Chief Antono . . . or both."

"I agree, Captain," said Farley. "I know Chief Tando was a renegade himself for a long time, but I don't think he could be that good an actor. He certainly seemed sincere when he signed that treaty, and it was obvious that there was a genuine respect in his heart for Dr. Logan for having saved his son's life."

Soon they were nearing the south edge of the forest, and suddenly both officers saw two pillars of black smoke in the distance just as Sergeant Jim Thatcher spurred his horse up beside Redmond and shouted, "Captain, look! Those Indians are at it again, for sure! *Two* fires!"

By that time, every man in the column had his attention on the pillars of smoke. One was off to their left, and the other directly ahead of them. What was actually burning could not be seen.

Redmond drew rein and signaled for the column to halt. He studied the ground and saw that the hoofprints of the Indian band

143

had split into two bands . . . one heading to the left, and the other moving straight ahead.

Redmond hipped around in the saddle. "Maybe we can catch the culprits this time. Lieutenant Farley, you take your half of the men and go see what you can find at the ranch up there on the left. I'll take the other half and head for the one directly ahead."

Farley made a snappy salute. "Yes, sir! Let's go, men!"

Soon Farley and his troops topped a steep hill where they could get a clear look at the ranch house that was aflame. The lieutenant put his horse to a faster run.

Every man had his eyes running from side to side, watching for any sign of the hostiles.

When they rode into the yard, there were two bodies lying facedown on the ground between a pair of trees some twenty yards from the house.

"Keep your eyes peeled, men," shouted the lieutenant as he slid from the saddle. Sergeant Connors hurried on Farley's heels toward the man and woman who lay on the ground with bullet holes in their backs.

When Captain Redmond and his troopers rode into the yard of the burning ranch house, they saw the rancher and his wife lying on the ground near the front porch, blood soaking their clothing, and two teenage boys lying beside them.

While the majority of the men kept their eyes on the surroundings for any sign of Indians, Captain Redmond and Sergeant Jim Thatcher left their saddles and hurried to the victims. It took only seconds to see that the rancher was alive, but the rest of his family was dead.

The heat from the blazing house was unbearable. Redmond called for two more men to help Thatcher carry the bodies away from the heat while he bent down and picked up the rancher. They carried the bodies some thirty yards from the house, and Redmond laid the rancher down next to the body of his wife, and said, "Sir, can you hear me?"

The rancher made a grunting sound, looked up at the uniformed man with dull, unfocused eyes, and nodded. "Yes. I . . . can hear you."

"I'm Captain Darrell Redmond. We're from Fort Junction."

The rancher nodded again. "My — my wife and — boys. Are they — ?"

"I'm sorry, sir. They're dead. It was Indians, wasn't it?"

145

The rancher swallowed with difficulty. "Yes. Utes."

"Do you have any idea where they were from?"

"I — I know who was — was leading them, because one of the savages called him by name."

"Who was it?"

"Chief Yukana."

Redmond looked at Thatcher and the other two men who stood over them. "Renegade, all right. Yukana." He looked back down at the wounded rancher. "Sir, there's a doctor in Central City. I'll have a couple of my men take you there."

The rancher's eyes were closed, and there was no more rise and fall of his chest.

The captain took hold of his arm. "Sir? Sir?" He bent over and put an ear close to the rancher's lips, then slid his hand down to the wrist, feeling for a pulse. After a few seconds, he looked at the other men. "He's dead."

At that moment, one of the men on horseback called out, "Captain, Lieutenant Farley and the other men are coming."

"Good," said Redmond. "We'll get on Yukana's trail right now. That's five ranches in two days!"

★ ★ ★

At Chief Tando's village some ten miles farther south, one of the warriors walking along the north edge of the village saw a large band of Indians coming from the north and called out to the others milling about that Ute riders were coming.

Moments later, Chief Yukana and twenty-four of his warriors came riding in, and were met by over a hundred warriors. Yukana asked to see Chief Tando, and was told that the chief and a few warriors had gone deer hunting that morning and had not returned.

Keeping his voice pleasant, Yukana told them he wanted to talk to Chief Tando. It was explained to him that the hunting party had gone in a northwesterly direction, and should be returning soon. Yukana thanked them, saying that he would try to find them so he could have a brief talk with Chief Tando, and they rode out.

The afternoon sun was almost halfway down the western sky when Chief Tando and his ten men were draping the carcasses of three dead deer over the backs of horses that had been brought along for that very purpose.

Subchief Nandano caught movement out of the corner of his eye, and focused on a large band of Utes riding toward them from the southeast. He called to Chief Tando, pointing them out, and said that the lead rider looked like Chief Yukana.

Tando took a deep breath. "It is Yukana, indeed."

When Chief Yukana and his band drew up, Tando and Nandano moved toward them, and they could both see that Yukana was not smiling.

The rest of Chief Tando's warriors stepped up behind him as he raised his hand to welcome Yukana and his men.

Yukana slid from his horse, stepped up to Tando, and said gruffly, "I wish to speak to you."

Chief Tando took a step closer and made a half-smile. "Of course. What is it about?"

Yukana's lips made a bitter curve against the bleak landscape of his cheeks. His thin, dark eyebrows pulled together over his angry eyes, and as he spoke, his voice was edged with indignation. "Word has leaked out from my Ute friends in a village near the village of Chief Ouray that Chief Tando has turned traitor and signed a peace treaty with the white government. Tell me. Is it true?"

"It is true that I signed a peace treaty, but not that I am a traitor."

Yukana's eyes bulged. "You are traitor just like Ouray and Ute chiefs like him who give in to the whites who come here without invitation, steal our land, and kill our game for their own bellies."

Tando slowly raised a palm toward Yukana. "I finally came to my senses and realized that all whites do not hate Indians. I made peace because of kindness some whites have shown toward us. I also told myself that since the number of white men is much larger than the number of Indians, that to continue fighting them would only result in more of my warriors being killed. The white man's army has far better weapons than do we. Especially because they have the Gatling guns that spit bullets so quickly. It is foolish to continue fighting them. Our people live better when we are at peace with them. The people of my village are very glad to be living in peace with the whites. Chief Ouray tried to get me to see this many grasses ago, but I was too stubborn to listen. I am glad that I finally came to my senses."

The venom in Chief Yukana suffused his cheeks with a bright-red tide of blood. His eyes flashed as he said, "I will not fight you, Chief Tando, because you are my Ute brother. I am ashamed of you and the other Ute chiefs who have turned traitor, but though it makes me angry, I will not fight you."

With that, Yukana wheeled, stomped angrily to his horse, and trotted northward, his warriors following on their horses. Tando cupped a hand beside his mouth and shouted, "Chief Yukana! Do not forget that the white man's army has much greater weapons than you do!"

Yukana did not look back.

Chief Tando and his men kept their eyes on Yukana and his warriors until they topped a ridge some three miles away, and disappeared.

They turned to the three horses who bore the dead deer, and started tying them in place, when all of a sudden, there was the sound of gunfire. Rifles barked, white men shouted battle cries, and Indians whooped as they fought back. Tando and his men stared at the ridge, seeing none of the action, then looked at each other when above the sounds of the barking rifles, they heard the deep-throated .58-caliber Gatling guns.

Soon the gunfire stopped.

Nandano laid a gentle hand on Chief

Tando's shoulder and said, "I am glad you made peace with the white man's government. We are living better lives now."

The other men agreed.

They finished tying the carcasses of the deer to the packhorses, mounted up, and rode toward their village.

It was almost four o'clock in Central City when Dr. Dane Logan finished with his sixth scheduled patient for the afternoon. He was standing over Tharyn at her desk, talking about the patient who had just left, when they both saw a big husky man in his late forties stagger past the large front window, holding his right jaw.

When the man opened the door and stepped in, Tharyn knew by the black dust on his face and clothing that he was employed at the Holton Coal Mine just west of town. He was still holding his right jaw, and it was obvious that he was in a great deal of pain.

As Dr. Dane moved toward him, the miner said in words that could hardly be understood, "Dogter Logad, do you rebeber be? I was one of the men who was trabbed with you in the mine in July."

Dane's mind flashed back to the hot day in July when there had been an explosion

151

at the mine, and how he went to the mine to do what he could for the injured miners. He had gone down into the mine to care for men who were injured and were unable to make their way out, and while down there — because of a cave-in — became trapped himself.

Smiling, the doctor said, "Sure, I remember you. Your first name is Rudy. I don't think I ever heard your last name."

Keeping his hand to his jaw, the miner said, "By las' dame is Louden."

Dr. Dane said, "I could understand you better if you weren't pushing so hard on your jaw. What happened to it?"

The miner eased up on the pressure he was putting on his jaw. "My last name is Louden. Nothin' really happened to my jaw. It's actually a tooth that's givin' me the pain. One of the men at the mine told me that like Dr. Fraser, you work on teeth since there isn't a dentist this side of Denver."

Dr. Dane nodded. "I have pulled a few teeth, but I'm not as good at it as a dentist would be."

"There ain't no way I can go to Denver, Doctor. Will you help me?"

"I'll sure try. Let's go into the back room."

Tharyn looked at her husband. "Would

you like for me to come, too?"

"Please. I just might need you."

Tharyn followed as the doctor led the suffering miner into the back room. He pointed to a straight-backed wooden chair that stood in front of an outside window where sunshine was shining through, and said, "Sit down on that chair."

While Tharyn looked on, the doctor went to the medicine cabinet and took the dental forceps and a headband mirror out of a drawer. He placed the mirror on his head, doused the forceps in alcohol, then moved to the miner and positioned himself so he could reflect the sunlight from the window into his mouth with the mirror. "All right, Rudy, open your mouth as wide as you can."

Rudy let out a groan as he opened his mouth. Dr. Dane looked in and studied what he saw closely. "Rudy, your upper gums are swollen on the right side, and they're oozing pus. It looks like the second molar is the problem. I'd say it's abscessed. But it *could* be the first molar." He raised the forceps toward Rudy's mouth. "I'm going to tap on the second molar with the forceps. If it *is* the second molar, it's going to hurt. Would you rather I anesthetize you first?"

Rudy shook his head. "Naw. Go ahead and tap on it. I can take it."

"You sure?"

"Positive. Go ahead."

Dr. Dane tapped on the second molar with the forceps.

Rudy jerked, howled, sprang out of the chair, and jumped up and down, while holding a hand to his jaw. Dane looked at Tharyn, who simply shook her head.

When Rudy settled down, Dr. Dane said, "It's the second molar, all right. You sure you want it pulled?"

The big husky man still held his hand to his jaw. "Yeah. I want it pulled."

"All right. Sit back down. But I strongly suggest that I use an anesthetic first."

Rudy plopped onto the chair, shaking his head vehemently. "No! If it got out that I allowed you to use anesthetic, the guys at the mine would never let me live it down. I can't be thought of as a sissy!"

Dr. Dane sighed. "Rudy, I understand this virile, rugged, masculine stuff. I used to live as a teenage orphan on the streets of New York City, so I know about your need to protect your he-man image. But this tooth is terribly infected. The infection goes all the way into the bone. I don't think you have any idea just how painful

154

this extraction is going to be. And when I get the tooth out, I'll need to suture the wound in order to minimize the danger of more infection. If it were me, no matter what . . . I'd take all the anesthetic I could get."

Rudy shook his head again. "Doc, in my lifetime, I've had a lot of serious injuries. Why, one time about five years ago, I had to set my own broken leg. This here tooth pullin' can't be as bad as that. Go ahead and yank it out."

Dr. Dane sighed. "Well, Rudy, it sounds like you know what pain is all about, but a minute ago when I tapped on that second molar, you hollered like a wild man. When I pull it, it's going to hurt a hundred times as bad. You'd better let me use the anesthetic."

Rudy shook his big head. "No, sir! I'm not givin' those guys at the mine any excuse to call me a sissy. As sure as anything, if I let you give me somethin' to ease the pain, they'd find it out. I'd never in this lifetime live it down."

"Tharyn and I would never tell anybody."

The crusty miner shook his head again. "It'd still get out somehow. Let's get on with it. I'm ready when you are."

"Okay. Go over there to the wash basin and wash your face real good. I don't want any coal dust getting in your mouth."

Rudy left the chair and did as the doctor had said. When that was done, the lack of a dental chair was overcome by the use of two straight-backed wooden chairs, one behind the other.

Tharyn stood by, ready to help if needed, as her husband placed Rudy on the first chair, then stood just behind him to the right, placing his left foot on the seat of the second chair.

"All right, Rudy," said the doctor, "lay your head back on my knee."

When this was done, Dr. Dane put his left arm around the patient's head and grasped his chin with his left hand. "This will give me leverage so I can hold your head still, leaving my right hand and arm free to handle the forceps."

"Makes sense," Rudy grunted.

"I'll give you one more chance to let me administer anesthetic."

"No means no, Doc."

Tharyn moved to where Rudy could see her. "Mr. Louden, my husband is only trying to save you some suffering."

"I understand, ma'am, but I can't let anybody ever think I'm a sissy. Do it, Doc."

Dr. Dane looked once again at the swollen gums. "Okay, Rudy. Brace yourself."

He pressed the tip of the forceps into Rudy's mouth and got a grip on the tooth. He gave a forceful yank, but the forceps slipped off, causing a powerful stab of pain.

Rudy stiffened as he ejected a wild scream, grabbed the doctor's left arm, then still screaming, fell on the floor. He rolled back and forth, holding his jaw and emitting loud groans and grunts.

Forceps in hand, Dr. Dane dropped to his knees and tried to hold the big man still. He was able to force his mouth open and almost got a grip on the tooth with the forceps, but Rudy was sixty pounds heavier than the doctor, and he could not hold him still.

"Rudy!" Dr. Dane said sharply. "Hold still! Let me get a grip on that tooth and pull it before this gets worse!"

The big man paid him no mind as he cried out in pain and thrashed about on the floor.

Dane looked up at Tharyn, and above the yelling and moaning of his patient, said, "Go out on the street and find me two of the strongest men you can! It's

157

going to take a lot of brawn to hold this man down! The adrenalin pumping through his body right now is making him as strong as a bull!"

Tharyn was wringing her hands. "Okay, honey. I'll be right back." With that, she bolted toward the door that led to the office.

When Dr. Dane let go of his patient and stood up, Rudy stopped thrashing, swallowed hard, and looked up at him, his face beet red.

The doctor said in a firm tone, "Rudy, stay right where you are. You want some anesthetic now?"

Rudy shook his head.

"You still want me to pull the tooth?"

Rudy nodded, biting his lips.

"All right. Then calm yourself. My wife has gone out on the street to get some help. I can't hold you down and pull the tooth at the same time. When the forceps slipped, they did some damage to the tooth. So it's going to hurt even worse when I clamp the forceps on it this time. You dead sure you don't want anesthetic?"

"Dead sure. I may scream and holler, Doc, but don't pay no attention to me. Just do what you have to do."

The sound of the front door of the office

158

opening and closing met the ears of both men, followed by the sound of three pair of footsteps.

Dr. Dane looked into the miner's eyes and said, "Sounds like reinforcements are coming."

Nine

The door opened, and both Dr. Dane Logan and Rudy Louden saw Tharyn enter the room with two rugged men behind her. Each one had a badge on his chest.

Marshal Jake Merrell and Deputy Len Kurtz looked past Tharyn as she led them to the spot where her husband stood over the thick-bodied miner, who was sitting on the floor.

Tharyn set her gaze on her husband. "These two were just passing by on the boardwalk when I stepped out the door. Will they do?"

Dane grinned. "Yes, they'll do."

As they drew up, the marshal looked down at Rudy with a frown. "I understand you came in here to get a tooth pulled, but you're puttin' up a fight when Dr. Logan tries to pull it."

Rudy cleared his throat nervously. "Well, it's just that he's givin' me a lot of pain when he tries to pull it."

Len Kurtz gave the miner a puzzled

look. "You mean even with the anesthetic, it still hurts so bad you can't take it?"

"Well, I — uh — didn't let him give me no anesthetic."

Jake Merrell chuckled. "Oh, sure. It's that weird thing among you miners. You boys have more fear that somebody will call you a sissy than you have of any physical pain. So I guess you're still not going to let Dr. Logan give you a pain killer?"

Rudy gave him a slanted grin. "That's right."

"But being afraid that somebody will call you a sissy isn't sissified, eh?"

Rudy scowled at him, then looked up at the doctor. "Let's get this over with. You want me to stay on the floor?"

"I do. Marshal, Deputy, I need you to get down here and hold Rudy down."

Both lawmen dropped to their knees beside the miner.

Dr. Dane knelt down at Rudy's head and looked at the lawmen. "Len, I need you to sit on Rudy's legs and hold them flat on the floor. And Marshal, I need you to hold both of Rudy's wrists above his head and pin them to the floor. Stretch his arms straight out and don't let him move them."

The marshal took hold of Rudy's wrists

161

and drew them all the way above his head. "Got him, Doc."

Len sat on the miner's stocky legs between the knees and ankles. "Got him, Doc."

Tharyn put a hand over her mouth and smiled.

Dr. Dane looked at Rudy. "Ready?"

"Yep."

The doctor put one knee on Rudy's chest and said, "Open your mouth and close your eyes."

The miner did as commanded. Dr. Dane pushed the tip of the forceps into Rudy's mouth and got a good hold on the abscessed second molar. He set his jaw and gave a hard yank. This time, the tooth came out.

Rudy bucked like a wild horse, screaming and yelling, but the two lawmen held him down. After two or three minutes, he finally went quiet and looked up at the doctor, who was standing over him with the bloody tooth between two fingers.

Dr. Dane bent over, holding the tooth so Rudy could get a good look at it, and said, "You'll need to get up on the table now, so I can stitch up the hole the tooth left and get the bleeding stopped. None of us here will let on to your pals at the mine how much you screamed and hollered."

Rudy's beefy features turned crimson as the lawmen helped him get on the table, and Tharyn placed a pillow under his head as he lay down.

The doctor went to work, and within fifteen minutes, the hole had been stitched.

"Okay, Rudy," said the doctor, laying needle and thread aside, "all done. I'll need to see you in a week to take the stitches out."

Rudy sat up and put a hand to the swollen jaw. "I guess it'll take a few days for the swelling to go down."

"Mm-hmm."

The miner slipped off the table and stood up. "How much do I owe you, Doctor?"

"My fee is three dollars."

Dr. Dane, Tharyn, and the lawmen made their way to the office, where Rudy gladly paid Tharyn the three dollars. He thanked Marshal Merrell and Deputy Kurtz for helping Dr. Logan, then holding his jaw, he stalked proudly out of the office.

Dr. Dane wiped a palm over his face. "Boy, am I glad that's over!"

The lawmen burst into laughter, and Dr. Dane and Tharyn quickly joined them.

When the laughter subsided, Dr. Dane picked up two of the three dollar bills Tharyn had laid on top of the desk, and handed one to each lawman. "You gentlemen deserve your share."

They had another good laugh, then the lawmen both said how glad they were that the peace treaty signing at Fort Junction went well. Merrell reminded the doctor that he and Len wanted him to come by the marshal's office soon and tell them every detail of the story. Dr. Dane assured them it would be soon, then the lawmen left.

Dr. Dane glanced at the clock on the wall behind Tharyn's desk and said, "Well, Mrs. Logan, let's lock the door, clean up here, and go home." He noted the single dollar bill that still lay on top of the desk. "You can put that dollar in your purse if you want."

"Well, Dr. Logan, Marshal Merrell and his deputy earned what you gave them, but I didn't do anything."

"But you were there to help me if I needed it."

"But —"

Dane picked up the dollar bill and placed it in her hand. "No arguments, ma'am. Put the money in your purse."

★ ★ ★

That evening while Dane and Tharyn were eating supper in the kitchen of their beautiful two-story house, Tharyn said, "Honey, as far as I know, you haven't told anyone except Marshal Merrell and his deputy about Chief Tando signing the peace treaty. Have you told anyone else?"

Dane shrugged. "No."

"Why?"

"Sweetheart, if it comes from me, people will think I'm wanting glory for my part in it. Before we left the fort, General Dayton said he was going to see that the whole story got to every newspaper in Colorado and Wyoming. Everybody in town will hear about it when the *Rocky Mountain News* shows up with the story in it. I figure it'll be in the *News* by tomorrow, or at least by Friday. I'd rather the people of this town learn about it that way."

Tharyn took a sip of coffee from her cup and nodded. "Okay, Dr. Humble Logan, I agree. It will be best if the people of Central City learn about it from the newspaper. Maybe you should at least have told Mayor Anderson."

Dane pondered her words for a moment, then said, "You may be right about that. Mike really ought to know ahead of time.

165

If it isn't in tomorrow's paper, I'll make it a point to go to his office and tell him the story."

"Good. And darling, I want to say once more how proud I am that you were the one the Lord used to bring about the change in Chief Tando."

Dane smiled at her comment, then said, "Chief Tando invited me to come back to his village any time I could. I'm definitely going to make time to do that. I'd like to talk to him about the Lord, and because of the way he feels toward me, he just might listen."

Tharyn's eyes lit up. "Oh, sweetheart, you're right! I think he would listen to you. Wouldn't it be wonderful if you could lead him to Jesus? He could very well be instrumental in bringing many of his people to salvation."

"I've been thinking the same thing."

When supper was finished, Dane lent a hand to help Tharyn with the dishwashing and the cleanup of the kitchen. That done, Tharyn put two cups of steaming coffee and a plate of oatmeal cookies on a tray. Dane carried the tray as they went to the parlor together.

Dane placed the tray on a small table beside the sofa, and as Tharyn sat down, he went to the fireplace and tossed in a couple more logs. He rubbed his hands together briskly as he headed back toward her. "The night air in late September is quite cool in Central City, Mrs. Logan."

She laughed. "Yes, Dr. Logan. Quite cool."

He lowered himself in his favorite chair next to the sofa where Tharyn sat, picked up his cup of coffee and a cookie, and sighed heavily. "I'm absolutely exhausted. Rudy Louden wore me out."

"I can understand that, sweetheart. Just observing it wore me out. Let's hope that the rest of his teeth stay healthy. I wouldn't want either of us to go through that again. He'd probably be just as stubborn about the anesthetic the next time."

"Without a doubt!"

The Logans talked further about Dane's desire to return to the Ute village and tell Chief Tando the gospel. They spoke of what a joy it would be to see the chief, his family, and the other people in the village open their hearts to Jesus.

When it was drawing near bedtime, Dane and Tharyn read their Bibles together and then prayed.

Tharyn prayed first, and after praying for many people, including their adoptive parents and their pastor and the church, she talked to the Lord about starting their family. Silent tears coursed down her cheeks as she told the Lord it would be difficult for Dane to find another nurse-receptionist to come to Central City to replace her when she was ready to give birth to their first child.

Tharyn felt Dane's firm hand on her shoulder as she prayed on, asking the Lord to show them His will about when they should start their family. She told the Lord that when that time came, Dane would need His leadership in seeking a new nurse-receptionist and the money to pay her sufficiently.

Tharyn closed her prayer by thanking the Lord for helping Dane to be the one to cause the change in Chief Tando's thinking.

As Dane prayed, he also went over the people and things they prayed about regularly, then said, "Lord, if this increasingly strong desire in Tharyn's heart to become a mother is because You are putting it there, then show us this for sure, and we will know that we are to start our family earlier than we had planned. If this is Your will, we know You will bless the practice sufficiently so we can afford to hire a lady full-time. I thank You that we are doing so well financially, and that we can already be thinking about turning it into a clinic and adding another doctor."

When Dane closed his prayer and opened his eyes, he saw the tears streaming down Tharyn's cheeks. He took her into his arms and said, "Sweetheart, don't concern yourself about the finances. I want to become a father as soon as the Lord is ready. Quite possibly He would have us hire the new nurse-receptionist so you can have our first child before we take the step to turn the practice into a clinic and hire another doctor. The Lord will provide when it's time."

Tharyn clung to him as she wiped tears from her eyes. "Darling, I want so very much to be a mother, but only when it's God's time. The desire has been inside me so strong ever since we got married, but somehow it grew stronger today when I got to hold little Lydia Marie in my arms."

Dane smiled and looked into her eyes. "I can understand that, honey. Well, it's getting late. We'd better head upstairs."

Half an hour later, Dane blew out the kerosene lantern that sat on the small table beside the bed and slid down into the covers. Tharyn cuddled up close to his back for warmth. After several minutes, she kissed the back of his neck and whispered, "I love this time of night. Everything seems so quiet and peaceful."

Dane did not respond.

A frown formed on Tharyn's brow in the darkness. "Sweetheart, don't you agree that this is the best time of the night?"

Then she heard his steady breathing and realized he was already asleep.

"Poor darling," she said in a faint whisper, "he has had a hard day. Bless him, Lord, and give him a good night's rest. Thank you for giving me such a thoughtful and wonderful husband."

Lying there snuggled up to Dane's back, Tharyn relived little Lydia Marie Miller's birth, and wiped tears on the sheet as she whispered, "Thank You, dear Lord, for giving Jack and Sally such a precious little girl. I will be so glad when we can have our first baby. I . . . I will be happy whichever it is, boy or girl. But somehow, Lord, I feel that our first child will be a girl. I've got to think about names, so when it comes time, I can tell Dane what I want to name our first girl."

Tharyn fell asleep thinking about her first child . . .

She was in her kitchen at midmorning one day, and while standing at the sink, she looked out the window into the backyard and smiled as she saw her little five-year-old daughter swaying back and forth in the swing her father had made for her and hung from a limb in one of the large cottonwood trees.

Tharyn felt impelled to step out on the back porch and watch as the little girl happily swung back and forth with her back toward the house. Her long dark brown hair, the same color as Dane's, fluttered in the air.

After watching for a few minutes, Tharyn stepped off the porch, walked around in front of the swinging child, and saw that she had dark brown eyes — exactly like her father's.

When the girl saw her mother, she flashed a big smile. "Mommy, will you push me so I can go up real high?"

Tharyn noted how beautiful the child was and marveled that she bore a strong resemblance to her mother. "Honey, it will be dangerous if you swing too high. I don't want you to fall out and hurt yourself."

"Daddy swings me real high. I'm a big girl. Come on, Mommy. I'll hold on tight."

Tharyn smiled and shook her head. "All right, Elizabeth Ann, but you make sure you hold on real tight."

Elizabeth Ann. What a beautiful name!

Suddenly Tharyn found herself sitting up in the bed, breathing hard and repeating the name *Elizabeth Ann* over and over.

Pale moonlight touched the curtains at the bedroom windows, giving just enough light to illuminate the room and to make deep shadows all around.

"Yes!" Tharyn said exuberantly, popping her hands together. "That's it! Elizabeth Ann Logan. It's beautiful!"

Dane stirred, rolled over, and opened his eyes. "Honey, shouldn't you be asleep? What are you clapping about in the middle of the night?"

A hand went to Tharyn's mouth. "Oh, I'm sorry, Dane. I didn't mean to wake you." She leaned over and hugged him joyfully. "I was just having such a wonderful dream, and it made me so happy!"

Dane rubbed his eyes. "Well, now that I'm awake, do you want to share it with me?"

"Yes! Oh, yes, I want to tell you about it!"

172

Tharyn shivered in the cool air and settled herself comfortably under the covers, placing her head on Dane's shoulder. "Darling, you know I don't believe in omens or things like that, but just before I dropped off to sleep, I was thinking about the first baby God will give us, and somehow I had a girl in mind."

"Oh, really?"

"Uh-huh. And this dream fell right into line with what I was thinking."

Dane twisted under the covers so he could see her face in the moonlight. "Okay, now you really have my attention. I'm wide awake. Tell me why this dream was so special. I want to share it, too."

Tharyn raised up on an elbow, bent down and kissed her husband's stubbled cheek. She lay back down and placed her head on his shoulder again. "Well, I dreamed that we had a girl first, and in the dream she was already five years old. She had dark brown hair and eyes just like yours, and she was absolutely beautiful. She . . . ah . . . did look a lot like me."

Dane snickered. "Well, she indeed would be beautiful, then."

"You're a flatterer. And you know what?"

"What?"

"Her name was Elizabeth Ann."

"And how did you learn her name?"

"Well, in the dream, I just walked up to her and called her Elizabeth Ann. And she called me Mommy."

"Hmm," said Dane. "I wish I could have been there, too. Elizabeth Ann, eh?"

"Yes! And that's what we will name our first baby girl! Ah . . . if that's all right with you."

"Sure it is. I love it. Elizabeth Ann Logan. I really do love the sound of it."

A thrill went through Tharyn's body. "It *is* beautiful, isn't it?"

"Most certainly. Now it's time for the future Elizabeth Ann Logan's mommy to get some sleep."

Tharyn raised up on an elbow again, kissed him on the lips, and said, "All right. Good night, future Elizabeth Ann Logan's daddy."

Ten

There was night music in the air around the village of renegade Ute Chief Antono as a dozen fires flickered their light on faces of braves and squaws and the tepees that stood close around the spot where the adults were gathered. All the children had been put in their blankets inside the tepees for the night.

Antono's village was situated in the Rocky Mountains a few miles due west of Chief Tando's village.

Above the sounds of the crackling fires and the few voices that could be heard in the village, the night music went on. There was the rhythm of the wind in the branches of the pines. Wolves howled in the mournful distance, and nearby owls hooted, underscoring the deep gurgling sound of the creek that ran past the village.

On each side of the village, two sentries were at their posts. At the east edge of the village, warriors Sudana and Hipto sat on a fallen pine tree, listening to the night music around them. Their ears, however, were alert to any unfamiliar sounds, and their eyes continuously searched the darkness for any sign of someone approaching.

A few clouds drifted overhead, partially covering the moon.

Suddenly Hipto stiffened as he heard sounds of hooves in the grass. "Do you hear that?" he asked his partner.

Sudana grasped his rifle, peering in the direction from which the sounds were coming. "Yes. It could be deer or elk, or even antelope. But I think it is horses."

Both men stood up, rifles ready, and suddenly they caught sight of what appeared in the dim moonlight to be ghostly shapes floating toward them.

The back of Hipto's neck prickled, the hairs rising.

"It is horses, and there are riders on their backs," Sudana said.

Sudana stepped forward first, then Hipto moved up beside him. At that moment, the clouds that partly covered the moon blew away, and the brighter light revealed two Ute warriors. As they drew up, one of them said, "Sudana, Hipto. It is Zaldo and Windano."

Sudana said, "You are traveling? You need a place to sleep for the night?"

"It is not like that," said Zaldo. "We must speak to your chief."

Sudana nodded. "We will take you to him. Please leave your horses here."

Zaldo and Windano slid off their horses' backs and walked with the sentries as they led them into the village. Soon they were moving past the fires, and some of the warriors recognized Zaldo and Windano and spoke to them.

Chief Antono was sitting on the ground by the fire in front of his tepee, his squaw beside him. Two other warriors and their squaws were seated around the fire with them.

All of them saw Sudana and Hipto coming their direction, and when Antono recognized subchief Zaldo and warrior Windano, he stood up. The other two warriors by the fire also rose to their feet.

"Chief Antono," said Sudana, "Zaldo and Windano have come here wishing to speak to you."

Antono nodded, with a friendly look in his dark eyes. "Come. Sit down here by the fire."

Antono's squaw stood up. "We squaws will leave so Antono may talk to Zaldo and Windano privately."

Antono thanked her, and as all three

squaws walked away, Antono told the other two warriors they could stay. He dismissed Sudana and Hipto that they might return to their post.

Antono picked up a fresh log and tossed it on the fire, then set his steady gaze on his guests. "What is it you wish to discuss with me?"

Zaldo's features were stony. "Chief Antono has not learned of what happened to Chief Yukana and many of his warriors today?"

Antono shook his head. "No. What happened?"

Zaldo explained that for the past few days, Chief Yukana had been leading his warriors in attacking white men's ranches, killing them and their families, then burning their houses. He explained that this was because Chief Yukana learned that earlier this week, Chief Tando had gone to Fort Junction — accompanied by Chief Ouray — and had signed a peace treaty with white man's government. In his wrath toward Chief Tando's turning traitor, Yukana had decided to show his hatred for the whites by attacking their ranches.

Antono smiled thinly. "I must say what Chief Yukana did was very good. I only learned of Tando becoming a traitor and signing the peace treaty this morning. Word came from some Ute warriors who live near Fort Junction. I will tell Chief Yukana how proud of him I am when next I see him."

Zaldo and Windano exchanged glances, then Zaldo looked back at Antono. "Chief, you will never see Chief Yukana again. He is dead."

"Dead? Chief Yukana is dead?"

"Yes. Earlier today, the chief sent Windano and me ahead to scout out the choicest ranches to attack. When we had found a good number, Windano and I rode back to join up with our chief and his band and make a report. Ahead, we heard the sound of gunfire. We galloped up close to the battle, left our horses tied to trees, and went in closer on foot. We arrived just in time to see the last of the warrior band go down under the fire of the white men's army. They had two of those guns they call Gatling."

Antono's features were gray. "And — and your chief was down?"

"Yes. A few of the soldier coats had been killed or wounded. We waited until the soldier coats had picked up their dead and wounded and rode away, then went down to the field of battle.

"Chief Yukana was still alive, but just barely. He asked if all the others in the band had been killed. We told him they had. With his last few breaths, Chief Yukana told us to come to you and tell you that he now believed that Chief Ouray had been right all along. All Utes should have made peace with the whites when Ouray and the majority of the Utes did. He also said Chief Tando did right when he signed the peace treaty. Chief Yukana told us to plead with you to make peace with the whites. It was the last thing he said before he died. That is why we have come, Chief Antono: to tell you what our chief said with his dying breath."

Grief showed in Antono's eyes. He held his gaze on Zaldo for a long moment, then said, "Your people know that their chief and those warriors are dead?"

Zaldo nodded. "Yes. The bodies are now at our village, waiting for burial tomorrow morning."

"And how do they feel about all of this?"

"They agree that we should have made peace with the whites when Chief Ouray urged us to do it. They are ready to make peace now."

Antono looked at his two warriors who

sat with him. "How do you feel? Have I been wrong to stand against the whites?"

The warriors looked at each other, then one of them said, "Chief Antono, when our warriors have been in battle with the white man's army, with many killed and wounded, there has been hushed talk in the village among the people. Many have said they wished you would make peace with the whites so there would be no more bloodshed."

"Why did they not say this to me?"

"Because they not only look up to you, Chief, but they *fear* you."

"You two have felt this way?"

"Yes, Chief," said the other warrior, "but we fear you also. This is why we have not told you how we feel. But has there not been enough blood shed by our warriors?"

While Antono ran his gaze between the two warriors, Zaldo spoke up. "Chief Antono, the soldier coats from Fort Junction are now patrolling with the guns called Gatling. It took them only a brief time to kill the band with Chief Yukana. Is it worth it to go on making war with them, and to have more of your warriors killed?"

Antono felt a weakness creeping over his stubborn will. After a brief moment, his face turned pale. He looked suddenly exhausted, and his eyes were like dead black coals. His voice was low as he said, "Chief Ouray has been correct all along. No, it is not worth it. Let us gather all of our people here right now. I will tell them that I will do the same as Chief Tando. I will go to Fort Junction and sign a peace treaty with the white man's government."

It was dawn the next morning — Thursday, September 22 — when Chief Tando and subchief Nandano lifted a groggy, feverish Latawga onto the frame of the buffalo-hide travois hitched by its pair of long poles to one of the pintos owned by Tando.

Leela stood close by her son, looking on with her face devoid of color. Two squaws flanked her, each holding a hand to comfort her.

The entire village was gathered at the scene.

The eastern horizon blushed pink above the majestic mountains. An eerie silence clung to the village as if the sight of the chief's ailing son on the travois meant he was going to die.

Medicine man Rimago stood over the chief's son, a worried look on his deeply lined face, as Chief Tando bent over and tied Latawga securely to the travois.

When Tando stood erect, Rimago looked at him with tears in his eyes. "I am so sorry, Chief Tando. This is all my fault."

Tando shook his head. "Anyone could have dropped the bottle, Rimago. It slipped from your fingers. You could not help it."

Rimago bit his lips. "If only it had landed on the soft earth instead of landing on that rock."

"I wish it had, Rimago," said Tando, "but since you have not been able to apply the medicine Dr. Dane Logan gave you, there is no choice. Latawga's fever is very high, and the wound in his leg looks very bad. Nandano and I must take him to Dr. Dane Logan immediately."

Standing close by, Nandano said, "Chief Tando, I am concerned that we are not taking a number of warriors with us in case we encounter trouble from white people who may not know that you have signed the peace treaty."

"We dare not appear to be traveling with warriors, Nandano. This would lead whites to think we are doing something against them as we have done for so many grasses. I can only hope if you and I come upon whites who show hostility toward us, that by seeing Latawga, they will believe that

183

you and I are taking my very sick son to Dr. Dane Logan in Central City."

Nandano nodded and walked to his pinto. As he was swinging onto the horse's back, Tando turned to his squaw and said in a tender tone. "Leela must not worry. Dr. Dane Logan will make him well. Latawga will not die."

Leela let go of the hands of the squaws and used both palms to wipe tears from her cheeks. She nodded. "Latawga will not die."

She then bent over her son and patted his sweaty cheek. "Latawga's father is correct. Dr. Dane Logan will make you well."

Tando squeezed Leela's arm, then stepped to his horse and mounted.

He and the subchief rode away with Nandano holding the reins of the pinto that bore the travois.

The people of the village looked on as Chief Tando, Nandano, and Latawga headed north. The horizon had changed from pink to molten gold, casting lengthy shadows as the sun lifted toward the sky.

Soon they entered a dense forest, and wove their way among the trees for over an hour. When they were nearing the north edge of the forest, Tando called for Nandano to stop. He slid from his horse and bent over Latawga, whose face was gleaming with perspiration. He looked up at his father with bleary eyes. Tando took a bottle of water from where it had been tied to the travois and gave his son a long drink.

When Latawga had downed all the water he wanted, Tando used a cloth he had tucked inside his buffalo hide coat to wipe the perspiration from his son's face.

Tando mounted his pinto again, and they headed down a gentle slope toward another forest.

When they were within less than a half-mile from the forest's edge, Tando was looking back at Latawga. Suddenly from the corner of his eye, he saw Nandano stiffen his body and pull back on the reins. His eyes were wide.

By reflex, Tando pulled rein, too. When he jerked his head around to see what had caused Nandano to stop, he saw a cavalry column of over thirty men riding toward them double file out of the forest, with two wagons bearing Gatling guns bringing up the rear. Metal from the rifles the troopers carried flashed in the sunlight and the column's guidon fluttered in the breeze blowing over the high country.

"Soldier coats!" gasped Nandano.

Tando squinted at the leader of the column, and a smile curved his lips. "Do not be afraid, Nandano. If you will look closely at their leader, you will see that it is Captain Darrell Redmond."

By this time, Captain Redmond had recognized the Indians, and was hurrying the column toward them.

When the men in blue drew up, Chief Tando raised his hand in a sign of peace, and Redmond did the same.

The soldiers looked on as their captain noted the travois attached to the pinto behind Nandano, and said, "Chief Tando, Nandano, who do you have on the travois?"

"My son, Latawga," responded the chief. "He is very sick. We are taking him to Dr. Dane Logan in Central City. Dr. Dane Logan will make him well."

Redmond nodded. "I am sure he will. We will not detain you. Just let me ask . . . have you heard about Chief Yukana?"

"We have not," said Tando. "What is this?"

Redmond told him how he and his men had been tracking Yukana and his warriors to put a stop to attacks on ranchers and their families. There was a battle, and when it was over, Redmond and his men rode away, leaving all of the Indians down — including Yukana.

Chief Tando shook his head. "I am sorry that Chief Yukana was doing this to the white ranchers and their families. I hope the rest of his warriors will stop making war against the whites."

"We have already gone to the village and talked to them. One of the subchiefs promised that they would no longer be our enemies."

"That is good. It seems, then, that there is only one Ute chief who still is at war with the whites . . . Antono."

"Yes. Does Antono know about you signing the peace treaty?"

Tando nodded. "Yes. He was very angry toward me, but said he would not fight me because we are Ute brothers."

"Well, I'm glad for that. I'm hoping that when Antono learns about Chief Yukana being dead, and his people making peace with us, he will think it over and do the same."

"This would be very good," said Tando.

"Very good, indeed, Chief. Well, I said I would not detain you, and I already have. Hurry and get your son to Dr. Logan."

In Central City, from the time Dr. Dane

and Tharyn opened the office at eight o'clock, the waiting room began to fill up. Some were patients with appointments, and others were walk-ins with emergencies.

At times, Dr. Dane needed Tharyn at his side in the surgical and examining room, but when she was at her desk doing paperwork, her mind often flashed back to her dream about Elizabeth Ann the night before.

The name was becoming even more precious to her, and as she thought about the dream, she relished her brief moment with the sweet child.

She told herself over and over that it was just a dream, but she was still determined that her first baby girl would be named Elizabeth Ann. She even told herself that her little girl might even look like the one in the dream.

At midmorning, Tharyn looked up and saw a couple come in with the man carrying a young boy who was quite pale and obviously hurting. As they stepped up to the desk, the man said, "Ma'am, is Dr. Logan in?"

"Yes, he is," Tharyn replied, noting that there was a white cloth around the boy's neck. "He is with some parents and their baby in the back room, but he should be finished very soon." She stood up, moved around the end of the desk, and looked at the pallid-faced child. "I assume there's something wrong here on his neck."

"Yes," said the mother. "Do you want to see it, ma'am?"

"I'd like to."

The boy winced and made a tiny cry as his mother removed the white cloth. Tharyn took one look at it and said, "That is one bad abscess! It will have to be lanced. Are you folks patients here?"

"We've been in a few times," said the father, "but it was when Dr. Fraser was here. Our names are Morton and Lillian Hall. This is Ronnie. He's nine years old."

At that moment, Dr. Dane had just finished examining Sam and Sherrie Drummond's week-old baby boy, and was walking out of the back room with them, saying what a fine, husky boy he was.

Tharyn rushed up and said, "We have a nine-year-old boy here with a real bad abscess on his neck, Doctor."

Dr. Dane excused himself to the Drummonds, and while they were getting ready to pay Tharyn their bill, Dr. Dane told Ronnie Hall's parents to bring the boy into the back room.

★ ★ ★

When Sam and Sherrie stepped outside, Sam's parents, Chet and Alice Drummond, were waiting for them in the buggy. Chet hopped off the driver's seat and took his grandson from Sherrie so Sam could help her into the buggy's rear seat beside Alice. When Sherrie was in place, Chet handed her the baby, then hurried onto the driver's seat. Sam climbed onto the driver's seat beside his father.

As they drove away with Sam at the reins, heading south toward their ranch in the mountains, Sherrie spoke up with elation in her voice. "Well, Grandma and Grandpa, you'll be happy to know that Dr. Logan says little Sammy Jr. is in perfect health."

Alice's face beamed. "That's wonderful!"

Chet turned around to take a quick look at the small bundle in Sherrie's arms. "Handsome little guy, too! Looks just like his grandpa!"

Sam chuckled. "Well, maybe he'll be fortunate and grow out of it."

The women laughed, and Chet gave his son a mock scowl.

Soon they reached the south edge of town, and were moving into open country

190

when suddenly Sam pointed ahead and said, "Look up there! Two Utes riding toward us! They've got a travois tied to that pinto behind them."

Sherrie gasped and said, "What are they doing, coming this way? Looks like they're heading right for town!"

Both Chet and Sam whipped out their revolvers.

"Utes!" Chet said, as if the word tasted sour.

Sherrie clutched her baby close to her heart, eyes wide.

"We should avoid a confrontation if possible, Chet," Alice said.

Chet bit down hard. "I don't want bullets flying with you ladies and little Sammy Jr. in the buggy, dear. We'll do our best to avoid any trouble, but we have to be ready in case these savages try anything."

The Utes were drawing near. When they saw the two men brandishing their guns, both of them raised their hands in a sign of peace, also showing that they held no weapons.

Chet signaled for them to stop, and both Indians pulled rein. The pinto pulling the travois behind them came to a halt.

Drawing the buggy to a stop, Chet held his gun in plain sight, the muzzle pointed

191

downward toward his feet. Sam did the same.

"You speak English?" Chet said.

Both Indians nodded, and the older one said, "I am Chief Tando, and this is one of my subchiefs, Nandano. My son, Latawga, is on the travois. He is very ill. We are taking him to Dr. Dane Logan in Central City."

Chet's cheeks became stony in the sunlight. "Dr. Logan doesn't treat Indians. It would be best if you let your own medicine men take care of your son."

Tando shook his head mildly. "You do not understand. Dr. Dane Logan treated my son a few moons ago when he was shot in the leg. He removed the bullet from the leg and saved his life. The wound is not healing. We need to have Dr. Dane Logan look at it."

Chet's features reddened. He turned to Sam. "This one on the travois has to be the one Doc treated and was gonna take home."

Sam licked his lips. "I'd say that's him, all right."

Tando looked puzzled. "You know about Dr. Dane Logan taking the bullet out of my son's leg?"

"Yes, I know about it," Chet said evenly.

"It was my son and I who shot at your son. He was with a band of your warriors who were trying to steal our cattle. Your warriors galloped away, and we saw a cavalry unit from Fort Junction chasing them."

Nandano felt his heart thump against his rib cage as he thought of the incident, which put him and the other warriors with him in the guardhouse at Fort Junction.

Chet went on. "Dr. Logan was at our house to deliver this baby in my daughter-in-law's arms when your band of warriors came onto the ranch and began to steal our cattle. My son and I did what anyone would do in the situation. We opened fire. Your son was the only one we were able to hit. Dr. Logan removed the bullet from your son's leg at our house. It was from there that he took him home to your village."

Chief Tando glanced at Nandano, then set his dark eyes on the older rancher. "May I learn your name, sir?"

"Sure. Chet Drummond."

"I need to take my son to Dr. Dane Logan, Mr. Chet Drummond, but it is important to me that I make an apology and explain something to you."

Chet glanced back at Alice. "What do you think?"

"I think we need to hear what the chief has to say."

Chet swung his gaze to Sherrie, who was still holding her baby close to her heart. "You agree?"

Sherrie nodded.

Chet turned to his son beside him. "Sam?"

"Sounds like something has happened to these Utes that we need to know about, Dad."

Chet looked at the Indians again, running his gaze between them, then let it settle on Tando. "All right, Chief Tando. We will listen."

Eleven

Chief Tando adjusted his position on the pinto's back, and the lines in his face seemed to grow deeper as he said, "Mr. Chet Drummond, I am truly sorry that my band of warriors went upon your land and tried to steal your cattle. Always, when my warriors made any kind of hostile move on the whites, it was by my orders. In spite of Chief Ouray's efforts to convince me that the Utes should no longer make war against the white men many grasses ago, I continued to lead my people to do so, as did a few other Ute chiefs. We were wrong. We did this because we believed that all white people hated us.

"My mind was changed about this when Dr. Dane Logan carried my wounded son home on his horse with him, and Latawga told me how Dr. Dane Logan had saved his life in two ways. First, when he kept you from killing him as he lay wounded on the ground; and second, when he removed the bullet from his leg, bandaged him up, and stopped the bleeding. By this, I knew that Dr. Dane Logan did not hate Indians. I appreciated him even more when I thought of how he brought my son home to the village, not knowing what we might do to him, just because he was a white man.

"Dr. Dane Logan assured me that all white men do not hate Indians, and I was quick to believe him. I want you to know that earlier this week, I traveled to Fort Junction with Dr. Dane Logan and Chief Ouray where I signed a peace treaty with your white man's government before General Joseph Dayton and Colonel Perry Smith. My people and I are no longer at war with the whites."

The Drummonds looked at each other, hardly able to believe what they were hearing.

Chet took a deep breath, let it out slowly, and said, "Chief, it is a bit difficult for me to believe that you have signed a peace treaty, but I sure hope it's true."

Tando nodded. "I can understand why you find my words hard to accept. And I think I see this in the rest of your family also. I must get Latawga to Dr. Dane Logan now, but I would like for you and your family to come with me and ask Dr.

Dane Logan if I am telling you the truth."

Sam looked at his father. "Dad, if he's willing to do this, he must not be lying. Let's give him the benefit of the doubt. Let's go with him and see if Dr. Logan backs up his story."

Alice and Sherrie had their eyes pinned on Chet as he rubbed the back of his neck and said to Sam, "I don't know, son. We could run into real trouble by escorting these Indians into town. There are plenty of other people in Central City who are wary of renegade Utes. It would be best if Marshal Merrell were to ride into town with them."

Alice leaned toward the front seat of the buggy. "Your father is right, Sam. It would be best by far if we could get the marshal to escort them."

Sam nodded. "Okay. I'll run into town, find the marshal, take him to Dr. Logan's office, let the doctor confirm that Chief Tando is telling the truth, then bring the marshal here so he can escort the Indians into town."

Chief Tando spoke up. "Mr. Chet Drummond, I want to get Latawga to Dr. Dane Logan very soon, but I understand why you are being cautious, and I understand why you want the town's lawman to know the truth and be the one to take us to Dr. Dane Logan's office. We will wait here until the marshal comes."

"I appreciate that, Chief," said Chet. Then to Sam and the women: "We'll drive back into town together and find the marshal."

With that, Chet snapped the reins, turned the buggy around, and drove toward town.

Almost half an hour had passed when Tando and Nandano were bending over the feverish Latawga. Tando was giving him water to drink, and Nandano was wiping his brow with the cloth when they looked up to see the Drummond buggy coming speedily with Marshal Jake Merrell riding beside it.

When they pulled up, Chet stepped out of the buggy while the marshal was dismounting. Chet introduced Marshal Merrell to Chief Tando and Nandano, then Merrell said, "Chief, I want you to know that I did not have to talk to Dr. Logan when Chet and Sam came into town just now. Dr. Logan already told me about you signing the peace treaty at Fort Junction. And I want to say, Chief Tando, that I am very glad that you and your people are no longer at war with white people."

Tando nodded. "We are glad, too, Marshal Jake Merrell."

Merrell smiled. "I'll escort you to the doctor's office so he can take care of your son."

The Drummonds headed for their ranch, and Marshal Merrell escorted the Indians toward town.

When Marshal Jake Merrell rode into town beside Chief Tando and Nandano, and their travois bearing the ailing Latawga, people along the street stopped and gawked.

Seeing the astonished and fearful look on their faces, Merrell called out, "All is well, folks! These are not hostile Indians!"

As they drew up to the hitch rail in front of Dr. Logan's office, Merrell ran his gaze over the faces of the gathering townsfolk and said, "Don't worry, folks. Chief Tando's son, here on the travois, needs Dr. Logan's attention."

While the marshal and the Indians were dismounting, an elderly woman said to her husband, "Do you think Dr. Logan will actually take care of a savage Indian?"

The old rancher shrugged. "Don't know,

Maisie. If Doc does see to him, he might jist git hisself into a heap o' trouble. People around here well remember the trouble some o' these Utes have caused us. Guess we'll have to wait and see what happens." A frown creased his leathery skin as he pondered the outcome of the situation.

Inside the office, Tharyn was at her desk when she looked up and saw the marshal coming through the door with the two Indians behind him. The younger one was carrying a pale, feverish Indian, who was younger yet.

Tharyn stood up, finding her knees a bit weak. "Good morning, Marshal. Looks like you have a very sick young man."

The marshal moved up to the desk. "Hello, Tharyn. I have Chief Tando and Nandano here. The sick young man is Chief Tando's son, Latawga. Dr. Dane no doubt told you about his taking a bullet out of Latawga's leg several days ago."

"Oh, yes."

Tando set worried eyes on the lady with the auburn hair. "My son's wound is very much infected. We need to have Dr. Dane Logan see him very soon."

"Of course, Chief. I am Dr. Logan's wife, Tharyn. I'll go tell my husband that you've brought Latawga here for treat-

200

ment. He doesn't have any patients back there right now." She wheeled about and quickly disappeared.

When she stepped into the back room, Tharyn found her husband working at the medicine cabinet, mixing powders in a bowl. He glanced over his shoulder. "Hi, sweetheart. Did I hear someone come in?"

"Did you ever! Remember Chief Tando's son, Latawga? You took a bullet out of his leg at the Drummond ranch, then took him to the village?"

"Of course. Are you telling me —"

"Yes! Jake Merrell just brought Chief Tando in with another Indian named Nandano, who is carrying Latawga. The chief said Latawga's wound is badly infected."

Dane dropped the two powder containers and hurried out to the office with Tharyn on his heels. "Hello, Chief Tando . . . Nandano. Mrs. Logan told me Latawga's leg wound is infected."

"Yes," said Tando. "*Very* infected."

"Let's get him in the back room and have a look." Dr. Dane smiled at the marshal. "Apparently you escorted them here to the office?"

Merrell nodded. "I'll explain it to you later. I'll be going now."

Tando expressed his thanks to the marshal for his help, then quickly followed Nandano, who carried Latawga into the back room.

Dr. Dane led them to one of the curtained sections and directed Nandano to place Latawga on the examining table.

Tando and Nandano stood close by as Dr. Dane looked at the sweaty Latawga, who was burning up with fever.

While the doctor was examining the infected wound, Chief Tando said, "Last Monday, when you left the bottle of carb—carb—"

"Carbolic acid," the doctor said without taking his eyes off the wound.

Tando nodded. "Yes. Carbolic acid. My medicine man, Rimago, was about to apply it to the wound that evening, as you had instructed him. But he accidentally dropped the bottle. It struck a rock on the ground and shattered."

Dr. Dane looked at him. "You should have let me know so I could supply Rimago with another bottle."

Tando bit his lower lip. "I suggested this to Rimago, but he felt that his own herbal concoction would take care of the infection. As the days passed, he could see that it was not working. Finally, last night,

Rimago said we should bring Latawga to you."

"I'm glad you did. You and Nandano can step outside these curtains here, and sit on a couple of those chairs over there by the wall."

When the Indians had done as directed, Dr. Dane bent over Latawga. "You just lie as still as you can, all right? I'll have you feeling better shortly."

Latawga looked at the doctor with dull eyes and nodded.

Dr. Dane went to work on Latawga to bring his fever down as much as possible before lancing the infected wound.

While he was working at his task, he heard the office door open, and Tharyn's rapid footsteps coming to the curtained section.

She moved in hastily and said, "Dane, we've got trouble outside in front of the office."

"What kind of trouble?"

"Apparently many people saw the Indians carrying Latawga in here, and they are out there on the street giving Marshal Merrell and Deputy Kurtz a hard time for letting them come into town. Mayor Anderson has been summoned."

Still occupied with his task, Dane

sighed. "Oh, yes. Mayor Anderson. I wish I'd had time to get to him and tell him about Chief Tando signing the peace treaty. Will you bring him in to see me when he arrives?"

"Of course." Tharyn paused before leaving. "Many of those people out there are really angry. Some of them may resent your caring for Latawga."

"Well, if they do, that's too bad."

Tharyn managed a smile. "You're absolutely the best, darling. The very best."

Dane took time to turn and look at her. He smiled widely, then went back to work.

Some twenty minutes had passed when Tharyn returned and stepped up to the curtained section where Dr. Dane was laboring over Latawga. "Honey, Mayor Anderson is in the office. I've explained to him what's happening in here. Do you want him to come in right now?"

"Yes. Please send him in."

Moments later, Mike Anderson stepped up to the opening of the curtains. "Hello, Doc. Your wife said you wanted to see me."

"Yes. Step in, Mike. I have to keep working here, but I need to explain something to you."

The mayor moved in, keeping some distance from the table where the patient lay.

While working on Latawga's wound, the doctor said, "I meant to get to you and tell you about this, Mike, but I just couldn't work in the time." He then told him about going to Fort Junction with Chief Tando and Chief Ouray, and of witnessing the peace treaty being signed by Chief Tando before General Joseph G. Dayton and Colonel Perry Smith.

Anderson smiled. "Doc, I'm really glad to know this. I'll go out there right now and tell that upset crowd about it."

The doctor looked at the mayor and said, "I'll be through here in about five minutes. I'd like to go out there and face the people with you."

Anderson grinned. "Sure. I'll wait."

It took just over five minutes for Dr. Dane to finish putting the bandage on Latawga's wound after lancing and draining it. He gave his patient a sedative, and told him to relax and let it work.

Then with Mayor Anderson at his side, Dane stepped out of the curtained section and approached the Indians, who immediately rose to their feet.

"Chief Tando," said the doctor, "I'm sure you could hear what my wife told me, and what Mayor Anderson and I have discussed."

Tando nodded.

"I would like for you to come outside with us and tell the crowd of people that you are no longer their enemy, and that you signed the peace treaty."

"I will do that, Dr. Dane Logan."

Dr. Dane turned to Nandano. "Will you stay with Latawga and watch over him? He should be sleeping soon, but I don't want him to be alone."

"I will do that."

"If there is any problem, you come and get me in a hurry, all right?"

"Yes."

When Dr. Dane, Chief Tando, and the mayor came into the office, Tharyn was standing by the outside door. Dane told her what the chief had agreed to do.

Tharyn smiled. "That will be good. Do you mind if I come out with you?"

"Of course not."

When the four of them stepped out onto the boardwalk, they heard Marshal Merrell telling a man to cool down and get a grip on his temper. Deputy Len Kurtz was at the marshal's side. Both lawmen turned to see the mayor, the doctor, the nurse, and the Ute chief step up close to them.

There was fire in the eyes of many of the people in the crowd. Fear showed in the faces of many others.

Mayor Anderson said loud enough for everyone to hear, "I want all of you to listen to what Dr. Logan has to say to you."

One middle-aged man, face beet red, yelled, "What if we don't want to listen to the doc? We just want those dirty savages out of our town!"

Merrell pointed a stiff finger at him. "If you continue to act like this, Stuart, you'll find out what the inside of my jail looks like. Now just pipe down and listen." The marshal then turned to the doctor. "All right, sir. The floor is yours."

Dr. Dane stepped forward a bit and said, "I ask that you give me your attention. If you will just listen, your anger and your fear will be gone."

The doctor then told them the whole story, starting with his being at the Drummond ranch delivering Sherrie's baby boy when the small band of Utes from Chief Tando's village tried to steal some of the Drummond cattle. He explained how Chet and Sam Drummond opened fire on them, hitting one warrior, and how the cavalry patrol from Fort Junction pursued the other Utes.

"I wish to explain," Dr. Dane went on, "that the warrior that was wounded was the son of Chief Tando. His name is Latawga." He paused for a second or two, then pointed to the Indian who stood a step behind him. "This man right here is Chief Tando. He will be speaking to you in a moment."

The crowd remained silent, for which Dr. Dane was glad.

Dr. Dane said, "Latawga's wound was in one of his legs. It was bleeding profusely. In order to save his life, I did the necessary surgery to repair and stitch up the wound at the Drummond ranch house. Latawga then asked me to take him home to the village, which I did."

A grim-faced man in his late forties named Elmer Dines said loudly, "Doc, how could you bring yourself to save the life of a savage Indian who was at war with white people, and who no doubt has killed many whites? He had just tried to steal cattle from the Drummonds. Why didn't you just let him die?"

"Well, Elmer, as a Christian, I couldn't just stand by and let Latawga die, even though he was an enemy of the whites. You are a Civil War veteran, Elmer."

"What's that got to do with this situation?"

"In the Civil War, when men on either side came upon wounded soldiers of the enemy army, they did what they could to give them medical attention, ease their suffering, and save their lives. Right?"

Dines's face was a mask of petulance. "Yeah."

"Why?"

Dines held his lips pressed tightly.

The doctor squinted at him. "I asked you a question, Elmer."

Dines cleared his throat. "Well, this was done in the Civil War because — because it was the humane thing to do."

"That's right. When I became a physician and surgeon, I took the Hippocratic oath, which states in the very first line, 'I swear I will prescribe treatment to the best of my ability and judgment for the good of the sick . . .' Elmer, it doesn't say 'for the good of the sick unless they are my enemies.' It says 'for the good of the sick.' As a Christian, as a human being, and as a doctor who was serious about my oath, I treated Latawga's wound because it was the right thing to do."

Another man in the crowd called out, "God bless you, Dr. Logan! From what

Marshal Merrell has told us, because of your compassion, Chief Tando and his people will never again make war against us!"

Chief Tando stepped up beside the doctor, raised his hand as if making a promise, and smiled.

Suddenly the crowd broke into cheers and people called out their blessings on Dr. Dane Logan.

Tharyn stood behind her husband and wept with pride and joy.

Mayor Anderson looked at Tharyn's tears, then stepped to the forefront and said to the crowd, "I'm so glad that God sent Dr. Logan and his dear wife to our town!"

Standing close by were Pastor Mark Shane and his wife.

People were cheering the mayor's words when Pastor Shane stepped on the boardwalk and asked the mayor if he could say something. Anderson motioned for him to do so, and took a step back.

"Folks," Shane said loud enough for all to hear, "I must say with Mayor Anderson that I am glad the Lord brought Dr. Logan and Tharyn to Central City. Together they are such a blessing to the people of this town and this part of the mountains."

There were loud cheers.

While the cheering was going on, Tharyn moved up and took hold of her husband's hand, smiling up at him.

Dane squeezed her hand, kissed her forehead, then turned toward the crowd. He waited for the cheering to subside, then said, "Folks, before we came out of the office, I asked Chief Tando if he would speak to you. He graciously agreed to do so. Please listen to him. When he is finished, you will all understand why I asked him to address you."

The chief stepped up beside the doctor, ran his gaze over the faces of the crowd, and cleared his throat nervously.

Twelve

Chief Tando ran his dark gaze over the faces of the crowd and saw a mixture of friendliness, hatred, and skepticism. His heart pounded wildly and felt heavy in his chest.

He cleared his throat again and said, "I . . . I wish to tell all of you how Dr. Dane Logan so deeply touched me, my squaw, and the people of my village." He turned and looked at Dr. Dane. "This white doctor not only did his best to save my son Latawga's life, but he actually brought him home, not knowing for sure what we — his avowed enemies — would do to him. He showed us genuine love.

"I want to say that it was Dr. Dane Logan's love and kindness to my son that showed me that all white people do not hate the Indians."

The chief drew a shaky breath. "I want to tell you that earlier this week I went to Fort Junction with Dr. Dane Logan and Chief Ouray. It was Chief Ouray who tried to persuade me to make peace with the white men many grasses ago. At Fort Junction, I signed a peace treaty before General Joseph G. Dayton and Colonel Perry Smith. My people and I are at peace with the whites, and you can all thank Dr. Dane Logan for it."

Several people applauded, calling out the name of Central City's physician.

The chief then turned and shook hands with the doctor white-man style. The people cheered, and the applause grew louder.

Mayor Mike Anderson stepped to the forefront again, shook hands with the chief, then waited for the applause and cheering to subside.

When he was sure everybody could hear him, Anderson said, "Well, folks, this has been a banner day in our town. And when the news spreads, there'll be banner days all over this part of the country." He paused briefly. "It's time, now, to get on with our business."

There was a rumble of voices as the crowd broke up and people began moving away.

Elmer Dines stepped up to the physician and said, "Dr. Logan, I want to apologize for my crass words about letting the Indian die. I was wrong."

Dr. Dane smiled at him and shook his hand. "Apology accepted, Elmer."

For several minutes Central City's citizens approached Dr. Dane and Tharyn individually and in small groups, speaking their words of love and appreciation for them.

Moments later, Nandano carried Latawga out of the office under Dr. Dane's guidance and placed him on the travois as the few citizens left looked on. In Latawga's hand was another bottle of carbolic acid.

Already feeling better, Latawga looked up at the physician and said, "Thank you, Dr. Dane Logan, for your kindness once again."

Dr. Dane smiled and laid a hand on Latawga's head. "You are very welcome. If you should need me again, your father knows to bring you back."

Chief Tando finished tying his son to the travois, then turned to Tharyn, looking at her with soft eyes. "I wish to thank you for being a helper to your husband."

She smiled and nodded.

Tando then turned to the doctor. "Dr. Dane Logan, I must agree with what was said here today by Mayor Mike Anderson and that other man. I am very glad that

214

white man's God brought you and your wife to Central City."

Dr. Dane glanced at Pastor Mark Shane, who was standing near with Peggy. Pointing with his chin at Shane, he said, "The other man, Chief Tando, is my pastor. His name is Mark Shane."

The preacher stepped up and offered his hand, and Tando shook it.

Dr. Dane felt Tharyn squeeze his arm. He looked down at her, and she smiled. He smiled back, then set his gaze on the Indian. "Chief Tando, I appreciate what you said about white man's God, but let me say to you that white man's God is also red man's God. There is only one true God, and He created us all."

Pastor Shane said, "Chief Tando, the one true God gave us a Book to guide us to Him, and to guide us through this life. We call it the Bible. You spoke of Dr. Logan's genuine love that was shown to you and your people, his avowed enemies."

Chief Tando nodded.

"I want you to know, Chief, that when Dr. Logan saved your son's life and brought him to your village — even though he was not sure what you and your people would do to him — that genuine love you saw was a result of what God's Bible taught him.

"Our Lord and Saviour, Jesus Christ, is quoted in God's Bible as saying to His followers, 'Love your enemies, do good to them which hate you.' The Bible also says, 'If thine enemy hunger, feed him; if he thirst, give him drink.' "

Tando met the preacher's steady gaze. "This is very good. I have never heard such words before."

Dr. Dane laid a tender hand on the chief's shoulder. "Chief Tando, I would like to talk to you sometime about my Lord and Saviour Jesus Christ and His Book."

The chief let a smile curve his lips. "This that I have heard today has captured my interest. You are welcome to come to my village at any time."

"Thank you. I want to come and look at Latawga's wound in a week or so. When I come, you and I can talk."

"I will look forward to your visit, Dr. Dane Logan."

The Logans and the Shanes stood side by side and watched as the Indians mounted up and rode south out of town.

Tharyn looked up at her husband with misty eyes. "I have a feeling the Lord is going to use you to bring Chief Tando to Him."

"Me, too," said Pastor Shane.

"I feel that way, myself," Dane said. "We'll pray to that end."

The two couples bid each other good day, and as Dane and Tharyn headed back for the office, he put his arm around her and drew her up close to his side. "Before I go to Chief Tando's village, you and I should spend a good deal of time praying about it."

"We will, sweetheart," she said softly.

As they passed through the door, Dane said, "I'll certainly need the power of the Holy Spirit when I talk to Chief Tando. He and his precious people are so steeped in their pagan religion, it won't be an easy task to break down their false beliefs. Their pagan gods are all they've known."

As Dane closed the door, Tharyn looked at him with her soft blue eyes. "Well, at least the chief is willing to talk to you about the Lord and His Bible, and that says a lot."

"It's so good to know that the Word of God is quick, and powerful, and sharper than any two-edged sword. It drew you to Jesus, and it did the same for me. God can use it to draw Chief Tando and his people to Jesus, too."

Tears misted Tharyn's eyes again. "It

takes prayer, too. And you and I will make it a matter of earnest prayer. Almighty God, alone, can do the necessary work in the chief's heart. And the fact that you took the time and the care to cultivate a friendship with the chief will speak volumes to him, I'm sure." Tharyn reached up and cupped his face in her hands. "Oh, Dane, I'm so proud of you. And you know what else?"

He frowned slightly. "What?"

"I am also thrilled to be your wife. God not only made you a physician and surgeon. He made you a missionary as well!"

Dane nodded. "Something He wants all Christians to be — telling everyone who will listen the good news of salvation. Since we have a few minutes before patients with appointments are due to come in, how about we pray together right now?"

They entered Dane's private office and knelt down at a worn leather couch. Hand in hand, the doctor and his wife lifted their heartfelt prayers to the God in heaven Who was able to draw souls to Himself through His Word.

The afternoon was a busy one, and between patients, Dr. Dane was reminded by his wife that he had several house calls scheduled for tomorrow, and that Dr. Robert Fraser was planning to be there all day.

Dane was wiping the microphone of his stethoscope with a clean cloth as Tharyn was speaking. He met her gaze. "I sure hope Dr. Fraser's back is doing better."

"I do too," she said, "but I really don't think he is going to be able to continue filling in here at the office much longer."

"His age is telling on him. He's going to have to retire completely, soon. I've been thinking about it a lot lately. I mentioned Dr. Tim Braden to you recently."

"Yes. He'll be finishing his internship at Mile High Hospital next May. Have you given more thought to trying to bring Tim here?"

"I have. We need to get back to our patients. I'll talk to you about it this evening."

It was nearly five-thirty when Dane and Tharyn closed the office and headed home. They put horse and buggy in their small barn, then entered the house through the back door and walked into the kitchen.

Tharyn looked around, and with a contented sigh, smiled at him and said, "Isn't it good to be home in our own little haven of peace and quiet?"

"It sure is, honey," Dane said, removing his coat and hanging it on a peg near the door.

"I know we have a busy schedule with our practice, but I intend to enjoy every moment when I can be home."

Dane grinned and let out his own sigh. "I'm with you, sweetheart. The patient load seems to grow daily, and my only free time is on Sunday, and that day is filled with church services and fellowship with our church family — which I love — but it would be nice just to have a 'free' day once in a while."

"Why don't you build a fire in the stove for me, then during supper, you can tell me all about your plan involving Tim Braden. I'm eager to hear about it."

Dane went to the stove, quickly built a fire, and told her he would build one also in the fireplace in the parlor. When he returned, he sat down at the table, which Tharyn had already set.

"I hope you don't mind some tomato soup and warm crusty bread with butter for your supper," she said, while she was at the stove.

"Sounds good. You know I'm not a picky

eater. After living on the streets of New York City, a hot bowl of soup and warm bread sounds like manna from heaven."

Stirring the soup in its pan, she looked over her shoulder and smiled. "I guess we'll never forget those hungry days, will we? We have so much to be thankful for. Starting, of course, with finding each other again after it looked so hopeless."

"That's for sure, sweetheart. My life just wouldn't be right without you."

Tharyn poured the soup into two bowls and set them on the table, then went back to the cupboard for the plate of bread. She stepped up behind Dane and kissed the top of his head. "If you'll lead us in prayer for the food, we can eat now."

Tharyn sat down, and they clasped hands over the table. Dane led in prayer, and when he finished, she said, "All right, tell me what you've got in mind about Tim. I'm excited to hear it, because my best friend will be coming with him if he does come."

Dane chuckled. "Of course. With Melinda here, you'd be elated, wouldn't you?"

"I'll say. All right, go ahead."

"Well, for sure our practice is growing steadily. I figure we won't be able to pay

Tim a big salary at first, but if you agree, I'd like to offer him the job as my assistant, then one day when we can afford to establish a clinic, I'd like to take him in as my partner."

Excitement showed on Tharyn's countenance. "Oh, yes, I wholeheartedly agree, darling! When you offer Tim the job, I think he'll jump at the opportunity. Oh, I'm so thrilled at the prospect of having Melinda living right here in Central City!"

Dane swallowed the piece of bread he was chewing. "Well, the next time we're in Denver, I'll talk to Tim about it and see if he's interested. If he jumps at the opportunity like you think he will, we'll make plans in a hurry. Since his internship at the hospital ends in early May, I'd like to have him and Melinda move here by the first of June."

"The first of June will be great!"

The Logans finished their supper and spent the evening in the parlor talking about how they would set up things at the office when Tim came to work for them. Intermittently, Tharyn brought up how she and Melinda would spend time together just enjoying each other's company.

At bedtime, they read their Bibles, then prayed together, spending extra moments praying for Chief Tando, that Dane's witness to him would result in his salvation.

Less than an hour after Tharyn had fallen asleep, she found herself dreaming. She was in her kitchen at midmorning on a bright, sunny day, and while standing at the sink, she looked out the window into the backyard. Her heart felt a warm sensation when she saw her little five-year-old daughter swaying back and forth in her swing.

This time the child was facing the house. Tharyn rushed out the back door and hurried toward the little girl, saying, "Elizabeth Ann, I just had to come out here and tell you that I love you."

Elizabeth Ann smiled and her dark brown eyes sparkled as she said, "I love you, too, Mommy!"

Suddenly Tharyn awakened with her heart pounding, and gasping for breath. Dane lay beside her, fast asleep.

"O Lord," Tharyn whispered, "someday, will You let me have a baby girl we can name Elizabeth Ann? Of course, I want to have a boy, too. It makes no difference which You give us first . . . a boy or a girl. But when You give us the girl, she is going to be my precious Elizabeth Ann."

223

★ ★ ★

The next morning — Friday, September 23 — Dr. Dane Logan left home early to begin his house calls. Some were as far as twenty miles from Central City.

When Tharyn arrived at the office half an hour before opening time and began preparations for the day, her thoughts were divided between the dream she had last night and the prospect of Melinda and Tim coming to Central City to live.

She thought back to the days when as young teenagers, she and Melinda lived in the alley in New York with the other orphans. She relived moments that were precious to her, both in the alley and on the orphan train that brought them to their new lives in the West.

Tharyn had the office and back room ready for the day by ten minutes before eight, and was sitting at her desk when she looked up and saw Dr. Robert Fraser come in.

The elderly physician smiled as he closed the door behind him and moved toward the pegs on the wall behind her desk. "Good morning, Tharyn."

She smiled in return. "And a good morning to you, my dear friend."

She noticed the dark circles under his

pain-filled eyes, and was aware of how slowly and deliberately he walked. "Dr. Fraser, are you having a bad day with your back?"

"Well, my dear, it's just one of those days. I didn't get much sleep last night. I couldn't find a comfortable position. I'll be all right, though. Don't you worry about me. I'm sure we have a full schedule, so I'm ready."

Tharyn left her chair and gave the dear old man a gentle hug.

He patted her back as she was hugging him and said, "Esther and I learned from neighbors last night about the incident that took place here at the office yesterday. She and I are both glad it turned out all right."

"Me, too. I was quite concerned at first because so many in the crowd showed such anger at Dane's having allowed Indians into the office." She smiled. "But praise the Lord, He made it turn out all right."

"Our God has a way of doing that, Tharyn."

"That He does. And you'll be glad to know that Dane and Pastor Shane talked briefly with Chief Tando before he left for home yesterday about the Bible and the Lord. He seemed interested. Dane is plan-ning to talk to him about Jesus when he

225

goes to the village to check on Latawga next week."

"Great! I'll tell Esther about it. We'll be praying for Chief Tando and his people."

The first patient of the day was coming toward the door from the hitch rail outside.

Tharyn looked at Dr. Fraser and thought, *I must ease his load as much as possible. Lord, would You please ease the discomfort in his back and help him through this difficult day.*

A smile was in place as she greeted the first patient. Dr. Fraser took the man into the back room, and moments later, more patients began coming in. There was a steady stream of them as the morning progressed.

It was almost eleven o'clock when the regularly scheduled stagecoach from Denver arrived in town. A few minutes later, Central City's Wells Fargo agent, Cliff Ames, came into the office with a copy of the *Rocky Mountain News* in hand. Tharyn and Dr. Fraser were talking together at Tharyn's desk.

Cliff unfolded the newspaper to expose the front page. "How about this?" he said with a smile.

Tharyn and the elderly physician noted the bold headline:

UTE CHIEF TANDO
SIGNS PEACE TREATY!

"Looks good!" said Tharyn.

"Let me read the article to you." Cliff read every word to them, which told of the peace treaty signed last Tuesday at Fort Junction, as reported by General Joseph G. Dayton. The article went on to praise Dr. Dane Logan of Central City, whose kindness and compassion to the wounded son of Chief Tando had led to the chief's signing the treaty.

When Cliff finished reading, Tharyn smiled. "My dear husband is going to be embarrassed by General Dayton's accolades."

Dr. Fraser laughed. "Well, Tharyn, dear, even if Dr. Dane does get embarrassed, he most certainly deserves those accolades!"

Thirteen

As the hours passed on Friday, people came into Dr. Dane Logan's office just to talk about the *Rocky Mountain News* article in the light of yesterday's incident over Chief Tando, Nandano, and Latawga being allowed in the office. Each time, Tharyn had to explain that her husband was out making house calls. The people then asked her to pass their comments on to Dr. Dane. Tharyn found herself extremely proud of her husband.

Late that afternoon, Tharyn was at her desk taking payment from a woman who had just been treated for a sore throat. As Tharyn placed the money into the cash drawer and thanked the woman, the front door opened and Tharyn saw Kirby Holton come in.

The wealthy owner of the Holton Coal Mine just west of town smiled at the woman and held the door open for her as she moved outside.

Tharyn smiled up at Kirby. "Hello, Mr.

Holton. Dr. Logan isn't in at the moment, but Dr. Fraser is here."

Kirby grinned and shook his head. "I don't need a doctor's attention today, thank goodness. I just came by to commend your husband for being instrumental in bringing about the signing of the peace treaty by Chief Tando. Last night I heard about yesterday's incident with the crowd and all, and I just read the article in the *Rocky Mountain News*. Dr. Logan did us all a favor, and I'm anxious to tell him how much I appreciate him for it. Will he be back soon?"

"Well, it will be a while yet. He's out making house calls. But I certainly will tell him that you came by."

"You go ahead and do that, but I'll come back tomorrow so I can talk to him personally. I'm very much relieved to know that the vicious Chief Tando is now at peace with us white folks. I hope Chiefs Yukana and Antono will soon give up their war on us also."

Tharyn nodded. "I've heard lots of people here in town talk about how hateful and brutal those two chiefs and their warriors are toward white people."

The door opened, and Tharyn looked past Kirby Holton to see Pastor Mark

Shane step in. The pastor closed the door and smiled at the mine owner. "Howdy, Mr. Holton."

Kirby nodded. "Hello, Pastor Shane."

"I just read General Dayton's report in the Denver newspaper, Tharyn. I came by to tell the good doctor once more how much I appreciate his part in all of it."

"He's not here right now, Pastor. He's making house calls today."

"Oh. Well, I have a busy day of visitation tomorrow, but I'll talk to him about it on Sunday." The preacher turned to Kirby Holton. "I keep looking for you to come to church, Mr. Holton. You promised me you would when I came to your house after your son Greg's funeral in July. Remember?"

Kirby avoided the preacher's searching eyes.

"And you also promised me you'd come to church on the other occasions when I came to visit you since then."

Kirby looked down at his feet and cleared his throat. "I . . . ah . . . I plan to come to church one of these Sundays."

Shane smiled. "Good. My people will welcome you with open arms. As you know, even some of your miners are members."

Kirby nodded and raised his eyes to once again meet the pastor's gaze. "Yes, sir. Well, I need to be getting back to the mine. I'll drop back by here tomorrow, Tharyn, and try to catch your husband."

"I'm sure it will mean a lot to him. I'll tell him you were here, and why . . . and that you'll be back tomorrow."

Kirby bid the pastor good day and hurried out the door.

While they were still discussing Greg's untimely death, Dr. Robert Fraser came out of the back room with a middle-aged man named Cletus Thornton, who was employed at the Central City Lumber Company. Thornton had cut his finger with a saw. The finger was wrapped with a large white bandage.

Tharyn told Thornton that she would send the bill for his treatment to the Lumber Company. He thanked her and left.

Dr. Fraser rubbed his chin and said, "Tharyn, was Kirby Holton here? I thought I heard his voice."

"Yes, he was. He had read the article in the *Rocky Mountain News* this morning, and he came by to compliment Dr. Dane."

The aging physician rubbed his chin again. "I wish Kirby would come to

231

church. If he would just hear some of your strong gospel preaching, Pastor, he might see his need to be saved, and do something about it."

"Kirby's a tough nut to crack, Doctor," Shane said. "I've been up to his big mansion on the mountainside several times since Greg died, but he brushed me off each time by saying he has his own religion."

Tharyn nodded. "Dane told me of two occasions when he talked to Kirby about the Lord and quoted Scripture to him, but he turned a deaf ear. You'd think with his wife having died several years ago, and then Greg dying just last summer, he'd be more concerned about facing death, himself."

"Seems to me," Dr. Fraser said, "that since both you and Dr. Dane have witnessed to him and he's turned a deaf ear, he's hardening his heart against the Lord."

Pastor Shane set his jaw and nodded. "It's so sad the way so many people harden their hearts toward the Lord and His Word. And they think they're right to do so. Proverbs 21:2 hits the nail right on the head. 'Every way of a man is right in his own eyes: but the LORD pondereth the hearts.' And when God ponders those hearts, He finds so much rebellion against Him."

Dr. Fraser nodded. "When it comes right down to it, I believe every motive we have and every important decision we make in this life is a *heart* matter. Our lives are shaped by what's in our hearts."

"You're right, Doctor. It is quite plain in Scripture that there's a big difference between the heart and the mind of a human being. In fact, that's exactly what I'm going to preach about on Sunday morning."

The elderly doctor's bushy eyebrows arched. "Really?"

"Really. My basic text is Proverbs 4:23. 'Keep thy heart with all diligence; for out of it are the issues of life.' God doesn't say to keep our *mind* with all diligence, but our *heart*. He doesn't say that out of our *minds* are the issues of life, but out of our *hearts* are the issues of life."

Tharyn smiled. "I'll be looking forward to hearing your sermon."

Dr. Fraser pressed a hand to his lower back, rolled his shoulders slightly to ease the pain he was feeling, and chuckled. "That's good, Pastor. God doesn't say that out of our *minds* are the issues of life. If we don't make and keep our hearts right with Him, we *are* out of our minds!"

At closing time, as the last patient was leaving, Tharyn was at her desk, and Dr. Fraser was standing over her. She noticed that he was pressing a hand to his back again. She was about to say something about it when both of them saw Dr. Dane pull up at the hitch rail in his buggy.

As the young doctor left the buggy, medical bag in hand, the elderly doctor said, "He looks a bit tired, doesn't he?"

"That he does."

"Well, I can understand. I had those long days of house calls for many, many years. It's wearisome on both the mind and the body."

Dr. Dane came through the door, smiled at both of them, and said, "Is this what I pay you two to do? Wait for the boss to arrive, and gawk through the window at him when he does?"

Dr. Fraser winked at Tharyn, pressed the hand to his lower back once more, and said, "I do love this young man. What would this town do without him?"

"I don't know," she said giggling, "but I certainly would be a mess without him!"

Dane smiled at her, then noted the lines of pain etched on his friend's face as he took his hand from his back. Placing steady eyes on the elderly man, he said, "Your back's hurting, isn't it?"

Dr. Fraser forced a grin. "A little."

Dr. Dane ran his gaze between them. "Has it been a busy day?"

"That it has," Tharyn said. "A *very* busy day."

Dr. Fraser forced another grin. "When you're my age, dear boy, even an *unbusy* day seems busy!"

"I know you'll be happy when you can retire completely," Dane said. "I can see the toll that coming into the office and helping us when you're needed is taking on you. I hope within a few months that need will be remedied."

Dr. Fraser looked up at him. "You mean you're considering hiring another doctor to come with you full-time?"

"I think it's about time, don't you?"

"Well, yes, I do. But until that happens, young fellow, I want to help you around here the same as I've been doing. And don't you start feeling sorry for me and try to get along without me when I'm needed, understand?"

Dr. Dane placed his hands on the stooped shoulders of his elderly friend and looked deep into his eyes. "I understand, and both of us appreciate it. But if on any given day we ask you to come in, and you're just not up to it, you tell us, all right?"

"I'll do that."

"Promise?"

"Yes, sir. I promise."

"All right. Tharyn and I will drop you off at your house on the way home. Okay?"

"Okay." With that, Dr. Fraser went to the hooks on the wall and exchanged his white frock for his coat and hat.

Dane helped Tharyn into her coat, and the three of them stepped out the door onto the boardwalk. The sun had dropped down behind the mountains to the west, and the air already had a bite to it.

Dane locked the door, and the elderly physician shuffled alongside them as Dane guided Tharyn to the buggy and helped her in. Dr. Fraser climbed in next to her. Dane climbed in beside Tharyn, took the reins in hand, and put Pal in motion.

Moments later, they drew up in front of the Fraser house. The aging physician stepped out, then turned and smiled at both of them. "Thanks for the ride."

"Our pleasure," said Dr. Dane. "You get yourself some rest this evening. And give our love to Esther."

"Will do. God bless you both."

They waited as Dr. Fraser shuffled his way toward the house, trying valiantly to hold his shoulders up, and mounted the porch. He opened the door, then turned and waved at them.

As they rode on down the street, Dane said, "Honey, I'm really concerned about his failing health."

"I am, too. If Dr. Tim accepts your offer, then that dear old man can fully retire and not place so much stress on himself. And I really do feel sure that Dr. Tim will accept your offer, don't you?"

Dane grinned at her. "Yes, I've gotten well enough acquainted with him to know what he's made of. He would fit in so perfectly here, and once we've gone over all the good things about Central City and this entire area, he'll see how well he could fit in. He's going to want to come. Melinda's love and devotion to you would be a factor, too. Another factor is that I really believe the Lord wants them to come here. I have peace about this whole thing."

On Saturday morning, Dr. Dane and Tharyn opened the office at eight o'clock, and within an hour, almost all of the chairs in the waiting room were filled.

It was just after noon when the last patients with morning appointments and the walk-ins were all treated for their ailments. Dr. Dane and Tharyn sat down at her desk to eat lunch, and were just finishing when they heard horses blow, and looked out the large front window to see a cavalry unit draw to a halt. Captain Darrell Redmond was in the lead. The captain said something to his men, dismounted, and headed toward the office door.

"Looks like we've got company." Dane opened the door just as the captain was stepping up on the boardwalk, and said, "Captain Redmond! Nice to see you!"

"You, too, Doctor. I have some good news I want to share with you, if you have a couple minutes."

"Sure. Mrs. Logan and I just finished eating lunch, and we have about forty-five minutes before the next scheduled patient is to be here."

Dr. Dane introduced the captain to Tharyn. Redmond greeted her politely, then said, "Dr. Logan, I felt that since you were instrumental in causing Chief Tando to change his mind about making war with the whites, you should know that the last two renegade Ute chiefs are no longer at war with us, either."

Dane and Tharyn looked at each other,

eyes wide, then the doctor said, "Chief Antono and Chief Yukana."

"Yes!"

"Tell us about them."

"Well, it's quite simple. On Wednesday of this week, my cavalry unit and I met up with Chief Yukana. He and a band of his warriors were killing ranchers in the mountains and burning their homes, and we were on their trail. There was a gun battle. We had some casualties, I'm sorry to say, but our Gatling guns made the difference. Chief Yukana and the whole band were killed. His subchiefs and his people have made peace with us, saying they want no more war."

"And Chief Antono?"

"Well, some of Yukana's men went to Chief Antono's village, told them about Yukana and his band being killed, and tried to reason with them and convince them to stop making war on the whites before the same thing happened to them. And it worked!"

Tharyn gasped. "Really?"

Redmond smiled. "Really. Just yesterday, Chief Antono and two of his subchiefs appeared at Fort Junction carrying a white flag. It was late in the afternoon, and I happened to be there at the time. Antono told the guards at the gate that he wanted to sign a peace treaty. Less than a half-hour later, Colonel Perry Smith and I sat down with Chief Antono, and he signed the treaty."

"Wonderful!" exclaimed the doctor. "Captain, this indeed is good news. Will you go with me to Mayor Anderson's office and tell him? He will see to it that word of this is spread all over town."

"Oh, yes!" said Tharyn. "This good news will make everything better in Central City!"

Redmond chuckled. "It's already made things better at Fort Junction, I assure you."

Dr. Dane patted Tharyn's arm. "Honey, I won't be long. I should be back before our first scheduled patient arrives."

"It's okay, darling. To coin a phrase that Captain Redmond will appreciate — I'll *hold the fort* till you get back."

Both men laughed as they went out the door.

Dr. Dane Logan did not quite make it back in time, but hurried to the back room to find his wife doing her best to make an elderly male patient comfortable while they waited for the doctor to show up.

Two hours passed, with the Logans caring for patients who were all talking about Chiefs Yukana and Antono. They were in the front office when they saw Kirby Holton come through the door.

Kirby was sporting a wide smile as he said, "Ah! The good doctor is in!"

Dr. Dane shook his hand, "Tharyn told me you were here yesterday, and why."

"I just had to come in and tell you in person how much I appreciated your role in bringing Chief Tando to make peace with us white people."

The doctor blushed. "Thank you, Kirby. There's more good news, too."

Eyes brightening, the mine owner said, "You mean about Chief Yukana being killed and his people making peace on Wednesday . . . and about Chief Antono signing the peace treaty at Fort Junction yesterday?"

"Yes. I knew it was all over town by now, but I didn't know if you had heard about it up at the mine yet."

"Two of my men came into town to get some lumber, and they heard about it at the lumber company. They hurried back to the mine with the news. This is really great!"

"The people of Colorado and Wyoming

can breathe easier about the Utes now," said Tharyn. "And I'm sure Chief Ouray is rejoicing, too."

Dr. Dane met Kirby's gaze. "So how are things at the mine these days?"

Kirby's face beamed. "Oh, listen, we're really doing well. We found a rich new vein a few days ago, and already it's producing even more coal than we had expected."

"I'm glad to hear that. You could use some good things happening there, after that cave-in last July and all the tragedies that went with it."

Kirby's brow furrowed. "Yes. And I want to thank you once more for how helpful you were in it all, Doctor. Especially when you were trapped down there yourself."

"I . . . I just wish I could have saved Greg's life, Kirby. But at least I'm glad I had the joy of leading him to the Lord before he died. I know he's in heaven with Jesus. That's the main thing."

Kirby slipped his pocket watch out of his jacket, glanced at it, and said, "I . . . ah . . . need to get back to the mine."

Dr. Dane looked him square in the eye. "Kirby, on that day when Greg was buried, I told you that unless you open your own heart to Jesus, you will never see Greg again. He's in heaven, but if you don't get saved, you'll spend eternity in hell. God's Word says so."

Kirby's hands trembled. His voice shook as he said, "I really must be going, Doctor."

"Both Pastor Shane and I have extended the invitation to you before, but let me ask again — will you come to church tomorrow? Tharyn told me what Pastor Shane is preaching about in the morning, and it sounds very interesting."

Kirby backed toward the door. "Tell you what. I'll try to be there in the morning."

Dr. Dane stepped toward him, chuckling. "When people say they'll *try* to make it to church, they seldom do. How about just saying you'll be there?"

Kirby stared at him silently.

The doctor said, "I very much appreciate your taking the time to come here and express your appreciation for my part in the Chief Tando surrender, Kirby. That's very nice of you. I want to do something nice for you. I want you to come to church and hear some good Bible preaching. Will you come?"

Kirby smiled nervously. There was a twitch in his cheek as he said, "All right, Dr. Dane. I'll be at church in the morning."

Fourteen

Dr. Dane and Tharyn Logan watched Kirby Holton move down the boardwalk. When he passed from view, Dane turned to Tharyn and said softly, "I want so much to see Kirby come to the Lord. Wouldn't it be wonderful if when Pastor is preaching in the morning, the gospel light shined down into Kirby's soul so powerfully that he would see that his 'religion' is only a humanistic thing, but the true gospel of Jesus Christ is the only way to heaven?"

Tharyn smiled and nodded. "It sure would. We'll pray hard for him tonight."

At that moment, they caught sight of Eric Cox pulling up in front of the office in his buggy. A woman sat slumped on the seat next to him, her head propped against his shoulder.

At first, they thought it must be his wife, Nelda, but when Dr. Dane hurried and opened the door, Eric was helping the woman sit up straight, and they could see that it was the Cox's neighbor, fifty-five-year-old widow Carlene Hughes.

In July, Dr. Dane and Tharyn had taken the Coxes to Mile High Hospital in Denver, where Dr. Dane did a hip replacement on Nelda. He had also led both of them to the Lord, and they were now faithful members of the church in Central City.

The Logans had met Carlene only once before when she came in for treatment of a rash several weeks earlier.

As Eric drew up, carrying Carlene like a child in his arms, her eyes were bulging, and she was breathing hard and biting her lips in evident pain.

Dr. Dane widened the door opening. "What's wrong, Eric?"

"I think she's having heart failure, Doctor. She's having severe chest pains."

"Let's get her into the examining room."

As Dr. Dane led Eric toward the back room door, Tharyn took hold of Carlene's hand, squeezed it, and said, "Hold on, honey. We'll take care of you."

When Carlene looked up at Tharyn, there was more than pain showing in her eyes. She was also quite frightened.

Dr. Dane led Eric to curtained section number one, and helped him place Carlene on the examining table. Tharyn placed a slim pillow under her head.

Dr. Dane looked at Eric. "Thank you for bringing her in. I'll need you to go to the waiting room while I work on her. We'll advise you of what we learn as soon as we have time to check her over."

Eric managed a smile. "I'll be anxious to hear your diagnosis, Doctor."

Tharyn had gone to retrieve one of her husband's stethoscopes from a nearby counter, and stepped in as Eric was walking toward the door.

Dr. Dane took the stethoscope from her, mouthed a *Thank you,* and began listening to Carlene's heart. Tharyn moved around to the opposite side of the table and watched her husband as he carefully moved the microphone from place to place on her chest, sides, and back.

At one point, he paused and glanced at Tharyn. "Honey, will you check her pulse for me, please?"

Tharyn took hold of Carlene's wrist and watched the second hand of the small clock that sat on the cart near the head of the examining table.

Carlene's frightened eyes were open, and she was watching both doctor and nurse as they worked on her. Dr. Dane said, "Carlene, have you ever had this kind of pain before?"

A sheen of perspiration covered the woman's pale face as she looked up at him. A look bordering on panic was in her pain-dulled eyes. "No. Not like this."

"Have you had any symptoms other than this pain?"

Carlene swallowed hard. "Well, I have been quite short of breath for the past few days, and my stomach hasn't been right for about that long. Sort of nauseated much of the time."

"Uh-huh," said the doctor, still listening closely to her heart. "But this severe pain just started today?"

She clenched her teeth for a few seconds, let out a short breath and drew in another one. "Yes. I had it some this morning, but it grew worse as the day went on. It became so unbearable a little while ago that I called out to Eric from one of my windows. He came into the house, took one look at me, and carried me to his buggy. He hitched up the horse in a hurry, and brought me here. He said Nelda was visiting some neighbors down the street. There wasn't time to try to contact her."

The doctor was still moving the microphone of the stethoscope around. He stopped, looked down at her with solemn eyes, and said, "What I'm hearing, along with what you just told me about your shortness of breath and nausea, goes hand in hand with what I believe is your problem."

Terror clouded the woman's face. "What is it?"

He looked at Tharyn, who had just finished checking the pulse. She said, "Her pulse is 198 beats a minute."

Dr. Dane took a deep breath and sighed. "Carlene, I must tell you that you have a very serious problem. It is called *angina pectoris,* which is coronary artery disease."

"Am — am I going to die?" she asked in a thin, plaintive voice.

Dr. Dane laid a hand on her arm. "I'm going to do everything I can to keep that from happening, Carlene. I'm going to put you on nitroglycerin." Dr. Dane turned to Tharyn. "Honey, would you bring a bottle of nitroglycerin to me with a cup half-full of water, please?"

Tharyn patted Carlene's hand. "Carlene, my husband knows what he's doing. Trust him." She then hurried out of the curtained section and headed toward the medicine cabinet across the room.

"Dr. Logan, I have heard of nitroglycerin being used for heart patients," Carlene

248

said, "but I've never understood why. How can an explosive help a person's heart?"

"It didn't start out as an explosive."

"Oh?"

"Nitroglycerin was first used by doctors in Europe, starting in late 1846, when they learned from an Italian scientist that when taken by mouth, it removed fibrous and fatty tissue deposits from the blood vessels in the heart."

Her frown was slowly fading. "Eighteen forty-six, huh? And it actually *removes* these deposits from the heart's blood vessels?"

"Yes. You see, if those deposits are not removed, they'll cause heart failure and death."

Carlene bit her lower lip. "You told Tharyn to bring a *bottle*. So nitroglycerin is a liquid?"

"Yes. It is a colorless, oily liquid having a sweet, burning taste. The Italian scientist I mentioned was a chemist. His name was Ascanio Sobrero. He first produced nitroglycerin in 1846 by adding glycerol to a mixture of concentrated nitric and sulfuric acids. It was eighteen years later — in 1864 — that Swedish scientist Alfred Nobel came up with nitroglycerin as an explosive. And nitroglycerin has been used to relieve *angina pectoris* here in America since 1850."

Carlene closed her eyes, swallowed with difficulty, opened them again, and asked, "Will the nitroglycerin you're going to give me save my life?"

"There is no way to guarantee it, but you most certainly will die if the arteries in your heart are allowed to clog up any more than they already have."

Tharyn entered the curtained section carrying the bottle of nitroglycerin and the half-full cup of water. As she set them on the cart, Carlene clasped her hands together, drew a shuddering breath and cried, "Oh, Doctor! I'm — I'm afraid to die! Help me! Help me!"

Dr. Dane started to speak, but Tharyn took the terrified woman's clasped hands into her own and squeezed them. "Please, Carlene, you're only making your situation worse. Dr. Dane is going to do everything possible to help you. Now, you need to calm down. As you've just heard, there is medicine for your problem, and my husband will do everything in his power to save your life and help heal you."

Carlene clenched her teeth, drew in another shuddering breath, and said with a tremor in her voice, "There — there really is a good chance that the nitroglycerin will keep me from dying?"

Tharyn bent low over her and gave her a reassuring smile. "You're going to get better. Just let the doctor do his work, and cooperate with him."

A serenity seemed to appear in Carlene's eyes. She nodded. "All right."

"Good girl," said Dr. Dane, then told Tharyn the exact proportions to use in mixing the nitroglycerin with the water in the cup.

When it was done, Tharyn handed him the cup. He took it, and said, "All right now, Carlene, I am going to lift your head a little and put the cup to your lips. Drink it slowly."

When she had drained the cup, he eased her head down and said, "Just relax now. You should be feeling less pain, and your anxiety should subside shortly. Nitroglycerin is a potent drug. In the medical world, we've been seeing great results from it. I'll check on you in a few minutes. I'm going out to the waiting room and explain this situation to Eric. I want to keep you here for several hours so we can watch you closely. I'll tell Eric to go on home for now, and to come back at five. If you're doing all right by then, he can take you home. Is there someone who can stay with you when you go home, so you don't have to exert yourself for a while?"

"Oh, yes. Even though Nelda still limps a little from the hip replacement you did on her, I know she'll spend time with me, and there are other neighbor ladies who'll come in when she can't."

"Good. Tharyn will stay right here at your side while I go talk to Eric. Be back in a few minutes."

When Dr. Dane entered the office, he found five people in the waiting room in addition to Eric Cox. He noted that two of the five had appointments, and asked the other three why they were there. When they told him, he could see that there was no emergency. He then explained that he had an emergency situation at the moment, but told all five he would get to them as soon as he could.

He then took Eric into his private office and told him that Carlene had coronary artery disease, and that he had given her nitroglycerin, which would remove the fibrous and fatty tissues from the arteries of her heart.

Like Carlene, Eric commented that he had heard of nitroglycerin being used on people with heart problems, and asked how an explosive could help a person's heart. Dr. Dane explained it as he had done with Carlene.

"Amazing," said Eric. "So Doctor, do you think that Carlene will live?"

"I believe we've caught it in its early stages, Eric. I feel quite confident that she will be all right. I wish we had a hospital, or at least a clinic, but we don't, and she sure couldn't take the trip to Denver, so we have to handle the situation the best we can. I want to keep her here at the office for observation for the rest of the day. Could you come back and get her at five o'clock? She told me that Nelda would stay with her until she's doing better, and there were other neighbor ladies who would come in and stay with her whenever Nelda couldn't."

"We'll see to it that she's taken care of, Doctor. I'll be here at five."

"Good."

"And, Doctor . . ."

"Mm-hmm?"

"Nelda and I have talked to Carlene about the Lord, but she thinks she's all right with God because she's a moral person and believes He exists. You might —"

"I'm already planning on doing that.

Tharyn and I could tell that she doesn't know Jesus as her Saviour the way she was showing such fear of dying. I'm going to talk to her about her need to be saved when I go back in there."

"Good. Well, see you at five o'clock. I'll have Nelda with me. When she finds out about this, she will definitely want to come along and help."

"I appreciate that."

"Oh, and thanks for telling me the nitroglycerin story. I have always thought it was Alfred Nobel who came up with it first as an explosive, then the medical world got ahold of it later. Good history lesson today."

The doctor chuckled. "Guess we all ought to learn something new every day."

"Well, I sure did today, anyway."

Moments later, Dr. Dane entered the back room, and as he moved toward the curtained section where Tharyn was standing over Carlene, he heard Carlene's voice pitched high with fear as she said, "Tharyn, I know Dr. Logan is an excellent physician and surgeon, but from what he told me about this disease, I'm afraid I'm going to die! Oh, please! Don't let me die!"

"Carlene, please get a grip on yourself," said Tharyn. "We're doing all we can for you. We both feel quite confident that you're going to be all right."

Dr. Dane drew up on the opposite side of the table from where Tharyn was standing. He told Tharyn of the five people in the waiting room, and named those who had appointments. He told her that he had explained to all five that he had an emergency on his hands, but would get to them as soon as possible . . . and that they were all willing to wait.

Tharyn said, "Good. We've got to help Carlene right now."

"Yes," said the doctor with concern evident in his voice. "I feel that helping Carlene with her fear of death is an emergency."

Tharyn nodded. "I do, too."

Dr. Dane then laid a gentle hand on the frightened patient's arm and spoke softly. "Carlene, a little while ago, you told me that you're afraid to die, and asked me to help you."

"Y-yes."

"As I was coming here into the back room, I heard you say again that you are afraid you are going to die, and I heard you begging Tharyn not to let you die."

"Yes! I'm very much afraid of dying, Doctor!"

"Let me tell you something. Even when I was a teenager, I used to have a horrid fear of dying. None of us wants to die, of course. But when I got born again, the fear of dying went away. I know now that if I should die, I would be in heaven with the Lord." He paused, glanced at Tharyn, then looked back down at Carlene. "Do you have that assurance?"

Carlene licked her lips. "I certainly *hope* I will go to heaven when I die."

Dr. Dane leaned down closer to her. "But if you only *hope* you will go to heaven when you die, you really don't have assurance, do you?"

She stared at him for a brief moment, then said, "Well, how can anyone do any more than hope? We all do wrong, so I guess it depends on how much wrong we do whether we'll be allowed into heaven when we die. I try to live as good as I can. I'm a moral person, and I do my best to treat other people right. But —"

"This is why you're fearful about dying, Carlene," spoke up Tharyn. "You think you might still come up short on your good deeds outnumbering your bad deeds when you go into eternity to face the almighty God."

"Well, I — I —"

"You *do* believe what the Bible says about there being a real burning hell, like there is a real wonderful heaven, don't you?"

"I do. And I certainly don't want to go to hell. But, Doctor, you said you *know* that if you should die, you would be in heaven with the Lord. How can you say you *know?* Are you perfect and without sin?"

"No, I'm not. But my going to heaven doesn't depend on my good works. God's Word says in Romans 3:12, speaking of the entire human race, 'They are all gone out of the way, they are together become unprofitable; there is none that doeth good, no, not one.' Did you catch the word 'all'? They are *all* gone out of the way. There is none that doeth good."

"Yes, Doctor."

"You see, Carlene, in the eyes of almighty God, there isn't one human being who does good. In ourselves, we can never deserve to enter heaven. We must be born again by receiving the Lord Jesus Christ as our personal Saviour. When we take Him into our hearts, He takes us into Him in a beautiful spiritual way, and places us in the family of God.

"When the heavenly Father looks at the

born-again person, He sees him in Christ, and He sees us righteous *in Christ,* not in ourselves. There's another verse in Romans chapter three that says, 'There is none righteous, no, not one.' Trying to miss hell and go to heaven by our own good works and our own righteousness will only land us in hell. We must come to the Father through His only begotten Son. There is no other way."

Carlene batted her eyelids and licked her lips again. "Dr. Logan, I have never heard this before. You did say that when you got born again, you lost your fear of dying. I've heard of this being 'born again,' but I know nothing about it. Will you help me?"

Dr. Dane looked at Tharyn, who had tears in her eyes, then looked down at Carlene again. "I sure will. Be right back."

With that, the doctor rushed to the medicine cabinet, took a Bible out of a drawer, and rushed back.

Tharyn said, "I want to be in here while you show Carlene what the Bible says, honey. But I should go out to the office and see if anyone else has come in. You go ahead and begin. I'll be back shortly."

"All right."

Dr. Dane opened the Bible as Tharyn hurried toward the door.

Carlene's eyes were glued on the tall, handsome physician as he flipped pages, then looked at her and said, "First, I want to read you a portion of Psalm 119:160. Listen to what the psalmist said to God. 'Thy word is true from the beginning.' Do you believe that, Carlene?"

"Yes, I do."

"Good. Then whatever I show you in this Book, you will accept as truth, right?"

"I sure will."

They heard the office door open and close, and rapid footsteps coming their way. Tharyn moved into the curtained section. "Still just the five. And they are being very cooperative."

"That's good to hear," said Dr. Dane. "I just read to her what the psalmist said about God's Word being true. And Carlene said she believes that."

"And I'm eager to hear it!" Carlene said with a lilt in her voice.

Fifteen

Tharyn Logan was praying under her breath as her husband flipped the pages of his Bible and said, "Carlene, a few moments ago I quoted Romans 3:12 to you, emphasizing the word *all*. 'They are *all* gone out of the way, they are together become unprofitable; there is none that doeth good, no, not one.' Now I want you to read another verse in that same chapter to me." He lowered the open Bible so she could see the page. "Read me verse 23."

Carlene focused on the verse. " 'For all have sinned, and come short of the glory of God.' "

"Did you catch the word *all?*"

"Yes."

"That means me, you, Tharyn, and all the rest of humanity, right?"

"Yes."

He flipped more pages. "Since we are all sinners in need of salvation and cleansing from our sin, God did a wonderful thing. He sent His only begotten Son so that we could be saved and cleansed." Finding his page, he said, "Let me read you 1 John 4:9. 'In this was manifested the love of God toward us, because that God sent his only begotten Son into the world, that we might live through him.' Who is God's only begotten Son, Carlene?"

"Jesus Christ."

"Right. Scripture says here that God sent Jesus into the world that we might live through *Him*. Not our good works. Not our religion. Not through church membership nor church ordinances, but through Jesus Christ. I want you to read another verse for me."

He flipped back to Romans chapter 6, lowered the Bible once again so she could see the page, and said, "Read me the last verse of chapter 6. Verse 23."

" 'For the wages of sin is death; but the gift of God is eternal life through Jesus Christ our Lord.' "

"Please note that eternal life is a gift. You can't earn a gift, can you?"

"No. If you earned it, it would be a wage, not a gift."

He smiled. "Right! And note also that this gift of eternal life comes to us *only* through Jesus. See that?"

"Yes."

"Good. Now . . . we're sinners, aren't we, Carlene?"

"Yes."

"And what are the wages we get for our sin?"

"Death."

"Yes. Physical death came upon the human race because of sin. But there is also *spiritual* death — separation from God. I told you when I got born again the fear of dying went away. Remember?"

"Yes."

"Now I want to read to you where that phrase 'born again' came from."

He turned back to John chapter 3 and explained to Carlene that the Lord Jesus was talking one night to a religious man named Nicodemus.

"Now listen to what Jesus said to him here in John 3:3. 'Jesus answered and said unto him, Verily, verily, I say unto thee, Except a man be born again, he cannot see the kingdom of God.' And again, down in verse 7, He said, 'Marvel not that I said unto thee, Ye must be born again.' So since Jesus said it, it has to be true, doesn't it?"

"It sure does."

Tharyn was still praying under her breath.

As he turned back toward the front of

the Bible, Dr. Dane said, "Now I'm going to show you why a person must be born again in order to go to heaven, the kingdom of God." He stopped at Genesis chapter 2. "Here, Carlene. Read me verses 16 and 17. In this passage, God has taken His first human creation, Adam, into the Garden of Eden."

Carlene nodded. " 'And the LORD God commanded the man, saying, Of every tree of the garden thou mayest freely eat: But of the tree of the knowledge of good and evil, thou shalt not eat of it: for in the day that thou eatest thereof thou shalt surely die.' "

"Do you remember the story, Carlene?"

"Yes. Satan came into the Garden of Eden and caused Adam and Eve to disobey God and eat the forbidden fruit. I've known that part of the story since I was a child."

"Good. Now look there again in verse 17. When did God say they would die if they ate the forbidden fruit?"

She looked down at the verse and studied it briefly. "Why, that very day."

"Do you remember the story well enough to tell me if God buried Adam and Eve that day?"

"Well, of course He didn't. They hadn't even had Cain and Abel yet."

"But God had warned Adam that he would die the very day he ate of the forbidden fruit, didn't He?"

"Yes."

"So if they didn't die physically that day, how *did* they die?"

"Oh, I see it. They died *spiritually.*"

"That's right. So Adam's spirit died, and so did Eve's. They were dead spiritually and cut off from fellowship with God. You and I are descendants of Adam, and in 1 Corinthians 15 it says that in Adam, all humanity dies. Adam and Eve died spiritually that very day, and years later, they died physically — all because of their sin in the garden.

"So, since the wages of sin is death — both physically and spiritually — we all come into this world as descendants of Adam, facing physical death and already dead spiritually. We were dead spiritually when we were born into this world. This is why Jesus said we must be born again. If we don't get born spiritually, we will go to hell when we die."

Tharyn touched Carlene's arm. "Do you understand so far?"

"I believe so."

"If you have any questions as we go along," said Dr. Dane, "feel free to ask."

"Well, just let me say something here."

"Of course."

"I believe in God, and I believe in Jesus, so my sins must already be forgiven, and I must have been born again and didn't realize it."

"Not so," the doctor said softly. "A person cannot be born again and not know it. You believe in God and His Son in your *mind* — your *intellect* — but in order to be born again you must believe in your *heart*. Let me show you."

He took the Bible from her hands, and while turning to the Gospel of John, said, "We saw that Jesus said in John chapter 3 that we must be born again to go to heaven, right?"

"Yes."

"You see, Carlene, this new birth also puts us in the family of God. As human beings born into this world in the image of Adam, we are God's *creation,* but we are not God's *child* until we have been born into His family. When we get born again, we not only become alive spiritually, but we also become God's children. Let me read it to you here in John chapter 1. Speaking of Jesus Christ, it says, 'He came unto his own, and his own received him not.' That is, He came to God's chosen nation of Israel, but they rejected Him."

"I see."

"Next verse. 'But as many as received him, to them gave he power to become the sons of God, even to them that believe on his name.' His name is Jesus, which means Saviour. To believe on His name is to believe that Jesus, alone, does all the saving of the soul all by Himself with no help from man. It says that only those who have received Him have become God's children. Do you see that?"

"Yes."

"All right. Next verse. Speaking of those who believing on His name have received Him, it says, 'Which were born, not of blood, nor of the will of the flesh, nor of the will of man, but of God.' They got born again, but it wasn't of blood. It doesn't come through family . . . bloodline. Just because a person's parents have been born again doesn't mean *they* have."

"Mm-hmm."

" 'Nor of the will of the flesh.' We can't give ourselves the new birth. 'Nor of the will of man.' This eliminates all mankind. There is nothing another human being can do to give you the new birth. So churches, religions, ministers, priests and such have no power to give a person the new birth. It is *God* who gives it. And He does so only when a person repents of his or her sin and, believing that Jesus is the one and only Saviour who does all the saving all by Himself, receives Him.

"Only those who receive Jesus get born again. They already have the *intellectual* knowledge of Him. They have Him in their *mind*. But that doesn't bring salvation. He must be received into the *heart*. In Ephesians 3:17, Paul said to born-again people, 'That Christ may dwell in your *hearts* by faith.' There is a big difference between our *hearts* and our *minds*.

"Believing in Jesus in our intellect — our *mind* — does not give salvation. We must believe in Him in our *heart*, the very center of our being. Now you're probably wondering how to believe in Him in your heart."

"I sure am."

He turned to Romans chapter 10, handed her the Bible, and said, "Read me verses 9 and 10."

She located them quickly. " 'That if thou shalt confess with thy mouth the Lord Jesus, and shalt believe in thine heart that God hath raised him from the dead, thou shalt be saved. For with the heart man believeth unto righteousness; and with the mouth confession is made unto salvation.' "

"Carlene, God says if you believe in your *heart* that He raised His Son from the dead, you will be saved. See that?"

"Yes."

"Then notice that God says it is with the *heart* that we believe unto righteousness — having all our sins forgiven and washed away. Not the mind, the intellect. And it's with the *mouth* that confession is made unto salvation."

"Yes."

"Now look at verse 13. What does it say?"

"For whosoever shall call upon the name of the Lord shall be saved."

"So do you see? You believe in your heart when you call on the Lord with your mouth and ask Him to come into your heart and save you. This is receiving Him. So this is what gives the new birth. Now look again at verse 9. God says you must believe in your *heart* that He raised His Son from the dead. This ties with God's definition of the gospel. Let me show it to you."

He took the Bible from her, turned to 1 Corinthians 15, and handed it back to her. "Look at the first verse, Carlene. What does Paul say he is declaring to the people at the Corinthian church?"

"The gospel. He says he had preached it to them."

"Right. And the gospel is found in verses 3 and 4. Read them to me."

" 'For I delivered unto you first of all that which I also received, how that Christ died for our sins according to the scriptures; And that he was buried, and that he rose again the third day according to the scriptures.' "

"Right. Now listen as I quote what Jesus said in Mark 1:15. 'Repent ye, and believe the gospel.' Repentance, Carlene, is a change of mind that results in a change of direction. When we come into this world, we are sinners headed for hell. We're going the wrong direction. When we hear the gospel and understand that we are lost in sin and are headed toward hell, we must change our mind about whatever religion or philosophy we cling to, and let it go. We must change our mind about Jesus Christ and turn around 180 degrees to Him in repentance. We must believe the gospel, ask for forgiveness for our sins, and ask Him to come into our heart and be our Saviour. Do you understand?"

"Yes, I do."

"Good. You see, in the gospel, we are told that Christ died for our sins. The Bible tells us that on that cross, He shed His blood as the Lamb of God. But He didn't stay dead. He arose from the grave, and is alive to save us from hell and to wash our sins away in His precious blood. When we repent, believing the gospel, and call on Him, receiving Him into our heart as our personal Saviour, trusting Him and Him alone to save us, we get born again. He saves our lost soul, cleanses us of our sins, forgives us, and makes us a child of God. We know this because the Scripture says so. Do you understand?"

"Oh, Dr. Logan, I most certainly do. I have never repented of my sin and received Jesus into my *heart*. I want to do this right now. Will you help me?"

Tears had already flooded Tharyn's eyes and now were cascading down her cheeks. She took hold of Carlene's hand as Dr. Dane said, "Romans 10:13 says, 'Whosoever shall call upon the name of the Lord shall be saved.' Let's bow our heads, and you tell the Lord you're coming to Him as a repentant lost sinner, trusting only Him to save you and cleanse you of your sins, and that you believe the gospel, and want Him to come into your heart and be your Saviour."

Tears flooded Carlene's eyes. She closed them, squeezing Tharyn's hand and weeping, and called on the Lord exactly as Dr. Dane had told her to do.

When she finished, Dr. Dane prayed for Carlene, asking the Lord to bless her, give her peace, and use her for His glory.

She smiled up at him, wiping away the tears on her face.

Tharyn wiped her own tears, bent over and kissed Carlene's cheek, and with quivering voice said, "Oh, Carlene, I'm so happy for you!"

Dr. Dane told her that he would let Pastor Mark Shane know what had happened here, and that the pastor and Mrs. Shane would come see her at home and guide her further concerning her new-found salvation and what the Lord expected of her now that she was a child of God. He quickly added that the very first thing would be to get baptized and unite with the church as soon as she was able to do so.

She sniffed and wiped away more tears. "Oh, yes. I want to do that just as soon as I'm feeling well enough."

Dr. Dane said, "Well, sweet wife of mine, we'd better see about those patients out there in the waiting room."

Tharyn bent down and kissed Carlene's cheek once more. "We'll be checking on you."

"Yes, we will," said Dr. Dane, taking hold of the curtain that surrounded the section. "You try to get yourself a nap now."

He started to close the curtain to give her privacy, but paused when she said, "Dr. Logan . . ."

"Yes?"

"Thank you for showing me how to be born again."

He smiled broadly. "My pleasure. You rest now."

With that, he closed the curtain, and took Tharyn's hand as they walked toward the office door together.

It was ten minutes before five when Tharyn looked up from her desk to see Eric and Nelda Cox pull up out front in their buggy. Tharyn was taking payment from a man who had just been treated by the doctor.

By the time the payment had been made and the man was walking toward the door, Eric pushed it open for Nelda. She still had to use a cane to walk, but was doing better at it day by day.

"How is Carlene doing, Tharyn?" asked Eric.

"Quite well," Tharyn said. "Her chest pains have eased considerably. Dr. Dane is with her. I'll go let him know that you're here. Please sit down in the waiting area."

Tharyn hurried away, and was back in less than two minutes. She moved up to the Coxes, and Eric rose to his feet.

Smiling, with her eyes brightening, Tharyn said, "I've got wonderful news!"

"Tell us!" said Eric.

"Dr. Dane talked to Carlene after you left, Eric, and led her to the Lord! She's going to be baptized as soon as she feels up to it."

While the Coxes were rejoicing, they saw Dr. Dane come into the office, steadying Carlene as she walked beside him.

Nelda stood up, leaning on her cane, and headed for Carlene with Eric right behind her. They expressed their joy in Carlene's salvation.

Tears filled Carlene's eyes as she said, "I want to thank you both for the times you tried to talk to me about being saved. The Lord had to get me over my stubbornness by letting me have this coronary artery disease."

"We're just glad you opened your heart

to Jesus," said Eric. "Now you're our sister in Christ."

She smiled. "Oh, yes! Thank the Lord, I am!"

"So tell us about Carlene's heart condition, Dr. Logan," said Nelda.

"All right. Let's everybody sit down over here in the waiting area."

When they were all seated, Dr. Dane said, "We know for sure that along with the use of the nitroglycerin, Carlene is going to need plenty of rest."

"I'm sure that's true," said Nelda.

Dr. Dane looked pointedly at his patient. "No more strenuous work for you, dear lady, until I say so. Since you have the Coxes, here, and the other neighbors you told me about, you must learn to let them help you. I'm sure they will be more than happy to pitch in."

"We sure will," said Eric. "And I know the other neighbors will."

Dr. Dane nodded. "Some days will be better than others, Carlene, and in time you'll be able to discern when and how much activity you can handle."

She smiled. "Yes, Doctor."

He rose from his chair and patted Carlene on the shoulder. "I feel quite sure that you will do just fine. Best of all . . .

now that you're personally acquainted with the *Great Physician,* you can depend on Him to help heal you of this problem."

Tears filmed her eyes. "Oh, yes! How wonderful to be personally acquainted with the Great Physician!"

Running his gaze from Carlene to the Coxes, Dr. Dane said, "Tharyn has written instructions for mixing the nitroglycerin with water. I'm sending a bottle of it home with her. She must have the prescribed dose once a day until I say differently. I'll come by the house periodically and check on her."

Dane and Tharyn walked outside with Carlene and the Coxes, and Dane helped Eric get both women into the buggy.

Doctor and nurse held hands as they watched the buggy pull away.

The Logans were about to enter the office when they heard their names called. They turned about to see Jack and Sally Miller in their buggy, moving toward them along the street.

Sally was holding a tiny bundle in her arms, wrapped in a blanket.

Dane looked down at Tharyn, a grin on his lips and a beam on his face. "Here we go. You're going to get your hands on little Lydia Marie, and we're going to talk some

275

more this evening about starting our family."

Tharyn giggled. "Get ready!"

He laughed. "Oh, I'm ready!"

Sixteen

Jack Miller swung the buggy up to the hitch rail in front of the office and smiled. "Howdy, Doctor . . . Mrs. Logan."

"Hello," said Sally. "I'm glad we caught you before you left for home. Little Lydia Marie has been asking to see her favorite aunt all day."

Tharyn stepped up to Sally's side of the buggy and opened her arms. "Well, let's not delay it any longer! Aunt Tharyn is eager to see her little niece. How's she doing?"

Sally turned the pretty baby's face toward Tharyn. "She's doing great."

Lydia Marie smiled and made a "goo" sound.

Sally laughed. "When she makes that sound, it means she's very happy."

"Of course," said Tharyn, taking the little bundle into her arms. "She's about to get hugged and kissed by her favorite aunt!"

While Dr. Dane was talking to Jack, he watched Tharyn cuddle Lydia Marie and kiss her chubby little cheeks.

After a few minutes, Jack turned to Sally. "Well, honey, I know our baby would love to stay here and get all this loving from her favorite aunt, but we'd better be heading home."

Tharyn kissed the baby one more time and handed her back to Sally. "Okay. That'll do till next time. Which will be to-morrow at church."

Sally laughed, looked down at her baby girl, and said, "More loving from your favorite aunt tomorrow, sweetie."

Lydia Marie smiled as if she understood.

Sally looked at Tharyn. "She says she is looking forward to it."

"Not as much as I am!"

While the Logans were driving toward home with Pal pulling the buggy, Dane turned to Tharyn and grinned. "Happy now?"

"Of course. But I'll be even happier when the baby I cuddle and kiss is Miss Elizabeth Ann Logan. Or, of course, Mr. Dane Logan Jr."

Dane laughed. "Well, I guess we need to keep praying about little Miss Elizabeth Ann Logan. Or, of course, little Mr. Dane Logan Jr."

★ ★ ★

That night, when the Logans were praying after reading their Bibles together, they both asked the Lord to guide them and to have His perfect will about when they should start their family.

Somewhere in the middle of the night, Tharyn found herself dreaming again.

In the dream, it was midmorning, and the sun was shining into the kitchen through a side window as Tharyn stood at the sink. She was looking out the window above the sink into the backyard, and a smile curved her lips as she fixed her gaze on her little five-year-old daughter who was swaying back and forth in the swing her father had made for her.

Little Elizabeth Ann was positioned on the swing seat so she faced the house. Her long dark brown hair fluttered in the air as she set her dark brown eyes on her mother and let go of one rope to wave to her. "Hi, Mommy!"

Tharyn felt a lump rise in her throat, waved back, and hurried out the door. When she stepped off the porch and headed toward the child, Elizabeth Ann dragged her feet to stop the swing, then hopped off and ran to meet her mother,

279

smiling and opening her arms.

When they came together, Tharyn swept her up in her arms. Before she could tell the child she loved her, Elizabeth Ann said, "I love you, Mommy! I love you so much!"

Tharyn felt warm tears fill her eyes and moisten her cheeks. "I love you, too, sweetheart! So very, very much!"

The warmth of the tears on her cheeks awakened Tharyn. She opened her eyes and sat up in the bed. Next to her, Dane was snoring slightly. Tharyn wiped the tears from her face and said in a low whisper, "Oh, Elizabeth Ann, I love you so much. So very, very much!"

She eased her head back down on the pillow, and this time whispered, "Dear Lord, You *are* going to give me my little Elizabeth Ann, aren't You?"

She dabbed at her eyes with the sheet, drying her tears. Moments later, she was asleep once again.

The next morning, when Dane and Tharyn arrived at church, they saw the Millers halfway down the aisle, talking to another couple. Tharyn's line of sight fastened on little Lydia Marie in her mother's arms, and her mind flashed back to the dream she had the night before.

Oh, dear Lord, she said in her heart, *I so very much want to be a mother.*

Dane stopped to shake hands with one of the men, who also greeted Tharyn. She returned the greeting warmly, then said in a low voice to Dane, "I want to go see Little Lydia Marie for a moment."

The Millers were alone, ready to choose a pew, when Dane and Tharyn drew up.

Sally smiled, looked at the baby in her arms, and said, "Well, Lydia Marie, your favorite aunt is here." With that, she handed the baby to Tharyn, who began talking to her as she cuddled and kissed her.

Dr. Dane and Jack shook hands, then observed Tharyn, who was overflowing with joy as she held the baby.

"You know, Tharyn," Sally said teasingly, "you're already spoiling this little one. Next time she cries and wants to be held, I'm bringing her to you."

Tharyn's eyes sparkled. "Oh, that would be fine with me! Anytime you need someone to take care of her, just bring her to me. If I'm at the office, I could put a bassinet right beside my desk." She caressed a soft cheek, gave it another kiss, and handed Lydia Marie back to her mother, thinking, *Someday I'll have my very own precious bundle! It can't come too soon!*

At that moment, Pastor Mark and Peggy came through a door beside the platform and greeted the Logans. Dr. Dane told them about Eric Cox bringing his neighbor Carlene Hughes to the office yesterday with chest pains.

Pastor Shane said, "I know the Coxes have been witnessing to Mrs. Hughes, but haven't been able to get anywhere with her."

"Yes, but praise the Lord, I've got good news. Tharyn and I witnessed to her at the office yesterday, and Carlene received Jesus as her Saviour. It took the fear of *angina pectoris* to get her to listen about her need to be saved."

"Great!"

"She said she wants to be baptized here in our church as soon as she's able."

"Wonderful!" exclaimed Peggy.

"I told her that both of you would be coming to see her soon."

Pastor Shane smiled. "Peggy and I will go see her tomorrow."

"Something else, Pastor . . ." said Dr. Dane. "Kirby Holton came into the office yesterday to commend me for my part in

Chief Tando's signing the peace treaty. While I had him there face-to-face, I invited him to come to church today. He promised to be here for the morning service."

The pastor smiled. "Well, I hope he keeps his promise! He's been a hard nut to crack."

"Tell me about it! Tharyn and I have been praying hard that the Lord will get ahold of him today."

At that point, the Shanes and the Logans spotted Eric and Nelda Cox coming toward them. Dr. Dane told them that he had spoken to Pastor and Mrs. Shane about Carlene Hughes being saved, and that they were going to visit her on Monday.

Eric looked at the Shanes. "She will be very glad to see you. We left her with some other neighbors this morning, who don't go to church. We'll be staying with her again tonight."

When Sunday school was over, Dr. Dane went out onto the front porch of the church building to watch for Kirby Holton. He had just shaken hands with a couple of church members when he saw Kirby pull his buggy into the parking lot, and he breathed a prayer of thanks to the Lord.

Dr. Dane waited on the porch, and when Kirby Holton mounted the steps, he shook Kirby's hand. "Welcome, my friend! Sure am glad to see you here."

Kirby was visibly nervous, but his uneasiness diminished some when they entered the building and he was greeted by other people he knew, including some of his own employees.

Pastor Shane spotted him, and hurried to him, giving him a warm welcome.

As the pastor headed for the platform, Dr. Dane said, "Kirby, would you sit with Tharyn and me?"

"Of course."

He guided his guest to the pew where Tharyn was already seated. She welcomed him with a wide smile, and Dr. Dane had Kirby sit on the aisle, then sat down between him and Tharyn.

The pump organ was striking up a song as the music director stepped before the choir, motioned for them to stand, and led them in a rousing gospel song to open the service. The congregation was then asked to stand, and the music director led them in a beautiful hymn about Christ's death on the cross.

The Logans noticed that Kirby Holton held a songbook, but did not sing.

During announcement time, Pastor Shane mentioned the article in the *Rocky Mountain News* about Chief Tando signing the peace treaty with the United States government, and asked how many had seen it. Hands went up all over the auditorium, accompanied by many an amen. Not wanting to embarrass Dr. Dane Logan, the pastor made only a passing remark about the doctor's part in the change of attitude toward white men that had taken place in Chief Tando's heart. He also made mention briefly about the renegade Chief Yukana's death, and the surrender of his people to the U.S. army — and the peace treaty signed by renegade Chief Antono at Fort Junction that week.

After the offering and a solo by one of the men from the choir, Pastor Mark Shane stepped up to the pulpit and opened his Bible. "My basic text this morning is found in Proverbs 4:23. Please turn in your Bibles and follow as I read it."

Pages were fluttering all over the auditorium as people flipped to the passage. Dr. Dane turned to the passage in his Bible and held it so Kirby could easily see the page.

The pastor read the verse loudly and clearly:

"Keep thy heart with all diligence;
for out of it are the issues of life."

He read it a second time for emphasis,
then explained that the "issues" in our
lives are what come out in consequences,
aftermaths, or results from what we do in
life. He added that our actions are determined by the condition of the heart.

He then compared the mind — the intellect, the brain, the seat of man's intelli-
gence — with the heart, the very center of
the soul, the core of the individual. The
pastor explained that as the physical heart
is the central organ of the body, so the
nonphysical heart is the central seat of the
affections and the center of the moral consciousness.

"From this moral center," he said, "flows
forth the issues of life. The currents of the
moral life take their rise in the heart, and
flow forth from it, just as blood is pro-
pelled and issues forth into the arterial
system in the body from the physical heart.
As physical life is centered in the physical
heart, so it is in the *spiritual* sense with the
heart, which is the center of the soul. Out
of that heart are the issues of life. It is the
emotional part of a person; the very per-
sonality and moral part of the person. This

286

is why God tells us to keep our heart with all diligence."

Pastor Shane pointed out that Genesis 2:7 makes it clear that man does not just have a soul. He *is* the soul.

"As I said a moment ago," he went on, "the heart spoken of in Proverbs 4:23 is the very center of the soul. It is the seat of our affections. It is our innermost being."

While the pastor was preaching, Dr. Dane noticed that Kirby Holton was listening intently.

"The Scripture says the issues of life are from the *heart*. The things that defile a person are from the *heart*. A person is basically what he or she thinks in their *heart*. The heart of man, therefore, is the source of his life, his activities, and his destiny."

Pastor Shane turned back several pages in his Bible. "The Bible says that God *knows* the hearts of men, *searches* the hearts of men, and *discerns the motives* of the hearts of men. Now go with me in your Bibles to Psalm 119:11. I want you to see what the psalmist wrote in this verse under the inspiration of the Holy Spirit."

When the sound of pages flipping ceased, Shane said, "Now look at this, and catch my emphasis on certain words. 'Thy *word* have I hid in mine *heart,* that I might not sin against thee.' Oh, Christians, hide the written Word of God in your hearts, not just your minds. You hide it in your mind when you memorize it, but you hide it in your heart when you not only memorize it, but let it take root in your very being. Listen closely to what I am about to say. The heart remembers things the mind forgets."

He paused as he swept his gaze over the faces of the crowd. "Did you hear what I said? The *heart* remembers things the *mind* forgets."

Dr. Dane Logan leaned close to Tharyn and whispered, "That's good! I never thought of it in that light before."

She smiled at him and nodded.

The pastor then returned to his original text, and after reading it aloud again, said, "Ladies and gentlemen, boys and girls, the 'heart' of Proverbs 4:23 is not only tied to the issues of life here on earth, but also is involved in the issues of *eternal* life."

Pastor Shane then took them to John 1:12, showing that to be born again, a lost sinner must *receive* Jesus Christ. He then took them to Ephesians 3:17, showing that Christ must dwell in their *hearts;* thus, He must be received into the individual sinner's heart . . . the very center of his soul.

He then quoted Jesus' words in Revelation 3:20: " 'Behold, I stand at the door, and knock: if any man hear my voice, and open the door, I will come in.' "

Running his gaze over the crowd, Shane said, "Jesus said He will come in *where?*"

Answers came back from the crowd: "Into the heart!"

The pastor smiled. "Yes! And before this sermon is finished, you who are here without Christ are going to feel Him knocking on the door of your heart. I implore you . . . don't turn Him away. Open your heart to Him!"

Dr. Dane noticed Kirby Holton nervously twisting in the pew.

Tears filmed Pastor Shane's eyes as he said with a break in his voice, "Lost friend, many people who planned on receiving Jesus as their Saviour *someday,* died before that someday came. Satan's greatest trick is to get you to put it off. Second Corinthians 6:2 says, 'Behold, *now* is the accepted time; behold, *now* is the day of salvation.' Your heart is pumping *now.* You are breathing *now.* But you have no assurance that this will be so *tomorrow.* Please do not leave here without opening your heart to Jesus.

"A wise Christian man once said, 'If we

put off repentance another day, we have a day more to repent of, and a day less in which to repent.' Another said, 'You cannot repent too soon, because you know not how soon it may be too late.'

"Let me tell you a story. A gospel preacher once was planning to preach on 2 Corinthians 6:2, which I just quoted to you. One night he dreamed that he was carried into the presence of wicked, evil spirits of Satan. They were assembled to devise means whereby they might cause more people to end up in hell. One said, 'I will go to earth and tell men that the Bible is all false; that it is not divinely inspired of God.'

" 'No, that will not work,' another said. 'I'll go tell people there is no God, no Saviour, no heaven, no hell.' At those words, a fiendish smile lighted upon their countenances.

" 'No,' said another. 'That will not do. We can only make a few people believe that. I will journey to earth and tell them that, yes, there is a God; that there is a crucified, risen Saviour; that there is a heaven and a hell. But I will tell them *there is no hurry. Tomorrow* will do. There is no need to repent and receive Christ until *tomorrow*.' And the other wicked, evil spirits voted to send him to earth."

Pastor Mark Shane asked everyone in the crowd to bow their heads. He prayed for those in the building who were lost, and asked God to convict their hearts of their lost condition and draw them to Jesus. He then had the congregation stand and began the invitation.

While the invitation song was being sung, Dr. Dane and Tharyn saw Kirby Holton standing there with his head bowed, gripping the back of the pew ahead of him and shifting his weight from one foot to the other.

With a prayer in his heart, Dr. Dane leaned over and spoke in a low tone. "Don't put it off, Kirby. If you're willing to go forward and receive Jesus, I'll walk down there with you."

With tears in his eyes, Kirby raised his head, looked at the young doctor, and said, "Let's go."

Tharyn choked up when she saw the two of them step into the aisle. "Thank You, Lord!" she whispered. "Thank You!"

When the doctor and the millionaire reached the front, the pastor took hold of Kirby's hand. "Why are you coming, Mr. Holton?"

Kirby wiped tears. "I want to be saved,

Pastor. Right now. I'm not putting it off till tomorrow."

The pastor smiled and set his tear-stained eyes on Central City's physician. "Dr. Dane, will you take him to the altar and lead him to Jesus?"

Face beaming, Dr. Dane said, "It will be my pleasure, Pastor."

As the invitation went on, three other people also came forward, and when they gave their testimonies after receiving Christ, there was great rejoicing in the congregation.

Moments later, when all four were baptized, there was more rejoicing.

Seventeen

Some two weeks passed.

On the morning of Monday, October 10, Dr. Dane Logan was standing at Tharyn's desk, talking to her about a patient who had just been treated, when they looked up to see Pastor Mark Shane come in. There were four more patients in the waiting room.

Both Logans greeted the pastor, who said, "I just came by to talk to you for a moment about Kirby Holton. If you're too busy, I'll come back later."

Tharyn rose from her chair and started around the desk. Meeting her husband's glance, she said, "I'll take the next patient on back to the examining room, Dane. Mr. Watson is next, and he needs you to check on his broken ribs."

Dr. Dane looked at the pastor. "You say it will only take a moment?"

"Yes. Not more than two or three minutes."

"All right, let's go into my office.

293

Tharyn, I'll be back there shortly."

When the two men stepped into the doctor's private office, Shane said, "I've noticed at church the past two Sundays, and on Wednesday nights, that Kirby has sat with you and Tharyn. Are you getting to know him better?"

"We sure are. In fact, he told us he wanted to sit with us because he wanted to get to know *us* better."

"Good. I've visited him twice at home since he got saved. He seems to be growing spiritually. I just wanted to see if you felt the same way."

"Oh, I sure do, Pastor. Kirby has gone out of his way to thank me for having a part in his salvation, and for leading his son to the Lord before he died. Over and over, he has spoken with joy about one day being with Greg in heaven. He tells me he's reading his Bible at least an hour each night. I'm very pleased with the progress he's made in his new spiritual life."

"Good. Then both of us are reading him the same. Well, that's all I needed to talk to you about." The pastor opened the door, then paused and looked over his shoulder. "It seems that almost every time I come in here, your waiting room is full. I guess your practice is still growing, eh?"

Dr. Dane grinned. "Yes, sir, it is. More and more people from surrounding towns and ranches are coming to me for medical treatment. The practice is growing steadily. One of these days I'm going to have to make a move toward setting up a clinic. I wish it could be a hospital, but at least we need to have a few beds so we can keep patients here overnight, and even longer after some surgeries. At this point, if they need extended medical care, we simply have to take them to Denver to Mile High Hospital."

"Well, I hope you can make a move toward setting up a clinic real soon."

"I'm going to have to. And I'm going to have to bring in a younger doctor to assist me, too. The load is getting pretty heavy."

"I can understand that. Dear Dr. Fraser is having a difficult time with his back. He's been asking Peggy and me to pray for him."

"Bless his heart, it's just getting harder and harder for him to work here at the office. And with this increasing load, I'm having my weary days, too. More and more, I'm having to make house calls, and so many of them are twenty and thirty miles away. And not only in the daytime, either. Just in the past couple of weeks, I've been awakened in the middle of the night three times to handle emergencies. I really need an assistant who can help me with the load."

As the two men stepped out of Dr. Dane's office, the doctor said, "You might be praying for me tomorrow, Pastor. I'm going to Chief Tando's village in the morning and taking a Bible to leave with him. If the Word can get into his heart, I feel that one day I can reach him for the Lord."

"I know he speaks English, but can he also *read* English?"

"Yes, he can. And so can his squaw, his son, and some of his people. So be in prayer, won't you?"

"I sure will."

That evening, after closing the office, Dr. Dane took Tharyn to one of Central City's cafés for supper.

While they were eating, Tharyn noticed her husband's weariness. "Darling, you look pretty tired. Maybe you shouldn't make that ride to Chief Tando's village to-morrow."

Dane wiped a palm over his eyes and shook his head. "I am a bit tired, but I'll be all right after a good night's sleep. I've just got to take that Bible we bought for the chief and give it to him. And I'm eager to talk to him about the Lord. The sooner I get started, the sooner he'll be saved. I'm sure it's going to take time to get the Word in his heart, and to see the fruit of my labors with him."

"Of course it will take time. But with the continual growth of the practice, I sure wish we already had Dr. Tim here to help shoulder the load. That would free you up for more rides to the Ute village. And not only that, but it would sure lift some of the pressure of the practice from your shoulders."

Dane grinned. "Well, honey, I'm just going to have to tough it out till next June or so. Don't worry about me. I'll be all right."

It was just past midnight and Tharyn was in the midst of her recurring dream about Elizabeth Ann when she was awakened by a loud pounding sound. She shook her head and listened to make sure the pounding had not been part of her dream. Then it came again. Someone was knocking on the front door.

She turned toward Dane. He was sound

asleep. Knowing he would want to be the one to go down to the door, she shook him and said, "Honey, wake up! Someone's knocking at the front door."

Dane moaned, raised up on an elbow, and shook his head. "What's that?"

"There's someone knocking at the front door."

"Oh. All right."

The doctor got out of bed, put on his robe by the pale moonlight coming through the bedroom windows, and the knock came again while he lit a lantern.

Tharyn put her head back down on the pillow and watched him leave the room in the circle of light from the lantern he was carrying.

Seconds later, she heard Dane's voice and a heavy male voice in conversation. Soon she heard footsteps on the stairs, and Dane came into the room. "It's Bart Jenkins, honey. Mary Ruth's baby has decided to come early. I'll be back as soon as I can. You get some sleep now."

"All right, sweetheart. See you when you get back."

He quickly took suit, shirt, and string tie from the closet, picked his boots up from beside a nearby chair, and headed for the door, still carrying the lantern. He paused at the door. "I love you, sweet stuff."

"I love you, too. Be careful."

Tharyn was still awake when she heard Dane hurry down the stairs a few minutes later. She heard the front door close, and soon was back to sleep.

It was almost noon the next day when Dr. Dane Logan sat in his saddle as Pal carried him down the long slope on the south side of Central City. The uneven rooftops of the town came into view, and he yawned. He thought of how he had arrived home at 4:30 after delivering the Jenkins baby, and Tharyn had hurriedly rushed him back to bed so he could get some sleep. She had tried to persuade him not to make the ride to Chief Tando's village, but he had insisted on doing so, and was up by six.

And now, as the sun was nearing its apex in the blue Colorado sky, he felt a deep weariness in his body. He raised his bleary eyes toward heaven. "Lord, I'm very thankful to be busy in my practice, but You know I'm going to need help soon."

Dane thought of Dr. Fraser, and how he was so willing to fill in for him when needed. "Lord, I appreciate Dr. Fraser's help so much, but I know his energies are very limited, and he needs to retire completely. I would look for another doctor to come and join me right away, but I feel so positive, Lord, that Tim Braden is the man I need. You've given me such peace about Tim. I know You have it all worked out, but until spring comes, I'm going to need You to give me extra strength as I carry on this practice."

Suddenly, Dr. Dane jerked in the saddle as Pal stopped in front of the office. Having been lost in thought and talking to the Lord, he hadn't realized he was already back in town.

He patted the horse's neck. "Good boy, Pal. I'm sure glad you know your way around here."

There were a couple of horses tied to the hitch rail. Heaving a big sigh, Dane slid from the saddle and led Pal to a spot at the hitch rail. He stroked the faithful gelding's long face, then headed for the office door.

When he stepped into the office, he saw Dr. Fraser and Kirby Holton standing at Tharyn's desk. He noted that there were no patients in the waiting room, then remembered that it was noon.

Tharyn hurried to her husband. She embraced him, kissed his cheek, and as the two men moved up close, asked, "How did it go with Chief Tando, darling?"

Dane ran his gaze to Kirby and the aging doctor, then looked at Tharyn. "It went well, honey. I had a long talk with the chief in his tepee about the true God. Leela and Latawga were also in the tepee. They sat silently and listened. Chief Tando had a hard time grasping the fact that there is only one true and living God, whose Son paid the penalty for the sins of the whole world on the cross. It's only natural that what I said puzzled him since the Ute religion has many gods."

"How did the chief react, though?" Dr. Fraser asked. "Did it anger him that you were, in essence, telling him that his gods do not exist?"

Dane shook his head. "At no time did he become angry or belligerent. He listened, as did his squaw and his son. When we had talked about as long as I thought I should for the first visit, I presented him with a Bible. As Tharyn knows, I had marked several passages for him to read over and over. He promised me he would do so. Well, we who know the Lord also know that faith cometh by hearing, and hearing by the Word of God."

Dr. Fraser smiled. "And we also know

301

that the Word of God is quick and powerful, and sharper than any two-edged sword."

Kirby had a surprised look on his face. "The chief can read English, Doctor?"

"He sure can. So can his squaw and son, and many of his people. When Chief Tando, Chief Ouray, and I were riding together to Fort Junction for the peace treaty signing, both chiefs told me about a white man who lived among the Utes in Chief Ouray's village many years ago. He taught Ouray and his people to speak and read English, and this was passed on over the years to the other Utes."

Kirby nodded. "Hmm. That's interesting."

"And what about your going back to talk to him again?" asked Tharyn.

"He's expecting me to come back in a few weeks so he and I can talk more about the one true God and His Son. He said he knew he would have questions to ask me after he had read from the Bible."

Tharyn's face was beaming. "Oh, I'm so thrilled to know that Chief Tando is actually showing interest! We must pray earnestly that the Lord will help him to turn his back on his heathen religion and open his heart to Jesus."

"This is marvelous," Dr. Fraser said. "Esther and I will be praying for Chief Tando."

"I will, too," said Kirby. He then looked at Dr. Dane. "I was in town to do some business at the hardware store, so I just came by the office to say hello. See you at church tomorrow night."

As Kirby was leaving, a female patient, Letha Trent, came in, followed by Western Union agent Charlie Holmes, who announced that he had a telegram for Dr. Logan from Dr. Matthew Carroll, superintendent of Denver's Mile High Hospital. Charlie handed Dr. Dane the brown envelope, and Dr. Fraser ushered Letha into the back room.

As Dr. Dane was opening the envelope, Charlie said, "I'll wait till you read it, Doctor, in case you want to send Dr. Carroll a reply."

Dr. Dane nodded and took out the telegram. Tharyn looked on with interest as her husband read the message.

As Dane read the telegram, his stomach seemed to roll over. *Oh, no. Another trip to Denver, when I'm already so tired.*

At once, his conscience troubled him. *Shame on you, Dane Logan! Remember your unfailing desire to be a physician and surgeon, when you were living on the streets of Manhattan, and all you went through to get your education? Remember the oath you took so solemnly at your graduation? Well, now is the time to live up to that oath!*

In his heart, the young doctor said, *Thank You, Lord, for speaking to my conscience and reminding me of where I came from. Please give me the physical strength and mental ability to make the trip and perform this task before me. Someday there will be many more doctors who will be able to execute a hip replacement, but in the meantime, I thank You for the training and ability to do so. Help me to be a success at this one.*

Tharyn was watching the play of emotions on her husband's face as he held the telegram and kept his eyes on it. She laid a hand on his arm. "Something bad, darling?"

He swung his eyes to his wife, and a smile erased the tired lines on his features. "No. Not bad at all. Dr. Carroll wants to know if you and I can come as soon as possible to do a hip replacement for a seventy-six-year-old man named Max Thurman."

Tharyn rubbed her chin. "Let's go over what we have scheduled this week yet."

304

"Well, we've got two surgeries scheduled, right?"

"Mm-hmm. Six-year-old Susie Waltham's tonsillectomy."

"And Horace Baldwin's fatty tumor cyst under his arm."

"Right. And, of course, you've got several patients expecting you to come for house calls."

"Then we could travel to Denver on Friday and do the surgery on Saturday."

"Sounds like a good plan. Then since we'd be there on Saturday, we could stay over and go to church Sunday with my parents and Melinda and Tim, and return on Monday."

Dr. Dane's eyes brightened. "Yes! That would give us a chance to talk to Tim and Melinda about you-know-what!"

Tharyn giggled. "The Lord knows so much better how to plan things than you and I do, darling. I ran into Nadine yesterday at the general store, and she's still open to fill in here at the office whenever she's needed."

"I figured so, but it's good to hear it." He turned to the Western Union agent. "Charlie, let me go talk to Dr. Fraser, and I'll be back to dictate a telegram for you to send to Dr. Carroll."

Charlie smiled. "I'll be here."

Two more patients were coming in, and Tharyn moved behind her desk to welcome them.

Dr. Dane found Dr. Fraser working over Letha Trent, who lay on an examining table in curtained section number two.

Dr. Dane stepped up beside the older physician. "How's Letha doing?"

"Just fine. She'll probably only need a couple more treatments."

"Good. You look better than when you were in last time, Letha."

She smiled up at him. "That's because I'm feeling better, Dr. Logan."

As Dr. Fraser kept working on Letha, Dr. Dane said, "Dr. Carroll's telegram was about an elderly man who needs a hip replacement."

"Well, Dr. Carroll knows where to find the expert for hip replacements, I'll say that," Fraser said.

"You sure know how to help a fellow's ego, don't you?"

The elderly physician chuckled and looked up at Dr. Dane. "Well, my motto is: *Always help a friend's bird.*"

Dr. Dane frowned. "I don't understand. What's a bird got to do with it?"

"Didn't you say I sure know how to

help a fellow's eagle?"

Dane shook his head and snorted. "You old coot! You never run out of them, do you?"

"Guess not. I've got a million more. Wanna hear some?"

Dr. Dane grinned. "Not right now. I've got to give Charlie a message to wire to Dr. Carroll. Tharyn and I talked it over. We've got some surgeries to do yet this week, and I've got some house calls scheduled. We figure we can travel over to Denver on Friday and do the hip replacement on Saturday. We'd stay over Sunday and come back on Monday. What do you think? I'm concerned about your back, so you'll have to tell me if you think you can fill in for me."

The kindly old physician grinned. "I'll take some extra salicylic acid each day. I'll be all right. It's important that the man in Denver has the hip replacement."

"You sure you'll be all right?"

"I'll be fine."

"I'll have Nadine come and fill in for Tharyn."

"Great!"

Dr. Dane's voice took on a serious note. "Now, doctor, I'm going to give you a special bonus in addition to your regular pay for filling in for me this time."

Fraser shook his head. "Son, it's not necessary for you to give me a bonus."

"Who's boss here?"

"Well, you are."

"Okay. Then as boss of this place, I hereby declare that you are going to get a bonus. No arguments."

Dr. Fraser saluted him military-style with a smirk on his face. "Yes, *sir!* Whatever you say, *sir!*"

"Good. Now you finish up on Letha. I've got a telegram to send."

In Denver, Dr. Matt Carroll was at his desk when his secretary entered his office and told him a Western Union messenger was there with a telegram from Dr. Dane Logan in Central City. The messenger told her a return wire from Dr. Carroll would be necessary.

When Dr. Carroll had read the telegram, he dictated a return message for Dr. Logan, saying the date was fine and that he would advise the Thurmans about it and also tell David Tabor that his daughter and son-in-law would be coming to Denver on Saturday.

On the way back to the hospital after talking with the Thurmans and David

Tabor, Dr. Carroll was approaching the federal building in his buggy when he saw Chief U.S. Marshal John Brockman and three of his deputies about to mount their horses at the hitch rail.

"Leaving town, John?" Carroll called out.

"That we are," Brockman replied. "We're about to go in pursuit of a gang of bank robbers led by Chick Barton."

"I haven't heard of the Chick Barton gang," said Carroll.

"They've operated only in Kansas for some time, but they've decided to come to Colorado. Yesterday they robbed banks in Byers and Strasburg. I got a wire from the marshal in Strasburg this morning. They shot and killed people in both banks, and eluded the Strasburg posse."

"So you're heading east to go after them?"

"No. They're west of here now. I just got a wire from the town marshal in Golden. The Barton gang robbed Golden's First National Bank an hour ago, and shot and killed a bank officer and a teller. They were last seen heading into the mountains."

"Well, I won't detain you," said Carroll. "Go get 'em."

"I plan to," Brockman said levelly, and swung into the saddle.

The chief and his deputies spurred their horses and galloped away.

Eighteen

Chick Barton and his gang were riding in a dense forest just south of the mountain town of Idaho Springs several miles west of Denver when the sun dropped over the peaks to the west. The shadows of the tall trees stretched eastward, and between them streamed a red-gold light from what was left of the sun's fire just above the horizon.

In the lead, Barton hipped around in the saddle and said, "Okay, boys, let's make camp for the night. We don't need to get any closer to Idaho Springs till tomorrow at noon. That's when we'll hit the bank."

Barton guided his horse into a small open area, dismounted, and said to his men as they were also dismounting, "Somebody's already been here not too long ago and left us some rocks stacked just right for a cookfire. All we gotta do is find us some wood. And that don't look too hard from where I stand."

Vincent Wagner set his eyes on the powerful, muscular Chick Barton. "Boss, I don't know about us buildin' a fire. Could be a posse from Golden on our tails. The fire would lead 'em right to us."

Barton rolled his wide shoulders. "This ain't Kansas, Vince. It ain't even the plains of eastern Colorado. We're in the mountains now, and this is October. I hear tell it gets plenty cold at this altitude even in the fall. I figure we can trade off through the night bein' on watch so's the other fellas can lay close to the fire. Most towns don't send posses, but if a posse did show up, whoever's on watch would hear 'em comin', wake the rest of us up, and we'd dash into the shadows and cut 'em down real quick."

"Sounds okay to me," spoke up Clete Lundy.

"I've been in this area before, years ago, and Chick's right," chimed in Ed Loomis. "It gets pretty cold here in these mountains even at this time of year. Don't worry about the fire, Vince. Like Chick says, if a posse does show up, we'll hear 'em comin' and make buzzard bait out of 'em."

Wagner shrugged. "Okay. Let's get us a fire going and make some coffee."

There was a small stream nearby. Three of the men moved around gathering wood for the fire while the other two led the horses to the stream and let them drink.

Darkness seemed to drop down swiftly. The unseen wolves around them began their haunting, mournful howls. The stars appeared, and soon grew brighter. The wind moaned through the branches of the pine trees that surrounded the gang.

By the time the fire was crackling, its blaze caused the shadows of the pines to appear as great, looming giants against the dark sky.

The five outlaws sat around the fire, drinking coffee from the pot that Ed Loomis carried in his saddlebag, while eating beef jerky and hardtack biscuits. The increasingly cold wind fanned the flames of the fire, whipping up flakes of white ash.

When the men had finished their meal, they took from their saddlebags the stuffed moneybags they had stolen from the bank in Golden, and sat down once again around the fire.

After counting the loot, they found that they had just over twenty thousand dollars to split among them. Chick Barton always took forty percent of the money from their robberies, and the other four divided up the other sixty percent.

Plenty satisfied with his portion of the

loot, Clete Lundy held it in his hands, looked at Barton by the light of the fire, and said with a smile, "Chick, I'm sure glad I hooked up with you!"

The other three quickly agreed.

Barton, who had his two front teeth missing, grinned. "Well, boys, I'm mighty glad we all got hooked up together. And it's only gonna get better. When we've cleaned out some more of the banks here in this part of the Rockies, we'll move on up north and clean out some Wyomin' and Montana banks. Time we've done that, we'll be rich enough to retire and live like kings wherever we decide to settle down."

There was more talk about becoming rich until finally they put more wood on the fire, and four of the gang members lay in their bedrolls while Vincent Wagner took the first watch. He sat near the fire, rifle in hand, tugging his hat down tight and pulling his coat collar up around his ears.

Just before noon the next day, the gang mounted up and rode into Idaho Springs. No posse from Golden had shown up.

Moving slowly along Main Street, they noted that there were many people along the boardwalks, going in and out of the stores and shops, and gathering in small groups to chat.

As they rode past the town marshal's office, they could see two men at desks inside. A sign that hung over the boardwalk told them that the marshal's name was Lou Hoffman.

A block and a half farther down the street, they hauled up in front of the Idaho Springs National Bank.

As they were dismounting, Barton said to Bud Finch, "As usual, I want you to stay here with the horses and keep an eye out for lawmen. If you see that marshal and any deputies comin' this way, come inside and let us know."

Finch nodded and slipped his rifle from the saddle boot.

There were few customers in the bank when the four men moved through the door. According to plan, Clete Lundy made his way to the small area where the bank officers had their desks. And as usual, at noon there was only one officer there to deal with customers.

The other three casually moved to the tables where customers could fill out deposit slips, write checks, or endorse checks.

As Clete Lundy passed through the small gate in the railing that surrounded the officers' area, he noted by the name-plate on the desk that the lone officer was a vice-president, and his name was Lloyd Smith. He looked to be in his midfifties.

Smith looked up at the stranger, smiled, and said, "May I help you, sir?"

Lundy whipped out his revolver, and pressed it against the vice president's forehead. He looked at him with eyes like a snake. "Yeah, you can help me."

Smith's eyes were suddenly wide with the horror of a sleeper awakened from a nightmare to find it real.

"See those three men headed for the tellers' cages, Mr. Smith?"

The terrified man gulped. "Y-yes, sir."

"Holler over there and get the tellers' attention. Tell 'em if they don't hand over all their money, I'll blow your brains out. And tell one of 'em to take the big guy into the vault with him and give him all the money in there."

Lloyd Smith quickly obeyed. The four customers who were in the bank stood frozen in place, eyes wide.

Moments later, with their free hands full of moneybags, and cocked revolvers in their gun hands, the three robbers headed toward the door.

Clete Lundy hurried away from the vice

president's desk to join them. Lloyd Smith took a revolver from a desk drawer, aimed, and fired.

The slug hit Lundy in the back of the head, and he fell to the floor facedown.

Barton saw the bank officer standing there with the smoking gun in his hand. He fired at Smith, hitting him in the chest, and Smith went down.

As the gang headed toward the door, two tellers pulled guns from drawers.

Outside, Bud Finch heard the gunfire inside the bank, and his nerves went rigid. At the same time, he saw the marshal and a deputy running down the street toward the bank, their badges flashing in the sunlight. People on the street looked on fearfully.

Finch raised his rifle and took aim at the lawmen just as Barton, Loomis, and Wagner came running out of the bank, moneybags in hand, firing back at the tellers inside. When they saw Finch shooting at the lawmen, who were firing back, they also opened fire on the lawmen.

People were scattering for cover as the thunder of gunfire rocked the street and ear-stabbing echoes clattered among the buildings. Women were wailing and screaming.

Bullets flew.

The two lawmen jumped behind a wagon for cover. The outlaws took advantage of it to mount their horses.

Marshal Lou Hoffman and his deputy once again opened fire.

In their saddles, the outlaws fired back. In the exchange of gunfire, the deputy went down. The marshal was hit in the upper left arm just after he put a bullet in the upper chest of Bud Finch, who doubled over in the saddle, but managed to stay on his horse as they galloped out of town to the northwest.

People rushed up to the marshal as he fired the last shot left in his gun in the direction of the fleeing bank robbers, then dropped to one knee. Others knelt over the fallen deputy, and one of the men called out, "Marshal, your deputy is dead!"

The Barton gang rode away from Idaho Springs with Bud Finch holding desperately onto the pommel of his saddle. After several minutes, Chick led them down a trail into a canyon and stopped beside a creek.

The three men dismounted, and Wagner and Loomis eased the bleeding Bud Finch from the saddle while Barton took a tin cup from his saddlebag and dipped it into the creek.

When Barton moved to the spot where Finch lay on the ground, Wagner said, "Chick, the slug hit him high enough that it couldn't have hit his heart or punctured a lung, but he's gonna bleed to death if we don't get him to a doctor. I just packed my bandanna against the wound to help slow the bleedin'."

Barton knelt down and placed the cup of water to Finch's dry lips. "Sip it slow-like, Bud. We lost Clete. I sure don't want to lose you."

Finch took a couple swallows, then asked in a weak voice, "Clete's dead?"

"Yeah. Bank officer shot him in the head."

Chick gave Bud more water, then looked up at Ed Loomis. "You're the only one of us who's been in this area before. You got any idea where we can find a doctor? Other than where we just were, I mean."

"The nearest town is Central City. It's about eight or nine miles to the northwest. There was a doctor there when I was in these parts before."

Barton nodded. "Now we've got to do some thinkin'. It's too dangerous to just take Bud into a doctor's office. The doctor will want to know how he got shot, and no matter what we tell him, he might be suspicious and insist on the law bein' brought into it."

"You're right about that, Chick," said Vincent Wagner. "Doctors are supposed to report any suspicious bullet or knife wounds to the local law."

"Best thing to do is hole up in some store where there are people we can hold hostage. We'll threaten to kill them unless a doctor comes in and tends to Bud's wound. After Bud is taken care of, we'll take a couple of the hostages with us for insurance. We'll threaten to kill them if lawmen or anyone else follows us."

The gang leader gave Bud Finch the last of the water in the cup, and rose to his feet. "All right, boys, let's get Bud to Central City."

They mounted up, with Vincent riding on Bud's horse with him. Ed was leading Vincent's horse as they rode out of the canyon.

In Central City at ten minutes after two o'clock, a group of ladies were gathering in front of the town hall for a quilting bee. They were chattering happily, anticipating the joy they always experienced when they got together for a bee.

Betty Anderson, the mayor's wife, was

always in charge of the sewing bees. Almost half of the women in the group were members of the church where Mark Shane was pastor. Betty inserted a key in the lock of the door, and told the ladies to go inside the building. She added that Mayor Anderson had already come into the building an hour ago and built fires in both stoves.

At the same time the ladies were filing into the town hall, Chick Barton and Ed Loomis were riding into town, looking for just the right store in which to carry out their plan. Vincent Wagner had stayed at the edge of town with Bud Finch, hiding in a grove of trees.

As Barton and Loomis rode along Main Street with people moving up and down the boardwalks and light traffic busying the dusty thoroughfare, Chick pointed off to the side and said, "Look over there, Ed."

Loomis immediately saw the sign beside the front door of the building that read: *DANE LOGAN, M.D.*

Barton said, "There's our doctor."

Ed grinned as he noticed a man and a woman coming out of the doctor's office. "Sure enough. Dr. Dane Logan doesn't know it, but he's about to get a new patient."

Suddenly Barton pointed up the street a half-block and said, "Look up there, Ed. See the town hall sign?"

"Yeah."

"Take a gander at all those women filin' into the buildin'."

Ed nodded. "Looks like some kind of women's meetin'."

Barton's eyes lit up. "Yeah, it's perfect! Let's go get Vincent and Bud. There's gotta be a back door. We'll go in that way and surprise 'em!"

Inside the town hall, Betty Anderson stood before the group of forty-seven women who were now seated at long tables with their quilting material spread out before them, needles and thread at hand.

"Ladies, it's nice to see such a good turnout today," Betty said. "May I remind you that this is a charity bee. We'll be donating these quilts to the less fortunate families who live in those shanties on the east edge of town. As I told you at our last bee, I know those poor folks could certainly use some extra bedding for winter, which is not far off."

The ladies nodded their heads. Betty sat down at the head table with Peggy Shane and two other women, and soon all the ladies were busy with their heads bent over the colorful material, their needles flashing in and out as they made their quilting stitches.

There was happy chatter as they worked, and everyone was having a good time.

Suddenly there was the sound of glass breaking at the back door of the building. A man's hand reached through a broken windowpane, grasped the knob, and flung the door open.

What had been happy chatter a moment before was now gasps and screams as the frightened women saw three men come in with guns drawn. One of them was also holding up a bleeding man who was leaning against him.

"Quiet, all of you!" roared Chick Barton, his voice cruel and menacing while waving his revolver. "Sit still! Don't move!"

The frightened group sat stock still, afraid to breathe.

"Who's in charge here?"

Betty Anderson lifted a hand. Fighting to subdue a quiver in her voice, she said, "I am, sir. My name is Betty Anderson. I am the wife of Mayor Mike Anderson."

"Mrs. Anderson, I want you to go right now to Dr. Dane Logan's office and tell him we have a wounded man here. He has a bullet in his chest and is bleeding bad. You tell the doctor I demand that he come instantly!" Barton glanced up at a large clock on the wall. "If that doctor isn't here in fifteen minutes, Mrs. Anderson, one of these women will die! You come back here with the doctor, too, or I'll still shoot one of these women!"

Betty rose to her feet shakily, fear showing in her eyes, and headed for the front door.

Barton called after her, "Mrs. Anderson, if you or the doctor bring the law, we'll spill blood all over the place! Do you hear me?"

"Y-yes, sir."

When Betty stepped out of the town hall, she was shaking like an aspen leaf in a cold winter breeze. "Dear Lord," she muttered, breathing heavily, "don't let those evil men hurt any of the ladies."

As Betty hurried along the boardwalk, people noticed the frightened look on her face and asked if she was all right. She hurried on without a reply, leaving them staring after her.

When Betty stepped into the doctor's office, Tharyn was at her desk. The waiting room was almost full.

"Betty, are you ill?" Tharyn said.

Betty bent over Tharyn's desk, and in a trembling whisper, said, "I'm not ill, but I must see Dr. Logan in private at once. It is a matter of life and death."

Tharyn studied Betty's eyes and said in an undertone, "Something really is very wrong, isn't it?"

Betty nodded. "Like I said . . . life and death."

Tharyn rose to her feet, rounded the desk, and put an arm around Betty's quivering shoulder. "Come with me," she whispered, and led her into the back room under the watchful eyes of the people in the waiting room.

Dr. Dane was working in curtained section number three on the broken arm of a ten-year-old boy. The curtain was not closed.

Tharyn seated Betty on a nearby wooden chair, patted her shoulder as if to say she would be right back, and stepped into the section.

The doctor had the boy's arm in a cast, and was just finishing tying the sling.

Tharyn said, "Doctor, Betty Anderson is here. She has an emergency she must tell you about."

Dr. Dane cinched the knot on the sling. "All right. I'm finished here. Would you take Raymond out to his mother while I talk to Betty?"

"Sure will," she said, extending a hand to the boy. "Let's go, Raymond."

As Tharyn and the boy headed for the door, Dr. Dane stepped up to Betty where she sat on the chair. At once he could see that she was very pale, and her forehead was clammy. Her eyes stared at him in horror. "Betty, what is it? What's wrong?"

She uttered a choked cry, strained to speak, and finally got it out. "There's real trouble at the town hall."

"What kind of trouble?"

Betty hastily told Dr. Dane about the four men who broke through the back door of the town hall and interrupted the quilting bee. "One of them has a bullet in his chest, Doctor, and the leader wants you there no later than six minutes from right now, or he is going to shoot one of the women! He warned me that if we brought the law in on this, they'd spill blood all over the place."

Dr. Dane dashed to the medicine cabinet, grabbed his black medical bag from a shelf, and hurried back to her. "I'll leave you here."

Betty stood up and shook her head. "No, Doctor! The outlaw leader said if I didn't come back with you, he would still shoot one of the women!"

The doctor shook his head. "I hate to let you go into danger again, but I guess there's no way around it."

"None. I can't let someone else die because I disobeyed that awful man."

When Dr. Dane and Betty entered the office, they paused at the desk. The doctor said in a low voice, "Honey, I can't explain anything right now. This is definitely an emergency, and we must go quickly."

With that, the doctor and the mayor's wife hurried out the door, leaving the patients in the waiting area looking on in bafflement, and Tharyn with a puzzled look on her face.

Again, people on the boardwalk saw the anxious looks on the faces of the doctor and the mayor's wife, and asked if something was wrong. Neither Dr. Dane nor Betty replied. They kept their hasty pace on down the street.

As they drew near the town hall, Dr. Dane prayed aloud, "Dear Lord, please help us. Don't let any of those ladies get hurt."

Betty was praying the same thing in her heart.

Unnoticed by the doctor and Betty,

Deputy Marshal Len Kurtz was across the street. His attention was on them as they dashed into the town hall with Dr. Logan carrying his medical bag.

"Hmm," Kurtz said to himself, "something must've happened to one of the ladies at the quilting bee. I'd better go see if there's anything I can do to help."

Nineteen

When Dr. Dane Logan and Betty Anderson entered the town hall, they found themselves facing the black muzzle of Ed Loomis's revolver.

Scowling at the tall, slender man with blazing eyes, Loomis noted the black medical bag in his hand and growled, "It's a good thing you made it, Doctor. In two more minutes, one of the women would've been shot."

Dr. Dane glanced at the table where he saw the wounded man lying, with the other two standing over him. From the side of his mouth, he said, "Betty, you go sit down."

Then, ignoring Loomis, he hurried toward the wounded man.

When Betty sat down in the chair where she had been earlier, Peggy Shane put an arm around her and squeezed her tightly. Tears were in Betty's eyes.

At that moment, Loomis glanced out the window by the front door and caught sight of a man heading toward the building, and the sunlight flashed off his badge.

Over his shoulder, Loomis said, "Hey, Chick! They brought the law with 'em! A guy wearin' a badge is comin' toward the door!"

Anger glinted in the outlaw leader's dark eyes. Over his shoulder, he told Loomis to lock the door, then he set his blazing eyes on the doctor and hissed, "You shouldn't have done that, Doc! Now blood'll be shed!"

Dr. Dane shook his head. "We didn't talk to any lawman. He must have spotted Mrs. Anderson and me coming into the building. She told me about your threat. I wouldn't go against it and put these women in any more danger."

Barton studied him for a brief moment, then said, "Okay, I believe you. Get busy on Bud." With that, he wheeled and headed toward the door where Ed Loomis was standing, gun in hand.

As he was drawing near the door, he heard the door handle rattle. Barton moved up to the door and called loudly, "Who is it?"

"Deputy Marshal Len Kurtz!" came the reply. "What's going on in there? Why is the door locked?"

Barton shouted back, "Well, Deputy Kurtz, my name is Chick Barton. There's a gang of us in here, and I'm the leader. We're holdin' guns on these women and the doctor, who's removin' a slug from the chest of one of my men. If you and your boss try to interfere, we'll start killin' women! You hear me?"

Kurtz's voice came back strong. "Barton, listen to me! You and your men can't hope to escape!"

"Oh, yeah?" blared the outlaw leader. "When we leave here, we're takin' two or three of these women with us. If you or anyone else tries to interfere, or if we're followed, you'll have some dead women on your hands! Now, you get outta here, or I'll shoot one of these women right now! And if you bring the marshal back with you, I'll kill *two* women! You got that?"

Silence.

"You gone deaf, deputy? I said, you got that?"

Ed Loomis looked out the window. "He's leavin', Chick."

Barton stepped up beside him and watched the deputy hurrying away. He scowled. "If he don't believe me, he soon will."

Loomis turned and looked at the

women. Fear was clearly etched on their faces.

Outside, Len Kurtz reached the middle of the street and broke into a dead-heat run. When he reached the marshal's office, he was glad to see his boss there. Quickly, he told the story to Marshal Jake Merrell.

The marshal sighed and said, "I've heard of the Barton gang. They've been active in Kansas, holding up banks, stagecoaches, and trains for three or four years. They are, indeed, bloody killers. Those women and Dr. Logan are in grave danger. For sure, they'll take some women with them when they go. They'll probably kill Dr. Logan once they don't need him anymore, too. Len, we've got to do something. Let's sit down here and come up with some kind of plan."

Even as Marshal Merrell was speaking, he noticed four riders draw up out front at the hitch rail.

Merrell's eyes bulged. "Hey, that's Chief U.S. Marshal John Brockman out there with some deputies!" Jake headed toward the door. "I don't know what they're doing here, but I'm sure glad to see them!"

Len was on his heels as he opened the door.

Brockman and his men were dismounting as Jake Merrell hurried up to the chief U.S. marshal and said, "Boy, am I glad to see you!"

Jake was about to tell him about the crisis at the town hall when Brockman pushed his black hat back a little on his head and said, "Jake, we're on the trail of the Chick Barton gang from Kansas. They held up banks yesterday in Byers and Strasburg. They shot people in both banks and eluded the Strasburg posse. I received a wire this morning that —"

"Chief, the Barton gang is here in Central City right this moment."

"They are?"

"Yes."

Jake quickly explained the situation at the town hall. He told Brockman of Barton's threat to shed blood if the marshal tried to interfere and his threat to take two or three women as hostages when they left and to kill them if they were followed.

Brockman took a deep breath and ran his gaze over the faces of his deputies. "We don't dare approach the town hall. It very well could get one or more of the women killed. We've got to be prepared to stop the gang when they attempt to leave. How long has Dr. Logan been in there working on the wounded gang member?"

"Just a few minutes. Not knowing what was going on in there, Len went to investigate when he saw Dr. Logan and the mayor's wife hurrying into the building. The ladies were having a quilting bee. Len figured there was some kind of medical emergency, and hurried across the street to see if he could help in any way. Chick Barton talked to him through the locked door and told him the doctor was removing a bullet from the chest of one of his men. It's going to take a while to get that bullet out and bandage him up so's he can travel."

"Good. Then we've got time to come up with a plan."

Jake nodded. "Let's go into my office and sit down."

At the doctor's office, Tharyn Logan was doing her best to care for the patients coming in. Some she had to tell to come back another time, and others she placed in the curtained areas of the examining and surgical room.

As time went on without the doctor appearing, Tharyn did her best to care for those in the curtained areas. She was able to handle the problems of most of them satisfactorily, and sent them home.

Meanwhile, at the town hall, Dr. Dane Logan worked to remove the slug from Bud Finch's chest. The doctor had used chloroform to put Finch under during the surgery.

Betty Anderson, although not a medically trained person, was doing what she could to assist the doctor.

After almost an hour of working on Finch, Dr. Dane began stitching up the wound. Chick Barton was standing close by. He kept his eyes on the doctor's hands as he asked, "He gonna be all right, Doc?"

"Yes. He will live."

Vincent Wagner was standing close by the table at a side window, watching for any sign of someone approaching the building. Barton glanced at Wagner, looked back at Bud, then at the doctor.

"How long is he gonna be under the influence of the chloroform, Doc?"

"I'd say he'll start coming around in a few more minutes. He should be fully awake in less than an hour."

Barton turned toward Wagner. "Vince, you heard what the doc just said. We need to leave here as soon as Bud's awake."

"Sure, Chick. We need to pick out what women we want to take with us as hostages."

"We'll do that in a few minutes."

Ed Loomis was still at the front of the building, keeping watch at the large window by the door. All three outlaws had holstered their guns.

While the women looked at the scene at the table, their hearts were pounding, wondering who among them would become hostages.

Dr. Dane finished the last stitch, knotted it, and let Betty dab at the blood around the wound with a wad of bandage material. He turned to Barton and said, "If you try to take Bud with you when you leave, he will die. Even when he wakes up, he'll be in no condition to travel."

Barton looked at him coldly. "We brought him here on a horse with one of us holdin' him in the saddle. I was just thinkin' that the best way to go would be to steal a wagon that's already hitched to a team of horses." He snapped his fingers and grinned. "Yeah! That'd be good, because we could take more hostages with us in a wagon than ridin' double on horseback."

Dr. Dane shook his head. "Barton, Bud won't be able to stand it, even in a wagon. Hard bumps are unavoidable, even on roads, but much more so if you're traveling through rough country. Either way, the bumps will cause the wound to start bleeding. He'll bleed to death if you do this."

Barton chuckled drily. "Don't give me that stuff, Doc. You're just tryin' to interfere with our escape. Bud's tough. He'll be all right." He frowned and looked Logan in the eye. "And why do you care if Bud dies, anyway? He's an outlaw."

Dr. Dane met his gaze head-on. "I'll tell you why. When I became a medical doctor, I took an oath in which I promised to protect human life. I promised to take care of the sick to the best of my ability. The 'sick' includes the wounded and the injured. The oath didn't specify whether it was good people or bad people . . . just sick human beings. Bud Finch is an outlaw, yes, but he's still a human being. As a doctor, I care about him, and I've done my best to save his life."

Chick Barton sneered. "Well, tell you what, Doctor. Since you care so much about Bud, we'll just make you one of the hostages when we go, so you can ride in the wagon and take care of him."

Dr. Dane noticed that Vincent Wagner was standing at the nearby window with his holstered revolver almost within arm's reach. He prayed in his heart, asking the Lord to help him, and started putting his

337

medical instruments back in the black bag. *Just one step and I can yank Vincent's gun out of its holster. I've got to make my move a fast one.*

He stole another look at Wagner's holstered gun.

While still dabbing at the little bit of blood oozing from around Bud Finch's stitches, Betty followed the doctor's eyes when they went toward the outlaw's gun.

When Dr. Dane looked back down at his patient, his gaze crossed Betty's eyes. He held his gaze on her and almost without moving his lips, he whispered ever so quietly, "Don't move."

Betty assented with a look of understanding.

As Dr. Dane was closing his medical bag, he inched his way closer to Vincent, who was looking out the window.

Suddenly he snatched the Colt .45 from the holster, snapped back the hammer, and stepped out of Vincent's reach. Vincent's eyes bulged as he pivoted around and gave the doctor a startled look.

Dr. Dane pointed the muzzle at an equally startled Chick Barton, who was going for his gun. "Don't do it, Barton!" he commanded.

Barton hesitated, noting the determined

look in the doctor's dark brown eyes.

"Lay it on the table, put your hands over your head, and take a step back," Dane said, and in the same breath, he shouted at Ed Loomis, who had been looking out the window by the front door. "Take that gun out of its holster, Loomis! Drop it on the floor and come this way with your hands up, or I'll shoot Chick!"

Barton had obeyed the doctor's commands, and his face was dead white as he looked down the barrel of the gun and again noted the determination flashing in the doctor's eyes. His pulse quickened as he called to Loomis while keeping his eyes on the doctor. "Ed, do as he says! He ain't kiddin'! He'll shoot me!"

The women at the tables looked on, still shaken by what they had already been through.

Loomis stood where he was, but made no move toward his gun. His hands hung loosely at his sides.

Vincent Wagner stood with his back toward the window, his eyes shifting back and forth between Loomis and Barton.

The doctor said, "Vincent, come over here and stand by Chick."

Wagner moved from the window and stood beside Barton.

Ed Loomis sneered at the doctor. "You wouldn't shoot anybody, Doc."

Dr. Dane kept Barton and Wagner in the corner of an eye as he looked at Loomis. "What makes you think so?"

"What about your oath? If you shoot Chick, or any of us, you'll be violatin' that oath. You swore to protect human life, didn't you?"

"I swore to protect human life, yes. And right now I'm protecting the lives of all these women. Do as I say, or I'll start by shooting you!"

The look in the doctor's eyes told the outlaws he meant business.

Barton bellowed with a quiver in his voice, "Ed, drop your gun and get over here! This guy ain't kiddin'!"

Reluctantly, Loomis removed his gun from its holster, dropped it on the floor, but remained where he stood.

Dr. Dane glanced toward Ed. "Get over here!"

In that split second, Chick Barton reached back, snatched his revolver from the table, and thumbed back the hammer.

But he was too slow.

The gun in the doctor's hand swung on him and spit fire as it roared.

Chick took the bullet in the shoulder. The revolver slipped from his fingers and clattered to the floor as he clutched the wound and collapsed.

Betty bent down and picked up the gun.

At the same time, Vincent threw up his hands, eyes bulging, and cried, "Don't shoot me, Doctor!"

Dr. Dane said, "Stand still, Wagner!"

He then swung his gun on Loomis, who was starting to bend over and pick up his weapon. "Don't do it, Loomis!"

The outlaw froze.

"Get your hands in the air and get over here!" the doctor commanded.

Loomis lifted his hands over his head and moved up to where Wagner stood, trembling.

The doctor then ran his gaze between Loomis and Wagner. "Get down on the floor, facedown!"

As they obeyed, Dr. Dane said, "Stretch your arms and legs out as far as you can, and don't flinch."

They quickly stretched out as commanded, and lay absolutely still.

The women were all on their feet. Dr. Dane looked at them and made a slight smile. "You can all leave now." Then to Betty Anderson: "Will you go to the marshal's office and let him know what's happened here?"

Betty handed him the gun she had picked up, and Peggy Shane said, "I'll go with you, Betty."

At the marshal's office, the lawmen were on the boardwalk, having come outside when the sound of the shot came from the direction of the town hall. Suddenly lawmen and townspeople alike saw the women running out the door of the town hall. Betty Anderson and Peggy Shane were ahead of the rest of them.

"Come on!" said Chief U.S. Marshal John Brockman, pulling his gun.

Marshal Jake Merrell, Deputy Len Kurtz, and the federal deputies all joined Brockman in running toward the women, guns in hand.

When the lawmen met up with Betty and Peggy, they were told what had happened, and the two women called Dr. Dane Logan a hero.

Brockman and Merrell led the way as they hurried toward the town hall and plunged inside.

Dr. Dane Logan, still holding the revolver in his hand, had the bleeding Chick Barton on the table next to the one where

Bud Finch lay. Finch was just starting to awaken from the effects of the chloroform. Ed Loomis and Vincent Wagner still lay spread-eagled on the floor.

The doctor looked up as the lawmen came charging in, and was surprised to see Chief Brockman and the other federal men. As they drew near, he said, "Hello, Chief. Glad to see you!"

The doctor gave his own explanation of what had happened, pointing out each outlaw as he named them.

Loomis and Wagner were handcuffed by Marshal Merrell and Deputy Kurtz, jerked unceremoniously to their feet, and ushered out the door to the jail.

Then Marshal Merrell and one of the federal deputies picked Finch up off the table. Merrell said, "Dr. Dane, we'll lock him up in the jail. You can come and check on him anytime you want."

The doctor nodded. "I'll check on him in a little while."

Dr. Dane then looked at his friend from Denver and said, "Well, Chief, we don't have a stretcher, but if you'll help me carry Mr. Barton to my office, I can remove the slug from his shoulder."

"Okay. Let's do it."

As the two men carried the wounded

outlaw leader down the street, a crowd gathered, and the people gawked at the scene.

In the crowd were some of the husbands of the women who had been held captive in the town hall, standing with their arms around their wives. In tears of relief, the wives had told their husbands what had happened in the town hall.

Tharyn Logan saw her husband coming along the street, carrying the bleeding man with the help of Chief Brockman. "Oh, thank You, Lord," she breathed. "Thank You that Dane is unharmed."

When Dane and Chief Brockman drew up, Dane said, "Honey, this is an outlaw gang leader who was holding all the quilting bee women captive in the town hall. I'll give you the details later, but I had to shoot him. Everything's all right now. The rest of the gang are in jail."

"I'm so glad *you* are all right, darling." Then she smiled at the federal man. "Hello, Chief Brockman. Nice to see you."

Brockman returned the smile. "Nice to see you, too, Tharyn."

Tharyn followed her husband and Chief Brockman into the examining room, where three patients were waiting for the doctor to show up. Chick Barton was placed on the table in section number four.

Moments later, Tharyn administered the anesthetic to the patient. As she assisted her husband in going after the slug in Barton's shoulder, with Chief Brockman looking on, Dr. Dane told her the whole story.

After the slug had been removed, Dr. Dane stitched Barton up and put his arm in a sling. Chief Brockman waited until the sling was tied securely, then said, "Doc, how soon can I take the gang and head back to Denver?"

"Well, Barton could go now if you took him in a wagon and laid him on a mattress or something just as soft. But Finch won't be able to travel for a couple of weeks."

Brockman nodded. "My men and I will take the outlaws' horses to Central City's livery stable and rent a team and wagon. We'll take Barton and the other two today. I'll wire you in a couple of weeks and see how Finch is doing, and if he can travel by then, I'll send two of my deputies to get him." He paused, ran his gaze over the faces of doctor and nurse, and added, "I have no doubt that when they face trial in Denver, they will be hanged."

Chick Barton was coming out from under the chloroform, and his mind was clear enough to assess what Brockman had just said. He began to weep. "I don' wanna die!"

Brockman set steady eyes on him. "The Bible says a man reaps what he sows, Barton. It also says the way of transgressors is hard. Nobody forced you to be a killer and an outlaw. You chose that path yourself."

Barton closed his eyes and swallowed hard, but did not reply.

The chief looked at doctor and nurse. "Barton and his gang have left a trail of innocent blood all over Kansas for over three years. Then they came to Colorado. They held up banks yesterday in Byers and Strasburg, and killed people in both banks. I received a wire this morning from the town marshal in Golden. The Barton gang robbed Golden's First National Bank shortly after it opened this morning and killed a bank officer and a teller.

"My deputies and I rode hard this morning to pick up the gang's trail. When we got to Idaho Springs, we found out that they had held up the bank there. They shot a bank officer and two tellers. Then when they came out of the bank, they were met by the town marshal and his deputy. There was an exchange of gunfire in which one of Barton's gang members was killed. That's when Bud Finch was wounded. Sad thing is, the marshal was shot in one of his arms, and the deputy was killed."

Dr. Dane shook his head. "I'm sure glad you and your gang are out of business, Barton."

Chick closed his eyes, rather than meet the doctor's gaze.

Brockman pulled a pair of handcuffs from his belt and said, "Doc, I'm going to cuff him to this bed. I know he's weak, but I don't trust him. I want to be sure he'll be here when we're ready to take him to Denver in an hour or so."

Barton gave the chief a sullen look when he cuffed a wrist to the iron frame of the bed, but said nothing.

Dr. Dane then said, "Tharyn and I will be traveling to Denver this Friday, Chief. Dr. Carroll sent a wire about a man who needs a hip replacement. We'll be doing the surgery on Saturday. We'll stay over Sunday, and come home on Monday."

Brockman smiled. "Well, good. You're welcome to stay at our house, but I'm sure Tharyn's parents will want you to stay with them."

The doctor smiled. "I'm sure they will, but we'd like to spend some time with you and Breanna and the kids while we're there."

"Well, we'll work that out when you get there. I know we'll see you at church."

"You sure will," said Tharyn.

"Well, I've got to get a wagon so we can head for Denver. Be back to get Barton in a little while."

When the chief U.S. marshal was gone, Tharyn took Dane by the hand and led him into an empty curtained section.

Puzzled, he looked at her askance and said, "What's this all about?"

She wrapped her arms around him, and her body trembled as tears filled her eyes. She stepped back so she could look at him, and wiped at the tears. "Darling, I had no idea of the danger you were in. They could have killed you."

"Sweetheart, I'm fine. The Lord was with me all the way. He knew I couldn't just stand by and do nothing."

She nodded and blinked at additional tears that were surfacing. "I know, darling. I know. But now that the threat is over, I'm just a little bit in shock over the danger you were in. I heard the shot, of course, as did everyone else in town. I didn't know where it had been fired until just before you and Chief Brockman came down the street, carrying that outlaw. I was so relieved to see you."

He kissed her forehead. "I love you so much."

Tharyn reached up and touched his cheek gently. "I love you so much, too. You certainly are the town hero now. Of course from that first frightening day when my parents were killed and you saved my life, you became my hero. You grew more heroic when I had to join you and the other orphans on the streets of Manhattan, and you protected me so well."

Dane placed a soft kiss on her cheek. "I hope I can always fill that role in your life."

She smiled. "Without a doubt, my love. Without a doubt."

It was midafternoon when the three federal men placed the handcuffed Chick Barton in the bed of the rented wagon on an old mattress, and helped Ed Loomis and Vincent Wagner in also. They were handcuffed as well.

Glenn Bell climbed into the wagon seat, took the reins, and they moved out with Bell's horse tied behind the wagon as Dr. Dane Logan, Marshal Jake Merrell, and Deputy Len Kurtz looked on.

The sullen outlaws sat beside Barton and kept their heads down while riding in silence.

Twenty

Marshal Jake Merrell, Deputy Len Kurtz, and Dr. Dane Logan watched in silence until the wagon, sided by Chief U.S. Marshal John Brockman and Deputies Casey Knight and Tyler Hufford on horseback, passed from view.

Merrell looked at the doctor and said, "Well, Len and I need to get back to the office. You know what?"

Dr. Dane shook his head. "No. What?"

"If you weren't such a good doctor, I'd say you ought to be a lawman. You sure handled those outlaws adeptly."

Len nodded and smiled. "You sure you don't want to give up medicine and put on a badge?"

Dr. Dane chuckled. "Positive."

Both lawmen laughed and headed up the street toward the marshal's office.

Dr. Dane turned to enter his office when he heard a familiar voice call out from behind him, "Hey, Dr. Logan!"

The doctor wheeled about and saw

Charlie Holmes hurrying across the street, waving a yellow envelope. "Telegram for you!"

As Charlie drew up, Dr. Dane asked, "Is it from Dr. Carroll?"

"Sure is. By what he says, Dr. Logan, you won't need to send a reply, so I'll get on back to the office."

"Okay, thanks, Charlie."

Dr. Dane quickly read the telegram and entered the office. He noted that the waiting room was almost full. Tharyn was just coming from the back room, and spotted the telegram in his hand. "From Dr. Carroll?"

"Uh-huh. Everything's set. The hip replacement is scheduled for ten o'clock Saturday morning. Max Thurman will be checking into the hospital just before noon on Friday morning, so we can stop in and see him before going to your parents' house. And Dr. Carroll says your parents are excited about us coming to stay with them."

"Good. I'm glad our plans fit with the hospital's schedule. And I'm so excited to see my parents!"

Even as she was speaking, the front door opened and Kirby Holton came in. Smiling, he said, "Dr. Logan, I just got word up at the mine about the town hall incident. You're amazing! I must commend you for your courage and quick thinking in capturing those outlaws. I understand you even shot the gang leader."

"He gave me no choice. All of those ladies were in grave danger."

"Is the gang leader going to live?"

"Well, I patched him up so the federal men could take him on to Denver. But to answer your question . . . Chick Barton is going to face a judge and jury in Denver, and because he's a cold-blooded murderer, he is not going to live long. He will face the hangman's noose."

"I see. Well, bully for you for stopping those low-down criminals. Could I take you and Tharyn to supper this evening?"

Dane looked at his wife. "That okay with you?"

Tharyn sighed and placed the back of her hand to her forehead. "It would be a blessing not to have to cook supper."

That evening in Central City's nicest restaurant, Kirby Holton talked to the Logans about what a joy it was to know he was going to heaven, and how much he enjoyed being in church.

"We're so happy for you, Kirby," said Tharyn.

Kirby grinned. "Thank you. Now, new subject. Dr. Dane, I've been amazed at how your practice has grown in the short time you've been here. Almost every time I go into your office, there are many patients in the waiting room. I know you make a lot of house calls, too. Do you ever get any rest?"

Before the doctor could reply, Tharyn said, "He gets very little rest, Kirby. Of late, he's even had people getting him out of bed at night."

Kirby nodded. "I know Dr. Fraser is not feeling well. I'm wondering how long he'll be able to fill in for you when you need him."

"That's been on my mind a lot," said the doctor. "The dear old man is having quite a bit of trouble with his back. But bless his heart, he's still willing to come whenever I ask."

Kirby took a sip of coffee and set the cup back in the saucer. "Aren't you going to have to bring in another doctor to help you?"

"Yes, sir. That's in the offing."

"Oh? Tell me about it."

Dr. Dane told Kirby of the plans he had for the new clinic when he could afford to buy a piece of ground and have a building built.

Kirby nodded. "Got any special piece of land in mind?"

"Yes, sir. I've got my eye on the vacant lot just down in the next block south on Main Street from the present office, between Hampstead's Clothing Store and the Central City Pharmacy. Being next door to the pharmacy would be a good thing."

"Sounds like it would be perfect. Any doctors in mind that you'd like to choose from?"

The doctor nodded. "There's a fine young Christian doctor who's interning at Mile High Hospital in Denver. His name is Tim Braden. He'll finish his internship next May. Dr. Tim is going to marry Tharyn's best friend, Melinda Kenyon, shortly thereafter. Tharyn and Melinda have been friends since they were orphans together on the streets of New York City as teenagers."

Kirby smiled and looked at Tharyn. "I'm sure it would make you happy to have her here in Central City."

She smiled broadly. "Words couldn't describe it."

Dr. Dane went on. "Tharyn and I are going to Denver on Friday. We're going to do a hip replacement at Mile High Hospital on Saturday. While we're there, I'm going to talk to Dr. Tim about coming to work with me in the practice, in view of becoming a partner when we establish the clinic. If Dr. Tim comes — and I really believe he will — Dr. Fraser can retire completely, which he needs to do."

Kirby smiled. "Sounds good. I hope it works out. I'd like to see you get the help you need, and I'd like to see Dr. Fraser be able to get the rest he needs."

At midmorning the next day, there was a lull in patient appointments, and Tharyn took advantage of the break to go to the general store and pick up some groceries. When she entered the store, the proprietor and his wife greeted her warmly, then the proprietor's wife said, "It's sure nice of Dr. Logan to give you up at the office so you can shop, Tharyn."

She paused and chuckled. "Well, it just so happens we're between patients at the moment. I dare not lollygag, though. More will be in soon."

Tharyn noticed there was a large cookie jar at the counter, where some children were enjoying free cookies. She moved down the long aisles between shelves, where other customers greeted her warmly, calling her by name.

Suddenly Tharyn heard a child gagging and choking at the front of the store. She looked up to see the proprietor running down the aisle of shelves. "Mrs. Logan!" he gasped. "We need you up front!"

Tharyn laid what goods she had in her arms on an empty spot on a shelf and ran to the front of the store. There she found a boy about six years old who was doing the gagging and choking. His mother's face was pale and she was holding him. "It's a chunk of oatmeal cookie!" cried the mother, setting fear-filled eyes on Tharyn. "Can you help him? Billy's turning blue!"

Tharyn grabbed Billy and tried to reach the foreign object with her fingers, but she could not. She picked Billy up by the waist with one hand, bent him over her thigh, slapped him hard between the shoulder blades, and said, "Cough, Billy! Cough real hard!"

Billy did so, and Tharyn continued to slap his back. Suddenly the chunk of oatmeal cookie came up, and the boy sucked in air. Tharyn let go of Billy so his mother could take hold of him.

The relieved mother wrapped her arms around her son, and with tears streaming down her cheeks, said, "Oh, thank you, ma'am! Thank you for saving Billy's life!

He would have died in a few more minutes!"

The proprietor said, "Mrs. Bates, you've heard that Dr. Dane Logan is now Central City's physician, haven't you?"

Mrs. Bates nodded. "Yes. We've been to Dr. Fraser many times, but haven't needed to see Dr. Logan so far."

"Well, this lady who saved Billy's life is Dr. Logan's wife. She's a nurse."

Mrs. Bates thanked Tharyn again for what she did.

Tharyn smiled and patted the boy's head as he clung to his mother. "To God be the glory. He made it possible for me to become a nurse, and He timed it just right so I would be here when Billy began to choke. Give the praise to Him."

When Tharyn entered the doctor's office, carrying two large paper bags, Dr. Dane was taking payment from an elderly male patient at her desk.

Tharyn looked up at the clock. "Sorry it took me so long. I'll explain in a moment, after I put these groceries down."

Dr. Dane grinned. "You don't need to explain. I already heard from some people who were in the store about you saving that little boy's life. They stopped in here to tell me about it."

"I just thank God I was there, honey. That precious little boy might well have died."

"The people who told me about it said you handled it like you were a well-trained physician." He chuckled. "Honey, you should have gone to medical school. You would've made a wonderful doctor."

Tharyn wrapped her arms around him and smiled. "But I don't want to be a doctor. I'm happy to be a nurse. But more than anything, there are two things I want to be — a wife and a mother. Half of this desire is already satisfied. Someday the other half will be satisfied, too."

Dane kissed the tip of her nose. "Well, it will be wonderful when little Dane Jr. comes into our lives."

Tharyn laughed. "Or little Elizabeth Ann."

The front door swung open, and they were surprised to see Chief Tando, Leela, and a limping Latawga come in.

Dr. Dane smiled. "Well, hello! Is something wrong with Latawga's leg?"

The chief, who was carrying the Bible Dane had given him, shook his head. "No. It is doing well. We have come to talk to you about Jesus Christ."

Both Dane and Tharyn felt their hearts jump.

The doctor smiled again. "We're so happy to hear this." He then introduced Leela to Tharyn.

Leela smiled and said, "Mrs. Dr. Dane Logan, I am so happy to meet you. My husband and my son told me that you are very beautiful. They did not lie."

Tharyn hugged her and said, "You are very kind."

Tando said, "Dr. Dane Logan, we have been reading this Bible you gave me. We know now that the Ute gods are false. We want to make the true God's Son, Jesus Christ, our Savior."

Dane and Tharyn were thrilled to see that the Holy Spirit had worked in the Indians' hearts — even as they had prayed.

Dr. Dane wanted Pastor Shane in on this and told them he would take them to the parsonage. Tharyn told him she would watch the office while he was gone.

At the parsonage, Pastor Mark Shane was thrilled to see the Indians and to hear that they wanted to be saved. Together the doctor and the pastor led them to the Lord.

Tando then said he wanted help getting

the message across to his people. He wanted them to become Christians also.

Pastor Shane told him that he would come to their village the next day and talk to as many of the village people as would listen.

The Indians rode away with joy in their hearts.

When Dr. Dane arrived back at the office, there were patients in the waiting room. Before he took the first patient to the back room, Dr. Dane first led Tharyn into his private office and told her that all three Indians had clearly understood the gospel and had received Jesus into their hearts, and that Pastor Shane was going out to the village tomorrow to preach the gospel to as many Utes as would listen.

Tharyn burst into happy tears, and together they praised the Lord for answered prayer.

In Denver on Friday, David and Kitty Tabor were at home to warmly welcome their adopted daughter and her husband when they arrived just after two-thirty. David explained that he was taking the afternoon off so he could be there when they showed up.

Tharyn hugged him and said, "Oh,

Papa, that was so sweet of you."

He hugged her tight. "That's because I so dearly love my daughter and this wonderful son-in-law of mine."

They were led into the parlor, and all four of them sat down.

Kitty said, "Well, let me fill you in on what's happening. The four of us, plus Tim and Melinda, have been invited for supper this evening at the Brockman home. Melinda and Tim are so eager to see both of you. Melinda volunteered to help Breanna, and they are already busy preparing the meal."

Tharyn laughed with glee. "Oh, this is so wonderful!"

David said, "John had told Breanna when he got home about the incident at your town hall on Wednesday. They passed it on to us. Of course, John also told Breanna about you two coming to Denver to do the hip replacement, and that you would be arriving this afternoon. Breanna took hold of that good news and made her plans in a hurry."

Kitty laughed. "That's Breanna for you!" Then she ran her gaze between Tharyn and Dane. "I know you've had an arduous trip from Central City. How about some coffee and chocolate cake?"

Dane grinned. "Sounds good to me! It indeed was a chilly ride all the way. But as always, the colorful trees in the mountains were a beautiful sight to behold."

"This is my favorite time of year," Tharyn said. "I love the crispness in the air and the quaking of the golden aspen leaves. Right now, Central City looks like a beautiful patchwork quilt with all of the brilliant colors. The sky today was such a clear canopy of blue. Of course, any day now the snow can come. But that's a lovely sight, too, and we look forward to it."

The foursome headed for the warm kitchen where Kitty already had the coffee on the stove. They sat down at the table, and she placed steaming mugs before her daughter and son-in-law and husband, along with plates containing large pieces of chocolate cake.

After devouring the delicious cake and downing a sufficient amount of coffee, Tharyn covered her mouth as she yawned.

From the opposite side of the table, Kitty said, "Tharyn, why don't you go on up to your old room and take a nice nap? There's plenty of time before we need to leave for the Brockman place."

Tharyn yawned again. "Are you sure,

Mama? I came here to visit with you and Papa, you know."

"Of course I'm sure. Your papa agrees." Then to Dane: "Why don't you take your luggage upstairs to Tharyn's old room and get some rest yourself? You both look pretty tired out. This is an extra good chance to rest before you tackle that hip replacement surgery tomorrow."

"Thank you, Mama, that sounds so good," Tharyn said around another yawn.

"Run along now," said David. "You two enjoy a nice nap."

Dane and Tharyn left the kitchen arm in arm.

When evening came, the Logans and the Tabors arrived at the Brockman place in the country. Dr. Tim had left the hospital early to be sure he was there before Dane and Tharyn arrived.

There was a sweet reunion between Tharyn and Melinda . . . and between Melinda and Dr. Dane, who had freed her from her captivity at the Ute village. Dr. Tim was very happy to see Dane and Tharyn again. The Brockman children, Paul and Ginny, asked to sit beside the Logans at the dining room table.

As the group was eating, they talked

about the recent peace treaties that had been signed with the Utes, and those who hadn't heard were thrilled to learn that Chief Tando and his family had become Christians.

David then turned to the phenomenal growth of the medical practice in Central City that they had learned about from the letters Tharyn had exchanged with her mother. Melinda and Tim, especially, wanted to hear the latest.

Dane explained that the growth had caused him to make plans to expand into a clinic with as many beds as seemed reasonable as soon as they could afford to buy property on Main Street and erect a new building. As Dane spoke, he noticed Dr. Tim's eyes light up at the mention of the new clinic.

The subject changed again as John Brockman brought up the incident at the Central City town hall on Wednesday. "I talked to Judge Claude Harper," said John. "The Barton gang trial will be held this coming Tuesday. There's no question in my mind that they will hang. And when Bud Finch is brought to Denver and faces trial, he'll also hang."

Tim told Dane and Tharyn that Chief Brockman had informed them all about the incident, and he commended Dane for his courage in capturing the gang.

When the enjoyable evening was over and the guests were leaving, Dane told Tim and Melinda that he and Tharyn wanted to talk to them sometime Sunday afternoon. Kitty overheard it, and invited Tim and Melinda for Sunday dinner, saying the four of them could go to the parlor and talk in private afterward.

The next day, Dr. Dane and Tharyn finished the hip replacement on Max Thurman just after one o'clock in the afternoon, with Dr. Matt Carroll and a hospital nurse present. While Tharyn and the nurse stayed with Max, who was still under the anesthetic, Drs. Logan and Carroll went to the surgical waiting room and informed Mrs. Thurman and other family members that the surgery was a success.

The church services the next morning were enjoyable for Dr. Dane and Tharyn. Along with the teaching and preaching, it was a blessing to see old friends, including Pastor and Mrs. Nathan Blandford.

After dinner at the Tabor home, the Logans and Dr. Tim and Melinda went into the parlor for their private talk.

Dane brought up the proposed clinic

again. He explained that Dr. Robert Fraser needed to completely retire as soon as possible, and set his eyes on the young intern. "Tim, I want to ask you something."

"Sure."

"Would you be interested in going to work for me in the practice after you finish your internship here?"

Melinda looked at Tharyn, who flashed her a smile.

Tim's face brightened. "You really mean it, Dane?"

"I sure do. And Tharyn is in full agreement with my offering the job to you."

"I'd be more than interested! I'd be delighted!" Tim closed his eyes for a few seconds, then looked at Dr. Dane. "I . . . I wish I had some funds to invest in the practice so it could become a clinic sooner."

"You don't need to say another word. I very well know how expensive medical school is, and how low the pay is when you're an intern."

Melinda took hold of Tharyn's hand. "Tim and I will be getting married right after he finishes his internship. That means —"

"Yes!" squealed Tharyn. "That means you'll be living in the same town I am!"

The two women hugged and gave praise to the Lord.

Dr. Dane told Dr. Tim what he could afford to pay him, and Dr. Tim told him it would be plenty enough for him and Melinda to live on.

Tim said, "Dane, I don't know how to thank you. This is so wonderful!"

Dane smiled. "When I was still a kid in the alleys of New York City, a kind old doctor befriended me. He's the one that I met when I first went to live on the streets. He and his wife had me in their home many times. They got me into church, where I first heard the gospel and learned of Jesus and His love for me. That precious old man led me to the Lord, Tim. Then later, he led everyone in our alley colony to the blessed Savior. But that's only part of what he did for me.

"Tharyn was hospitalized due to the trauma of losing her parents. I was trying to find a way to pay her hospital bill. Dr. Harris, the one I just mentioned, paid the bill for me, and when I offered to pay him back, his comment was, 'You don't owe me anything. But when you're a physician and find a young doctor in need, you help him out. That's what a fellow physician once did for me, and now I'm passing it on.'

"Tim, I will never forget that generous man. He took special care of all of us orphans, got me a job at a pharmacy, and was a great strength to me. Now it's my turn to carry on this most worthy tradition."

Tim had tears in his eyes. "Thank you, Dane. I appreciate your attitude so much. And when the time comes, I too will pass along this kindness to another struggling young doctor."

"Good for you, Tim! We need to always care about others." Dane paused, then said, "Now let me add this — whenever we can afford to buy a lot on Main Street and have the building built, I'll make you a partner. Your income will increase as the clinic grows."

Tim was thanking Dane as Tharyn and Melinda embraced each other, agreeing how wonderful it was going to be to live close to each other again.

The Logans then told Tim and Melinda that they would love their church and Pastor Shane's preaching.

Dane said, "We'll stay in contact with you by mail, and keep you posted as to the progress of our plans for the clinic."

Melinda asked about housing in Central City. Dane told her there were usually some houses and apartments for rent in town, but if there weren't any available at the time they came, there were always rooms in boardinghouses.

Tim said, "Well, my internship will be finished on Friday, May 5. We've set the wedding with Pastor Blandford for the next day. We won't be able to go on a honeymoon, so we'll come to Central City on Monday, May 8, 1882."

Dane's face beamed. "Really? May 8?"

"Yes, sir."

"For some reason, I had the idea it would be later in May when you finished your internship. I figured if you were willing to come to work for me, it would be in June. Well, Tharyn and I will be here for the wedding, that's for sure. The four of us can travel from Denver to Central City that Monday together."

Tim and Melinda smiled at each other, then Tim said, "We just set the date with Pastor Blandford a couple of days ago. We were going to write you, but we'll tell you right now. I'm sure glad you two are wanting to come to the wedding, because Dane, I want you to be my best man."

Melinda took hold of Tharyn's hand and smiled. "And Tharyn, I want you to be my matron of honor."

Dane and Tharyn smiled at each other, and then Dane said, "Tim . . . Melinda . . . we are thrilled at this. We will gladly grant your requests!"

Twenty-one

It was three minutes till noon in Central City on Monday, October 17, when Dr. Robert Fraser and Nurse Nadine Wahl watched their last patient for the morning walk out the door.

Nadine was sitting at Tharyn's desk, and Fraser was standing in front of it, rubbing his lower back. She looked at him with compassion and said, "Hurting again?"

"Mm-hmm. I took some more salicylic acid when I was in the back room with Mr. Austin. The pain will ease up in —"

Nadine looked up and saw him staring out the window.

"Oh! It's Dr. Dane and Tharyn!"

Dr. Dane was helping Tharyn out of their buggy.

Dr. Fraser shuffled to the door and pulled it open as the Logans were crossing the boardwalk. "Well, if it isn't the handsome hero of Central City and his beautiful wife. Welcome home!"

Dr. Dane chuckled as they passed

through the door. "Well, you got half of it right. Tharyn most certainly is beautiful!"

"Well, if I can only get one half right, that's the half I would choose!"

Nadine had left the desk and stepped up to them as Dr. Fraser closed the door. "Yes, welcome home. How did the hip replacement go?"

"Just fine," said Dr. Dane. "No complications at all. And what about Bud Finch, Doctor? How's he doing?"

"He's doing as well as can be expected. I stopped at the jail to check on him on my way to the office this morning. It's my opinion that it will still be a full two weeks before he can be transported to Denver to stand trial."

Dane nodded. "The trial for Barton, Loomis, and Wagner is to be held tomorrow. Chief Brockman is dead sure they'll hang."

There were a few seconds of silence, then Tharyn said, "We've already been home. We unpacked the luggage, changed clothes, and ate lunch so we could handle the office for the rest of the day and let you two go to your homes and get some rest."

"Well, that's mighty nice of you," Dr. Fraser said, "but after making the trip this morning, you're probably pretty tired yourselves."

"We'll be fine," said Dr. Dane. "And before you go, I want to give you the good news."

Fraser's bushy eyebrows raised. "Good news?"

"After Dr. Tim Braden finishes his internship the first week of next May, he and Melinda are getting married. They'll be coming to Central City immediately after their wedding, because I'm hiring Dr. Tim to work for me. Do you think you can still fill in for me until then?"

Fraser smiled. "The Lord giving me strength, I sure will. But Dane, my boy, you have no idea how happy this makes me. There are some days when my back hurts so bad I don't think I can get out of bed, let alone take a step. It will be such a relief to Esther and me when I can retire completely and give this old body some rest."

"I know it's been rough on you these past several months. And I'm so grateful that you've stayed on to help me as much as you have. I'm a young man yet, but the load of this practice tires *me* out. So I can just imagine how worn out you must feel. I deeply appreciate all that you've taught me, and even more, I'm glad for the special friendship between us. It won't be long now, and we can give you a proper, complete retirement party."

Dane hugged his friend, and Dr. Fraser pounded him on the back.

When the two men released each other, Dr. Dane said, "My plan is to establish a clinic with four beds to begin with, but eventually I'd like to have ten or twelve beds. As soon as we can afford it, we want to buy one of the vacant lots on Main Street and have a building built. I've got my eye on the vacant lot in the next block south of us, between Hampstead's Clothing Store and the Central City Pharmacy."

Nadine smiled. "Oh, yes! It would really be good to have the clinic right next door to the pharmacy! With all of these plans, when you and Tharyn start your family, you'll need a nurse to take Tharyn's place. I wish I were younger so I could do it, but I know an excellent nurse in her late thirties who presently works at the hospital in Colorado Springs. She's a widow, with no children. Her name is Susan Coulter. She's a fine Christian and lives next door to my sister in Colorado Springs. They both go to the same church. I've gotten to know her quite well since I visit my sister often. Susan has been here to visit me twice, and has fallen in love with Central City. She's told me that she would very much like to live here."

"Nadine, I just might need another nurse even before we start our family," Dr. Dane said, "if we can get the vacant lot purchased and the clinic under construction within a year or so. I'll keep Susan in mind."

Dr. Fraser and Nadine then left the office, and Tharyn checked the appointment book to see when the next scheduled patient would be in. She told Dane it wouldn't be for another half hour.

"All right," he said. "I'll take a quick drive over to the parsonage. I want to find out how it went for Pastor Shane at Chief Tando's village on Friday."

When Dr. Dane Logan returned to the office, Tharyn was not in sight, but he noticed two men sitting in the waiting area. He knew Steve Bittner, the manager of the land office in Central City. The other man was a stranger.

Tharyn had taken a patient into the examining room, and returned to see if her husband was back just as Steve Bittner was introducing him to Todd Eckman, who owned the Central City Construction Company. As they shook hands, Dr. Dane said, "Mr. Eckman, I've been past your office many times, and I've seen some of the houses you've recently built in town, but I've never laid eyes on you until now. I'm very glad to meet you."

Eckman replied that he had seen the doctor on the street several times, and had heard many good things about him.

Running his gaze between the two men, Dr. Dane said, "What can I do for you?"

Steve Bittner smiled. "We are here about what we can do for *you,* Doctor."

Dr. Dane glanced at Tharyn, who was waiting near the back room door, then said to the men, "You have my curiosity up, but could you give me a few minutes? I have a patient who needs my attention."

Both men smiled, and Steve Bittner said, "Go ahead. We'll wait."

Twenty minutes later, the patient was gone, and Dr. Dane approached the men where they were seated in the waiting area and sat down, facing them. Tharyn sat at her desk and listened.

"Dr. Logan," Steve Bittner said, "now that you and your wife own the vacant lot down the street between Hampstead's Clothing Store and the pharmacy, I need your signatures on the deed to make it legal."

"As soon as you and I can get together on the exact dimensions and floor plan for your clinic, Doctor," Todd Eckman said, "we'll get the construction started. Winter's coming, but if we can get started soon, we still should have it done by early April."

Dane shook his head. "Gentlemen, what are you talking about? We don't own the lot between the clothing store and the pharmacy. I sure wish we did. And . . . and we very much want to have a clinic building built, but there's some mistake here. I —"

"There's no mistake, Dr. Logan," Bittner said. "Kirby Holton said you would probably be a bit stunned, but believe me, there's no mistake."

Tharyn left her desk and sat down beside her husband. "Excuse me, gentlemen, but I've got to hear this from up close."

Both men smiled. Bittner said, "You're welcome to hear it up close, ma'am. You most certainly are involved here. You see, this past Friday Kirby Holton purchased the vacant lot and put it in both of your names. He then engaged Mr. Eckman to construct the clinic building to your specifications, guaranteeing that he will foot the entire bill."

Dr. Dane wiped a palm across his eyes. "Gentlemen, I'm overwhelmed."

Bittner leaned toward the Logans. "Mr. Holton left for Denver this morning to catch a train to Chicago. He'll be back a week from Thursday. He asked us to come to you as soon as you got back from Denver so we could get things started."

Dr. Dane chuckled and shook his head again. He looked at Tharyn. "Kirby had to have been on that stagecoach we met on the road this morning."

"He no doubt saw us, too," Tharyn said. "Bless his heart. This is wonderful."

Steve Bittner opened his briefcase and took out the deed. "I need you both to sign this for me."

They walked to Tharyn's desk, where they used her pen and ink to sign the deed.

While Bittner was blowing on the ink to dry it, Todd Eckman made an appointment with Dr. Dane for the next day at the construction office so they could make plans for the clinic building.

When the two men had gone out the door and started down the boardwalk, the

Logans turned and stared at one another, hardly able to believe what had just transpired.

Dane scrubbed a palm over his eyes again. "Honey, I did hear right, didn't I? Those two men . . . they did tell us that Kirby Holton bought us that choice property and that he's going to pay for the construction of our building. Didn't they?"

"Yes, sweetheart. We both heard the same thing. What a miracle this is! I'm . . . I'm still completely stunned by all of this!"

Dane wrapped her in his arms, and with tears of joy and gratitude streaming down their faces, he said, "O dear Lord, we praise You for this unexpected and marvelous blessing! Please bless Kirby abundantly for his generosity."

When they had both brushed away the last traces of their tears, Dane said softly, "We've come a long way from the streets and alleys of Manhattan, my love. Only by the matchless grace of our wonderful God are we where we are today."

"Amen to that," Tharyn whispered past the lump in her throat.

They embraced again, then Tharyn asked, "What did Pastor Shane tell you about his visit to Chief Tando's village?"

"Well, he said most of the people showed

interest in the newfound faith of the chief and his family. Pastor said he'll be going to the village periodically to preach the gospel to them. He knows it's going to take some time to get the seed of the Word planted in their hearts and to see more people saved."

"Well, I'm happy to hear that most of the people showed interest. I just know in my heart that many of them are going to become Christians."

"I feel the same way."

On Tuesday, October 25, the Eckman Construction Company began work on the clinic building, and the people of Central City were glad when they read the sign at the site that informed them what it was.

Late on Thursday afternoon, Dr. Dane and Tharyn entered the Wells Fargo office and found the assistant agent behind the counter.

"Hello, Wally," said the doctor, as they approached the counter.

"Howdy, Dr. Logan. Howdy, Mrs. Logan. What can I do for you?"

"We know the Denver stage usually comes in about five-thirty, and the chalkboard behind you says that's what it's supposed to do today. Is that right?"

"Yes, sir. The wire from the station in Denver said it left on time."

"And is Kirby Holton aboard?"

"I believe so," said Wally, turning to pick up a sheet of paper near the telegraph key. He looked at it and nodded. "Yes, sir. Mr. Holton is listed as one of the passengers."

"Good. So it should be here in about fifteen minutes, right?"

"Oughtta be. Unless they ran into a problem along the way."

"Well, we'll just sit here and wait for it, if that's okay?"

"Sure is. Oh . . . uh . . . by the way, Dr. Logan, I want to thank you for doing that surgery on my foot. It's feeling a whole lot better now, and my limp is almost gone."

Dr. Dane smiled. "Good. Just don't let another horse step on it."

"Don't you worry. I'm a whole lot more careful since I got stepped on."

Dane and Tharyn sat down on a bench across the room and began talking about the new clinic and the four beds they would start out with.

Tharyn said, "So did you and Mr. Eckman plan room for more beds, like you wanted to do?"

"Mm-hmm. They'll each have their own small room, just like the first four will.

That area will be unused until we need it. There'll be a dozen beds once we're using all the space."

"That's almost a small hospital, isn't it?"

"I guess you could say that."

Abruptly, Wally called from behind the counter. "Stage is here, Dr. Logan. I can see it coming up the street."

The Logans headed for the door. When they stepped outside, the stagecoach was slowing down and veering toward the driveway where it would pull up in front of the office. Dane took Tharyn by the hand and led her to the spot where the stage would stop.

Just as the driver guided the six-up team off the street, both of them caught sight of Kirby Holton looking at them through the window where he was sitting. He smiled and waved. They returned the smile and waved back.

As soon as the stage came to a halt, Kirby jumped out, followed by three more men. He stepped up to the couple, and before he could say a word, Dane and Tharyn were pouring out words of appreciation for his generosity.

Kirby's eyes sparkled as he told them how glad he was that he had the funds to do this for them. He then asked, "Are Dr.

Tim and his bride coming to Central City?"

"They are!" Dane exclaimed. "He accepted my offer in a hurry, and Melinda is more excited about moving here than he is. They'll be here in early May."

Kirby's smile spread from ear to ear. "Good! I'm going to have a house built for the Bradens. It will be my gift to them. Will you write to them and tell them for me?"

Tharyn found her voice first. "We most certainly will write and tell them. We've been checking into housing here the past couple of days, and were surprised that right now, at least, there are no houses for rent, and no apartments. We decided if it stayed this way, Tim and Melinda would have to start out in a boardinghouse. We talked about inviting them to stay with us, but we figured they'd rather have the privacy of their own room."

Kirby grinned. "Well, now you can put your mind at ease. It will give me great pleasure to provide them with a comfortable house. I'll have it ready before they get here. It won't be huge or fancy, but they'll be happy in it, I'm sure." He paused. "Oh, by the way, Tharyn, I know you're busy, but in the next week or so, could you write down some ideas that would help me design the house so Melinda will be happy with it? I know women think differently than us men when it comes to things like this."

Tharyn laughed. "I'll do that, sir. I recall that when we were just teenage girls, Melinda used to talk about her dream house. I remember some of the things she likes. Oh, this is so wonderful!" Even as she said that, Tharyn gave the startled Kirby Holton a big hug. "Thank you for doing this for Tim and Melinda!"

Dane was in the parlor reading a newspaper while Tharyn was in the kitchen preparing supper.

Tharyn was humming a happy tune as she prepared the meal, and at one point, looked at her reflection in the small mirror on the wall by the cupboard and gave herself a private smile. "When are you going to tell him, Tharyn?"

Not more than two minutes later, as she was stirring gravy at the stove, a wave of nausea hit her. She took a deep breath and felt beads of perspiration on her forehead. She sat down on one of the chairs at the kitchen table and gulped in one deep breath after another. When her breathing returned to normal, she stayed on the chair waiting for the nausea to pass.

This came in a minute or two.

She rose from the chair, and on her way back to the stove, she looked again at her reflection, and a self-satisfied grin beamed on her face. Before pouring the gravy into a bowl, she placed her hands on her tummy. "I've got to tell him tonight. It just has to be tonight. Later tonight."

Soon she called her husband to the kitchen, and as they were eating, Dane said, "Honey, we need to write Tim and Melinda soon and let them know about the house."

Tharyn nodded. "I'll write the letter on Sunday afternoon and mail it on Monday."

Dane noticed an unusual sparkle in her eyes. "What's up, sweetheart?"

"What do you mean?" she asked, giving him an innocent look.

"There's a special . . . light in your eyes."

She smiled and opened her hands, palms up. "Well, darling, if there's a special light in my eyes, it's because I'm so happy."

"Oh, sure. I know it will mean a lot to you to have Melinda living here."

"It sure will."

Later that evening, at bedtime, Dane had

already slipped between the covers, and Tharyn was in her robe, brushing her hair at the dresser mirror. Unaware that Dane was looking at her reflection in the mirror, she winked and gave herself a secret smile. *It's almost time to tell him!*

She was surprised when she heard Dane say, "What are you grinning about?"

She ran her gaze to his reflection in the mirror. "I'm smiling because I'm happy."

"Because Melinda is coming to Central City?"

She turned and walked toward him with another smile on her lips. As she drew up beside the bed, she said, "I'm happy about Melinda coming, yes . . . but I'm even happier about someone else coming. Someone who will live right here in this house."

Dane sat up straight, eyes wide. "You mean — ?"

"Mm-hmm. I didn't know for sure when we were in Denver, so I didn't say anything. But I know for certain now. Little Dane Jr. or little Elizabeth Ann will be born in late April or early May."

Dr. Dane Logan was dumbstruck, then a look of pure joy passed over his face. He jumped out of the bed, kissed her, and wrapped her in his arms. "Oh, Tharyn, God is blessing us with such a precious little gift! Let's right now dedicate this child to Him!"

"Yes," she whispered, and they knelt together at the side of the bed, holding hands and giving praise to the Lord and asking for His wisdom in raising the child for His glory.

When they stood up, both wiping tears from their faces, Dane said, "Honey, it just hit me. Since the baby is to be born in late April or early May, neither you nor the baby will be able to make the trip to Denver. We won't be able to go to Tim and Melinda's wedding."

"You're right. You could go, but we couldn't."

"I wouldn't go without my wife and baby. Tim and Melinda will certainly understand, even though they'll have to find another matron of honor and another best man."

"Of course they'll understand. I'll write the letter to them, as I said, on Sunday afternoon. They'll be disappointed, I'm sure, but the good news about the house will more than make up for it. I'll also write to your parents and to mine and let them know that I'm expecting our baby."

During the latter part of the next week,

letters came from the Logans in Cheyenne and the Tabors in Denver, happy to learn that Tharyn was with child.

A letter also came from Tim and Melinda, saying they were sorry Dane and Tharyn wouldn't be able to make it to the wedding, but assuring them that they understood. They offered their sincere congratulations about the baby and said they were also very excited about the house Kirby Holton would build for them. They added that they had already sent a telegram to Mr. Holton to express their gratitude.

Dr. Dane wrote to Nadine Wahl's friend Susan Coulter and offered her a job, saying he needed her to start as soon as possible. A letter came from Susan the next week, accepting the offer, and she arrived in Central City by stagecoach three weeks later. Being widowed also and having a large two-story house, Nadine Wahl took Susan into her home.

Twenty-two

Winter came with the normal cold weather in the Colorado Rockies, and plenty of snow.

Dr. Robert Fraser, in spite of days when his pain-wracked body made it difficult, continued to fill in for Dr. Dane Logan whenever he had to be out of the office. The elderly physician was looking forward to May, when Dr. Tim Braden would come to work for Dr. Dane, and he could completely retire.

It was nearly five o'clock on Friday, March 3, 1882. Tharyn Logan was at her desk, accepting payment from a rancher that her husband and Susan Coulter had just treated for a cut on his hand. When the rancher was going out the door, Dr. Dane and Susan came from the back room and drew up by the desk.

Tharyn looked up at Susan and smiled. "I'm leaving everything in and on the desk just like it is, Susan. I know you've gotten used to it this way, so it's best that I take none of my personal supplies with me."

"Quitting your job isn't easy, is it?" Susan said softly.

"It's hard, but the joy of the baby in my womb is prevailing over the difficulty I'm having giving up my job."

Dane stepped behind the desk and hugged her. "Honey, little Dane Jr. will be worth it."

"Yes, sir, little Elizabeth Ann will be worth it, all right!"

Susan laughed. "You two! Go on home now. I'll clean up."

From his pulpit the next Sunday, Pastor Mark Shane reported on the progress in his ministry to the Indians in Chief Tando's village. As of that date, over a hundred had now become Christians.

There were joyful smiles, along with many amens.

As the month of March moved on, there was continual correspondence between the Logans and Tim and Melinda, who were pleased to hear about the progress in the construction of the clinic building and their new house. In every letter from Tim and Melinda, they spoke of how excited they were about coming to Central City.

They also wrote of how happy they were to know that Tharyn and her unborn child were doing well.

In one letter, Tim wrote on the last page: "I hope the baby's father won't be too nervous to do his job when the time of birth comes. I've seen many a father terribly shook up when his baby was being born!"

Tharyn and Dane had a good laugh over those words.

On Monday, March 20, Dr. Dane received a letter from the president of Northwestern University Medical College, asking him to come and be the speaker at the graduation ceremony of the class of '82 on Friday, May 26. The president said in the letter, "As you know, Dr. Logan, the alumni paper, which we publish every quarter, has kept the readers up to date on the growth of your practice, of your upcoming clinic, and of your successful hip replacements. You are the man we want this year."

Dane was thrilled at the invitation, as was Tharyn. However, since the baby was due in late April or early May, they agreed that mother and baby would not be able to make the long trip with him to Chicago that soon after the baby's birth.

Dane sent a wire, accepting the invitation to be commencement speaker.

In early April, with the clinic building nearing its completion, Dr. Dane hired another nurse. Mary Edwards was a Christian and a close friend of Susan Coulter's from Colorado Springs. Mary was also given a place to live at the Wahl house.

During the second week of April, Susan Coulter volunteered to begin staying in the Logan home every night till the baby came, in case Dr. Dane should be called away. The Logans gladly accepted her offer, and Susan started on Monday night, April 17.

The following Thursday, Dane awakened at the usual time and slipped out of bed, not wanting to disturb his sleeping wife. Tharyn had experienced a restless night, and he wanted her to get as much sleep as possible.

He dressed quietly, then went downstairs to build a fire in the kitchen stove. He knew that Susan would come down from her room soon to prepare breakfast, as she had done the last two mornings. He was surprised to find her already in the kitchen. She had a fire going and oatmeal and scrambled eggs cooking on the stove.

She smiled at him, and said, "Good

morning, boss. Is Tharyn not coming down for breakfast?"

Dr. Dane shook his head. "No, she's still asleep. Had a bad night."

"Oh. You don't suppose she's beginning labor, do you?"

"Hard to tell. If so, she can alert the neighbors, as planned, and have one of them come get me."

Doctor and nurse ate breakfast together, then as Susan was cleaning up the kitchen and washing the few dishes, he went upstairs to look in on the expectant mother. She was still sleeping.

Moments later, Dr. Dane and Susan drove away in his buggy.

When Dr. Dane came home for lunch, he found Tharyn in the kitchen making beef sandwiches. She left the cupboard, opened her arms, and they enjoyed a sweet kiss.

Dane lightly patted her swollen belly. "How's it going, sweetheart? I thought after the restless night you had, maybe the baby was coming. Even though it is a bit early yet."

"Wel-l-l-l, it could be. I'm not sure. I've been rather uncomfortable ever since I got up this morning. No definite pain or contractions. Just an uneasy feeling."

"You sure could be in the very early stages of labor. Especially with your first child."

She smiled. "Well, I guess we'll find out, won't we?"

That afternoon, Tharyn lay down on the bed and soon fell into a fitful sleep. When she awoke, she felt a bit better, and went down to the kitchen to prepare supper.

After supper that evening, the Logans and Susan spent some time in the parlor together. By bedtime, Tharyn was feeling queasy.

Dane and Tharyn prayed together, and after Dane had doused the lantern, they talked about the baby coming. Soon Dane was asleep, tired after a busy day at the office.

Tharyn lay wide awake beside him, her mind on the baby who would soon be born and once again feeling quite uncomfortable and a bit nauseated.

The hours seemed to drag by as she heard the grandfather clock downstairs chime on the hour. She had just counted three chimes when a sharp stab hit her lower back and clawed its way around to her belly. She put the knuckles of a clenched fist into her mouth and waited for the pain to pass.

It began to ease some. She took a deep breath, then relaxed and waited to see what would happen next. A few minutes had passed since the pain had hit her, and she began to slip off to sleep.

Suddenly another pain, every bit as severe as the first one, knifed its way through her body.

This time, she moaned softly. Dane rolled over and laid a hand on her in the darkness. "What is it, love?" Without waiting for a reply, he placed both hands on her stomach, noting its rigidity. "You're having pains."

"Yes."

"How many so far?"

"Two."

"How far apart?"

"A few minutes. Four or five, I think."

Just then, another contraction jolted her.

When she finally relaxed from that one, Dane said, "Well, sweetie, I believe this is the real thing. I'm going to awaken Susan. We'd better get ready. Soon we're going to see our first child face-to-face."

He kissed her cheek and got out of bed.

Dr. Dane and Susan hovered over Tharyn as the hours passed, and her contractions came closer and closer together.

Dawn came, and by that time, the contractions were coming one on top of another. It was almost an hour after sunrise when the baby was about to be born. Susan was holding Tharyn's hand as the pain grew worse, and from his position, Dane said with excitement in his voice, "Keep taking those short breaths, honey, and keep pushing. You're doing great!"

Tharyn closed her eyes and gritted her teeth. Gripping Susan's hand, she gave one long final push. There was sudden relief, and as she tried to take a deep breath, she heard a slap and the shrill cry of the newborn baby.

Gasping for breath, Tharyn opened her eyes and looked at Dane, who had the wailing infant cradled in one arm while picking up a towel. Weakly, she said, "What do we have, honey?"

Wiping mucus and blood from the baby's face and body, Dane looked at his weary wife and smiled. "We have a handsome baby boy! Just a few minutes, and you can hold him."

Dane finished with the towel and handed the wailing little boy to Susan so she could take him to the washroom next to the bedroom.

Dane leaned over Tharyn, hugged her, and together they rejoiced and praised God for His goodness.

Dane did some clean-up work, then took a stethoscope from his medical bag on the dresser and hung it on his neck. He helped Tharyn into a sitting position with pillows at her back, and a few minutes later, Susan entered the room with the baby wrapped in a small blue blanket. He had stopped crying. She smiled as she placed him into his mother's waiting arms.

Tharyn looked at him with adoring eyes and felt her heart enlarge to encompass her new son. She gently gathered him close and felt a warmth run through her at the sight of God's precious little gift. She ran her gaze to Dane as she stroked the baby's soft cheeks. "Oh, darling, little Dane Jr. is absolutely beautiful. What a marvelous miracle he is!"

Dane smiled from ear to ear. "That he is, sweetheart. Well, now that you know he has two eyes, one nose, one mouth, ten perfect fingers and ten perfect toes, do you mind if I check him over?"

Tharyn's smile matched her husband's. "If you insist."

Dane took the little guy into his arms and gazed at him with adoration, then laid him down at the foot of the bed to examine him more closely. He glanced at Susan. "Would you help Tharyn freshen up? I'm sure she would feel better."

While Susan was assisting Tharyn with a washcloth and a pan of water, Dane opened the blue blanket and gently ran his fingers over his son's tiny body, stopping to probe here and there. He warmed the microphone on the stethoscope with his hand, then placed it on the baby's chest. After listening for a half-minute or so, he turned the baby over and placed the instrument on his back.

Holding it there, a frown formed on his brow.

Tharyn had her eyes on him, and she was quick to pick up on her husband's troubled look. "What is it, Dane? What's wrong?" There was a quiver in her voice.

Looking from his son to his wife, he put on a smile. "Just a little irregular heartbeat. Nothing for you to concern yourself about, sweetheart. He's a couple of weeks or so early, you know. I'm sure it'll clear up in a day or two, and he'll be fine."

Dane Jr. puckered up and a demanding cry erupted. Dane forced a smile. "He wants his mommy."

He wrapped the baby back in the blanket

and placed him in his mother's arms. Tharyn looked into the tiny face and cooed and talked to him.

Dane told Tharyn and Susan that he wanted to stay with mother and baby for the day, and he would go ask Dr. Fraser if he would fill in for him. He told Tharyn he would stop by the Western Union office and send telegrams to her parents and his, advising them that they had a little grandson. He would also stop by the parsonage and let the Shanes know that little Dane Jr. had been born.

Susan went to the kitchen and cooked breakfast while Dr. Dane walked to Dr. Fraser's house and told him and Esther of little Dane Jr. being born. He explained to Dr. Fraser that the baby's heart was not sounding quite right, and asked if he would fill in for him so he could stay home for the day. He wanted to keep a check on the heart. Dr. Fraser told him he would.

When Dane returned home, Susan had fed Tharyn and was eating her own breakfast. He told her that Dr. Fraser would be at the office by the time she got there. He ate a quick breakfast and went upstairs.

When Dane entered the bedroom, he noted that his son was asleep in the cradle they had bought a few weeks earlier.

Tharyn was sitting up on the bed with her back against the pillows. She managed a smile.

"So he's napping already, eh?" Dane said.

"Mm-hmm. I fed him his breakfast, so he's sleeping with a full tummy."

"Good. I'll check him over when he wakes up. The telegrams are on their way, and Dr. Fraser is filling in for me all day. Pastor and Jenny will be by later. I told them about the irregular heartbeat."

As the day wore on, Dane checked the baby's heartbeat and became increasingly concerned that all was not well. He noticed that little Dane was very lethargic at times, and unusually fretful at other times.

The Shanes came by a little before noon and prayed with Dane and Tharyn for the baby. Both the pastor and Jenny tried to encourage the Logans.

In early afternoon, Tharyn looked on with concern as her husband once again laid the infant beside her on the bed and listened to his heart.

The growing sounds of irregularity were mixed with a sound that Dane could not identify. He had delivered many a baby during his internship at the hospital in Cheyenne, during the time he worked in his father's practice, and since he had come to Central City. He had not encountered a sound like this.

Lord, he said in his heart, *I feel so helpless. There's so much in the medical profession that we don't know yet. Help me to do all I should for my little son.*

Trying to mask from Tharyn his concern for the baby, he listened again to the rapidly beating heart. A wave of fear welled up within him. He placed the baby in Tharyn's arms, doing his best not to show the fear he felt, and said, "Maybe he'll sleep some more now."

Dane sat down on a chair beside the bed.

Tharyn held the baby close, looking lovingly into his eyes, and cooed to him some more, doing her best not to reveal her own fear. As young as baby Dane was, he found his thumb, popped it into his mouth, and fell asleep.

Dane leaned close, setting his gaze on the baby's face. "That's a good boy, son. You get some sleep. Maybe it will help heal you."

Tharyn frowned. "Do you really think it will?"

"It might. The Lord did give us sleep to help strengthen our bodies."

Some twenty minutes had passed when the baby awakened and started fussing. Dane was alarmed at his ashen appearance, and though his little son opened his mouth to cry, only a small, mewling sound came out. He jerked, coughed twice, whimpered, and went limp.

Tharyn's eyes widened and her breathing became tense as Dane massaged their son's little chest, and even pressed his lips to the baby's mouth and blew.

But little Dane Logan Jr. did not move and did not breathe.

His face ashen as he held the little body, Dane looked at Tharyn through his tears and drew a short, shuddering breath. "He's dead, honey."

Tharyn's whole body stiffened and her throat went tight. She became aware of the weight of her heart, like a stone in her chest.

Dane cradled the lifeless little form in one arm and wrapped the other one around her neck, pulling her close. "I'm so sorry, sweetheart. I couldn't save him. There was something wrong with his little heart. It just wasn't strong enough to keep beating."

Great wet sobs shook Tharyn so hard that her chest felt as if it had been pierced with a sharp blade. Her throat felt hot and raw. She sagged against Dane, her face twisted in a grimace, and cried between sobs, "No! No! Not my baby! No-o-o!"

Her body was shaking all over. As she continued to sob, Dane held her close, their tears mingling. His voice cracked as he said, "Sweetheart, the Lord had a reason for little Dane to be born with a faulty heart. We may not understand what that reason was till we get to heaven, but we must trust Him in this. Our God doesn't make mistakes."

Tharyn was trying to stop shaking and sobbing.

Dane squeezed her tight with the arm that held her. "Honey, our little boy is in heaven with Jesus now."

Tharyn sniffled and reached for the life-less little body. Dane relinquished it into her arms. She gathered the body to her breast as tears ran down her cheeks, dripping off her chin. She cooed to him like she had before, kissed both cheeks, and gazed longingly at his tiny face, trying to commit everything about him to memory.

The funeral was held the following Tuesday in order to allow both sets of grandparents to make the trip to Central

City. Melinda Kenyon had come with the Tabors and stayed close to Tharyn during the service.

Most of the town had gathered at the cemetery. While Pastor Mark Shane delivered the brief message at the grave site, his wife was also as close to Tharyn as she could get.

The tiny white coffin looked so forlorn as it sat on a cart next to the yawning grave.

The pastor's words of comfort found deep root in the grieving parents' hearts as they stood, flanked by their own parents and friends, holding hands.

That night at bedtime, with both sets of parents and Melinda Kenyon staying in guest rooms at the Logan house, Dane and Tharyn entered their own bedroom, again holding hands.

Tharyn's eyes went to the spot where the cradle once stood.

It was gone.

She looked up into her husband's eyes questioningly.

He laid his hands on both her shoulders. "Honey, when you were in the parlor with our mothers just before we went to the funeral, I took the cradle and put it in the

404

attic. Both of our dads were with me. They agreed that the sight of it would just tear at your wounded heart every time you looked at it. If God wills, that cradle will one day hold another child. Do you understand?"

Tharyn wrapped her arms around him. "Yes, darling, I understand. You did the right thing. Thank you for being so thoughtful and kind. No one will ever take baby Dane's place, but with this mother's heart beating in my breast, I do pray for more children in this family."

Dane kissed her cheek. "I know you know the verse that says, 'As for God, his way is perfect.' We will trust Him to have His way concerning our future children."

"Yes, we will," she agreed softly.

"I need to talk to you about my trip to Chicago."

"Yes?"

"I want you to go with me. It will help occupy your mind."

She smiled. "Always thinking of me, aren't you? Of course I'll go with you."

The Tabors, the Logans, and Melinda Kenyon stayed for another day, then headed for their homes.

On Monday, May 1, the new clinic was opened with Mayor Mike Anderson presiding over the opening ceremony.

The newlyweds arrived in Central City on Monday, May 8. Melinda was a real comfort to Tharyn over the loss of the baby.

Dr. Tim and Melinda moved into their new house with Kirby Holton there to help them. On Tuesday, Dr. Tim started work in the clinic. He was very much liked by Susan and Mary.

On Saturday morning, May 27, Dane and Tharyn were at Chicago's railroad station, waiting for their train to arrive from New York that would carry them to Denver. Tharyn was still talking about what a great speech Dane had made at the commencement ceremony, and how so many people had come to him to comment on it.

Soon the train pulled in, and as it rolled to a stop, both of them saw that the last two coaches were filled with children — boys in the last one, girls in the one just ahead.

Tharyn said, "Dane, it's an orphan train!"

"Doesn't that bring back some memories. We're going to ride an orphan train again!"

When the orphans and their Children's Aid Society sponsors, including the nurse who was traveling with them, got off the train to stretch their legs, the Logans approached the sponsors and introduced themselves. They told them how they had both gone out West on different orphan trains when they were teenagers.

The sponsors were pleased to meet them, and the nurse said she was always glad to know when there was a doctor aboard their train. Dr. Dane told them that his wife was a certified medical nurse.

One of the sponsors told the Logans that in Topeka, the orphans would be on display for the first time before prospective foster parents.

The train arrived in Topeka on Sunday afternoon. Dr. Dane and Tharyn got off to watch the orphans line up, and memories flooded their minds.

Tharyn's attention was drawn to one little girl with dark brown hair and dark brown eyes. Pointing to her, she said, "Honey, look at that little girl. Her hair and eyes are exactly the same color as yours."

Dane smiled. "She's a pretty little thing, isn't she?"

"I'd guess she's about five years old. Wouldn't you agree?"

"Yes, I think you're right."

Suddenly Tharyn thought of Elizabeth Ann in her recurring dream. She had dreamed it again while in the hotel in Chicago the night before. This little girl very much resembled Elizabeth Ann.

When it was time for the children to get back on the train, only two teenage boys had been chosen.

Soon the train pulled out.

During the night, one of the Children's Aid Society women entered the coach where the Logans were riding in a seat near the front. As with most of the passengers in the coach, they were both asleep. Lanterns burned low at both ends and in the center of the coach. Cora Stevens awakened Dr. Dane, who was seated on the aisle. Tharyn woke up also. Cora told Dr. Dane they had a little girl with a fever. She explained that the nurse was in the boys' coach tending to a very sick little boy, and asked if he would come and look at the little girl. He picked up his medical bag and followed her.

Tharyn was about to fall asleep again when she felt Dane sit down beside her. When she opened her eyes, she was astonished to see that he had in his arms the girl she had pointed out to Dane in Topeka. She could see that the child was feverish. The child opened her eyes briefly, set them on Tharyn, then closed them again.

Keeping his voice low, Dane said, "I gave her some powders. The fever isn't dangerously high. Her name's Beth Martin, and she is indeed five years old."

The child opened her eyes again and set them on Tharyn. Tharyn patted the top of her head. "Hello, Beth. I'm Dr. Logan's wife."

Beth let a weak smile curve her lips and closed her eyes again.

Dane explained that Beth's father was killed in a New York City riot before she was born. Her mother died of pneumonia last winter. Cora told him that since awaking with the fever, Beth kept calling for her mommy. Cora thought if Mrs. Logan would hold her, it would help.

Tharyn smiled. "Of course."

She took the child into her arms and kissed her cheek. For a few seconds, she thought of her dead little boy.

Beth opened her eyes, looked up at Tharyn, and this time her smile was stronger. "Mrs. Logan . . ."

"Yes, honey?"

"My mommy died. I miss her. Will you be my new mommy?"

Tharyn felt her heart lurch in her breast. She cuddled the child close and said, "So your name is Beth Martin."

The little girl nodded. "My real name is Elizabeth Ann, but everybody calls me Beth."

Tharyn hugged the child tightly and felt tears well up in her eyes.

Dane's head jerked around when he heard the little girl's words. He saw the tears in Tharyn's eyes.

Tharyn looked over the little orphan girl's head directly into her husband's eyes and gave him a smile like none he had seen since their son died.

"Darling," she said softly, "did you hear that? Her name is Elizabeth Ann."

Dane smiled. "Isn't that something?"

In Central City on Monday afternoon, May 29, Pastor Mark Shane and his wife pulled up to the Wells Fargo office in their buggy at 3:15. The stage carrying the Logans was due to arrive at 3:30.

Peggy said, "Mark, Tharyn was handling little Dane Jr.'s death pretty well by the time they left for Chicago, don't you think?"

He nodded. "The Lord was giving her peace as only He can do."

Moments later, they saw the stage coming down the wide, dusty street, and climbed out of their buggy. When it pulled up in front of the office, Dr. Dane saw them through the window and smiled.

As the Shanes approached the stage, two men who were sitting opposite the Logans stepped out, followed by the doctor. They watched as Dr. Dane turned around, reached through the door, and picked up a little girl. He held her in one arm while he helped Tharyn down with his free hand.

The pastor and Peggy looked behind the Logans to see if the little girl's parents were following. There was no one else inside the coach.

The Shanes moved up to them and Mark said, "Welcome home! Who's this pretty little girl?"

"This is Elizabeth Ann Martin," Dr. Dane said. "She's an orphan."

Tharyn spoke up. "The train Dane and I were on from Chicago turned out to be an orphan train. We got acquainted with Elizabeth Ann on the trip, and the Lord laid it on our hearts to bring her home with us. She's God's special gift to us. Before we got off the train in Denver, we signed

411

Children's Aid Society papers as her foster parents."

"That's wonderful!" Peggy said.

"Tomorrow, we'll take her to the Gilpin County judge and legally adopt her," Dr. Dane said. "She wants us to call her Beth Ann, so Beth Ann, say hello to Pastor and Mrs. Shane."

Beth Ann smiled. "Hello."

The Shanes welcomed Beth Ann, as did everyone who met her in the days that followed, including both sets of grandparents, who came to visit shortly after they heard of her arrival.

Beth Ann and her new parents grew closer every day, and Tharyn thanked the Lord daily that though in His wisdom He took little Dane Jr. to heaven, He gave her little Elizabeth Ann, even as she had dreamed.

Twenty-three

On Tuesday afternoon, September 26, the September 25 edition of the *Rocky Mountain News* arrived in Central City on the stagecoach from Denver. The paper reported that Cheyenne and Shoshone warriors were attacking white settlements, farms, and ranches in the Medicine Bow area in northern Colorado and southern Wyoming.

Mary Edwards left the Logan Clinic on an errand to the pharmacy next door for Dr. Dane Logan. She purchased a copy of the newspaper at the pharmacy, and when she returned to the clinic, she was telling Drs. Dane Logan and Tim Braden and Nurse Susan Coulter about the attacks.

The office door opened, and Western Union agent Charlie Holmes came in, carrying a yellow envelope. "Dr. Logan, I have a telegram here from a Dr. Thomas Watson in Glenwood Springs."

Dr. Dane thanked Charlie as he handed him the envelope, and said, "Better wait till I read it, Charlie. I might need to have you send a reply for me."

"Sure, Doctor."

Dr. Dane took the telegram out of the envelope, and his staff watched as he read it.

When he finished, he said, "Dr. Watson has a sixty-nine-year-old female patient who needs a hip replacement as soon as possible. He wants to know if I can come to Glenwood Springs and do the surgery."

Mary said, "I've heard of Glenwood Springs. Where is it?"

"A hundred miles west of here," Dane replied.

"Can you get to Glenwood Springs by stagecoach?" Dr. Tim asked.

"I can, but I'm not going to. I can get there much faster on horseback. I'll leave tomorrow at dawn. That'll get me there about four o'clock in the afternoon. I can rest up and do the surgery the next morning."

Dr. Dane dictated his message to Charlie, telling Dr. Watson he would be coming by horseback and would be in Glenwood Springs by late afternoon tomorrow. He would plan on performing the surgery Thursday morning. He added that he would bring an ivory ball and his own surgical instruments.

★ ★ ★

When Dr. Dane arrived home that evening, his little girl was waiting beside her mother at the stove, her eyes dancing. She ran to him, opening her arms, saying, "Daddy! Daddy!"

He hugged and kissed Beth Ann, then hugged and kissed Tharyn, saying that whatever they were having for supper sure smelled good.

Beth Ann helped her mother put the food on the table while Dr. Dane washed his hands at the sink.

They sat down together, held hands while Dr. Dane prayed over the food, and began eating. Dr. Dane told Tharyn about the hip replacement he would be doing in Glenwood Springs, and that he would be riding Pal and leaving at dawn tomorrow morning.

Tharyn said, "Beth Ann and I will miss you, but you must go and perform the surgery."

"I sure will miss you, Daddy," Beth Ann said. "When will you be back home?"

"If all goes well with the surgery, it'll be sometime Friday afternoon, sweetheart."

At dawn the next morning, Tharyn kissed her husband good-bye and watched him ride away on Pal.

At noon, Dr. Dane stopped for lunch in the busy town of Vail, which was surrounded by towering mountain peaks.

In the café, he overheard two local men talking at an adjacent table. He learned that nearly all the troops from Fort Junction had been sent to the Medicine Bow Mountains area to join troops from Fort Laramie to put down the Cheyenne and Shoshone uprising. The stagecoaches running between Denver and Grand Junction would not have the normal military escorts, but the army authorities believed that since the renegade Utes were now at peace with the whites, the stagecoaches should still be safe.

After lunch, Dr. Dane mounted up and continued along the road westward. After half an hour, he rode into a small unnamed settlement and dismounted in front of a blacksmith shop, where he let Pal drink from the water trough.

While Pal was slurping water, Dr. Dane noticed a wagon pull up with one of the horses limping. On the wagon seat was a young man and his wife, who was holding a small boy, who obviously had a fever.

The man hopped out of the wagon, and Dr. Dane heard him say, "Honey, I'll tell

416

the blacksmith we're in a hurry and get him to put a new shoe on immediately."

The young woman nodded. "Please tell him we need to get Tommy to the doctor as quickly as we can. This fever is getting worse."

As her husband hurried into the blacksmith shop, Dr. Dane left Pal at the water trough and drew up to the wagon. "Ma'am, pardon me, but I couldn't help but hear what you and your husband were saying. Your son has a fever?"

"Yes. We're taking him to Dr. Bill James in Wolcott. We had to stop because one of these horses just threw a shoe."

"I'm a doctor, ma'am. My name is Dane Logan, and I have the Logan Clinic in Central City. I'm on my way to Glenwood Springs to do hip replacement surgery on a lady there. Would you mind if I look at Tommy?"

"I'd be glad for you to look at him." She spoke to the boy. "Tommy, this man is a doctor. He wants to have a look at you."

Dr. Dane took the boy from his mother's arms, helped her down from the wagon seat, and carried him to the rear of the wagon. He lowered the tailgate and laid him down. The mother stepped up close to observe.

In less than half a minute, Dr. Dane looked at the mother and said, "Ma'am, Tommy has a wood tick burrowing under his skin right here in the small of his back. I need something hot to put close to the tick's head so it will back out from under the skin. I'm sure the blacksmith has a hot iron in his shop. Let's take Tommy inside."

He cradled the boy in his arms and entered the blacksmith shop with the mother on his heels.

Unbeknownst to Dr. Dane, two young men had been standing nearby, looking on, and eyeing Pal.

One said to the other, "Now's our chance, Roger."

"All right, Eddie. Let's do it."

They hurried to Pal and led him to their own horses. They mounted up, and with Roger holding Pal's reins, trotted away.

Moments later, when Dr. Dane Logan came out of the blacksmith shop to get his medical bag, he was shocked to see that Pal was gone.

He dashed back into the shop and told the parents his horse was missing, along with the medical bag. "I've got to go look for him," he said with strain in his voice. "Tell you what. Take Tommy home and wash the spot where the tick had been in strong lye soap. That'll prevent any infection."

The blacksmith spoke up. "Doctor, I have some lye soap over there at the wash basin. We'll wash the spot right here."

"Good. I have to go now."

The parents spoke their appreciation to him, and Dr. Dane hurried outside. He ran to the road and looked both directions. There was no sign of Pal.

He would just have to go on to Glenwood Springs, wire Dr. Tim to send him another ivory ball by stagecoach, and use Dr. Watson's surgical instruments. Now he needed to see if he could borrow a horse from some rancher down the road.

As he started walking westward, anger welled up in him over the theft of his horse. Pal would not have just run away.

Soon he noticed dark clouds gathering in the sky ahead of him, and a wind from the west was picking up.

After the doctor had covered a couple of miles, he heard the rattling sound of harness and wheels and the pounding of hooves behind him. He looked over his shoulder and saw a stagecoach coming with the six-up team churning up dust.

As the stage drew near, Dr. Dane waved at the driver and shotgunner. The driver drew rein, and the stage was brought to a halt.

Looking up at both men, he said, "Howdy, gentlemen. I'm Dr. Dane Logan from Central City. I was riding my horse to Glenwood Springs to perform a hip replacement surgery at the hospital there, but somebody stole my horse a few miles back. Do you have room for me? I need a ride to Glenwood Springs."

The driver grinned. "Sure, Doctor. We have five people aboard, so there's room for one more. We won't charge you anything either. Hop in."

"I'll be glad to pay you."

The driver shook his head. "It's all right. The ride's on Wells Fargo. Hop in."

Dr. Dane thanked him, climbed inside, introduced himself to the other passengers, and commented about the oncoming storm.

One of the men said, "Could be a bad one, Dr. Logan. I've seen some real bad snowstorms hit these mountains before, in early fall."

The stagecoach soon passed through the small town of Eagle. Seven miles farther down the road, it drew into the town of Gypsum. When they reached the west end of town, Dr. Dane saw a sign that told him it was now seventeen miles to Glenwood Springs.

They were some five miles west of Gypsum with the stage rolling along the narrow road with a deep canyon on their right. Suddenly the driver and shotgunner saw a band of whooping Indians coming at them on their pintos from a dense forest off to the left.

The driver hollered down to the passengers inside, as he sped up the horses. "We've got Cheyenne warriors coming after us!"

As the Indians drew near, they opened fire with their rifles.

The shotgunner raised his double-barreled shotgun to fire at the attackers. From inside, two of the male passengers began firing out the windows.

The Cheyennes swung onto the road behind the stage, and were coming up fast. Just as the shotgunner fired and blew an Indian off his horse with a 12-gauge blast, a bullet chewed through the rear of the coach and hit one of the women in the back of the head. She collapsed, and it took Dr. Dane only seconds to check on her and discover that she was dead.

Some of the galloping Indians drew up alongside the coach. The shotgunner used his second barrel to blast one of them off his pinto, but Cheyenne rifles barked. Both the shotgunner and the driver fell off the racing stagecoach, bouncing limply on the road.

Another Cheyenne bullet hit the lead horse on the right side of the harness. When the horse stumbled and fell, the other horses lost their footing. The stage careened over the edge of the road and plunged down into the canyon.

The Indians brought their horses to a halt and watched as the stage and team crashed at the bottom of the canyon, beside a swift-moving river. They looked at the shattered stage, the dead horses, and a couple of male bodies that were visible on the ground near the wreckage.

The Indians laughed and rode away.

In the bottom of the canyon, two teenage boys had been riding their horses along the bank of the river. They saw the plunging stagecoach, the screaming, pawing, falling horses, and the awful crash at the bottom.

When the boys drew up to the bloody sight, they looked at the male and female bodies inside the shattered coach, and the two men that lay on the ground next to the wreckage. They dismounted, and while they were stealing the men's wallets and the women's purses, they noticed that two of the men on the ground were breathing, though unconscious. They rode away in a hurry.

Roger and Eddie rode onto the small acreage where they lived, some five miles south of the main road. Roger was still leading the stolen horse. As they approached the cabin, Eddie cupped a hand beside his mouth and shouted to his little brother, who was watching them from a window, "Hey, Buddy, we got you a new horse!"

Fifteen-year-old Buddy came running out, while putting on his coat. When he ran up to the stolen horse, he noticed a black bag tied to the saddle. He stepped into the stirrup and swung into the saddle, telling himself he would throw the bag away later.

Pal instantly let out a shrill cry and started bucking. Buddy flew out of the saddle and landed on the ground. The horse galloped away and quickly vanished from view.

Eddie snapped his fingers as his little brother was getting up. "Oh, well, Roger and I will find you another one."

Nearly two hours had passed when Dr.

Dane Logan first became aware of the gurgling river. He heard birds chirping above the sound of the whining wind, and tried to open his eyes. The black edge of unconsciousness swirled at the edge of his mind, attempting to pull him back where he had been.

He placed a hand to his forehead, squeezed his temples with thumb and fingers, and finally was able to force his eyes open. He felt a large knot on his forehead and felt warm moisture. He looked at his hand and realized that the knot was trickling blood.

His right knee was hurting severely. He tried to sit up, and when he did, he passed out and fell back to the soft ground of the riverbank.

A short time later, he regained consciousness again, and once more, sat up. His brain started to swirl. He closed his eyes and let his mind clear.

He opened his eyes again and looked around him. A man that lay near him was unconscious, but breathing. He became aware that the heavy clouds above were lightly spitting snow, which was being swirled around by the wind.

Dr. Dane rose painfully to his feet and limped toward the wrecked stagecoach, noticing that the horses were dead. He looked inside the wreckage. Just like the horses, the men and women inside were dead.

He staggered back to the man who lay close to where he had lain, and looked down at him. The man was breathing no more.

Dr. Dane noted a small pool of water next to the river. He limped to it, and lay down to splash water on his face.

The image that was reflected back to him caused him to jerk his head. The man whose face he saw was a stranger! He moved his head slightly to make sure it was *his* reflection.

Nothing about his own reflection was familiar. How could he not know his own face?

He blinked and wet his lips with his tongue. *Who am I? What am I? Do I have a family? Where is home? Where am I right now?* He could answer none of those questions.

He reached to his left hip pocket for his wallet. It was gone. He tried the other hip pocket, and when he found it empty, he patted his coat pockets. No wallet. No identification.

He sat down on the ground and examined the painful knee. After squeezing it and bending his leg back and forth, he said aloud, "It's only a sprain. It'll heal quickly."

His pulse thudded in his ears. "How do I know that?" he asked himself aloud.

He limped back to the wreckage of the stagecoach and searched among the bodies, but every wallet and purse was gone. He went to the man who had been breathing earlier and went through his pockets. No wallet.

As snowflakes struck his face, driven by the wind, he palmed them away and said, "Dear Lord, I need Your help. I —" He gasped. "I remember I'm a born-again Christian! Jesus is my Saviour!"

Scripture verses began coming to mind. Aloud, he said to himself, "Why can I remember these Scriptures, and that I am a Christian . . . but not remember who I am or what my occupation is?"

Another Scripture came to mind. *Thy word have I hid in mine heart that I might not sin against thee.*

He shook his head. "Heart. Heart. Heart."

More Scripture scratched at his memory. *Keep thy heart with all diligence; for out of it are the issues of life.*

He shook his head again. "Heart. Heart. What is it about that word?"

Suddenly a voice that seemed familiar echoed in his head: "The heart remembers things the mind forgets."

Again, Scriptures ran through his mind: *Thy word have I hid in mine heart . . . Keep thy heart with all diligence . . .*

He tried again to remember his name.

Nothing.

Do I have a family?

Nothing.

Where is home?

Nothing.

I had to have been on that stagecoach. But I don't remember being on it.

He wiped more snowflakes from his face. "Lord, You know who I am, and You know the answers to these questions. Please help me."

Dane realized that it was snowing harder. The wind was stronger, too. He looked up toward the top of the canyon. There was what looked like a trail, winding its way to the top, but it was covered with snow.

He limped toward the trail and started climbing.

The wind-driven snow was partly blinding him, and the steep trail was slippery, but he kept struggling upward. He continued to slip and slide, and his knee burned with pain. At one point, he stopped to catch his breath, then continued to fight his way upward. After stopping to catch his breath a few more times, he looked up and saw that he was only a few feet from the top.

He summoned all his strength, and seconds later gained level ground. Rising to his feet in the snow, he ran his gaze around, and finally made out what appeared to be a road. Hunching his shoulders against the frigid wind, and wiping snow from his eyes, he began walking eastward.

After a while, he saw a sign lightly coated with snow, but he could read it. The sign told him it was five miles to Gypsum.

His heart pounded. The town's name was familiar!

Moments later, a rancher came along the road behind him and pulled up beside him. "Looks like you could use a ride, mister."

Dr. Dane smiled at him. "I sure could use a ride!"

When Dr. Dane had seated himself, the rancher said, "Where you going?"

Dr. Dane shrugged. "I don't know."

The rancher frowned. "You don't know?"

"I'll explain," Dr. Dane said, gesturing

for him to put the wagon in motion.

The rancher did so, and Dane told him about the stagecoach and the bodies at the bottom of the canyon. He pointed out the knot on his forehead, which by then was an angry shade of red, explained that his memory was gone, and said he was the only one who lived.

The rancher said, "Well, sir, my name is Jim Nelson, and I'm on my way to Vail. I'll take you to the doctor there, since there are no doctors in the small towns between here and there."

"I appreciate your kindness, Mr. Nelson."

"It'll be best, though, if we stop and let you tell the town marshal in Gypsum about the stagecoach and the bodies in the canyon."

"Yes. I need to do that."

Nelson looked at him with puzzlement. "So you don't have any idea why you were on that stage?"

"None at all. All I can say is that I'm thankful to be alive." He touched the knot on his forehead. "I must have hit my head a good lick, though."

Nelson chuckled. "I guess so."

It was getting dark and snowing even

harder when they arrived in Vail. The wind was fierce. Jim Nelson took the amnesiac to Dr. Bruce Stanton's house behind his office on Vail's Main Street, and left to keep the appointment he had in town.

Dr. Stanton took the amnesiac into his office, treated the knot and the cut on his forehead, examined his knee, and listened to his story.

Dr. Stanton told him there were many kinds of amnesia: hysterical amnesia, which was caused by some powerful emotional shock; disease-caused amnesia; selective amnesia, in which the brain blocks the memory of repugnant events; and traumatic brain injury amnesia, which is caused by a severe blow to the head.

Dr. Stanton looked at him compassionately. "This is what you have, sir."

"I see. Let me tell you something, Doctor. One thing that I do remember is Scripture."

Stanton's eyes brightened. "Scripture? The Bible."

"Yes, and I remember that Jesus Christ is my Saviour."

Stanton's eyes grew brighter yet.

"I remember these two Scriptures especially. 'Thy word have I hid in mine *heart,* that I might not sin against thee.' And

'Keep thy *heart* with all diligence; for out of it are the issues of life.' I also have a familiar voice that echoes in my head, Doctor, that says 'The heart remembers things the mind forgets.' The heart, versus the mind, Dr. Stanton."

Dr. Bruce Stanton smiled. "There definitely is a difference between the heart and the mind, my friend. I want you to know that my wife and I are born-again Christians."

Dane Logan smiled. "Well, wonderful! Doctor, will I ever get my memory back?"

"Because your eyes and speech are clear, your trauma must not have been severe. Your memory will probably come back gradually, but it could come back all at once. You must avoid exertion and get plenty of rest." Dr. Stanton paused, then said, "My wife and I will keep you in our house until it clears up and you know where your home is. I think it will only be a few days."

"Well, dear brother in Christ, I appreciate this more than I can ever tell you."

"It will be our pleasure, my brother. I'm going to take you to my pastor tomorrow. I want him to hear that with all of your loss of memory, you still remember Scripture and that you are a Christian, although you cannot remember your name, your occupation, or anything about your family or your home."

Twenty-four

It was snowing hard in Central City on Thursday morning.

At the Logan Clinic, Dr. Tim Braden left Mary Edwards in the back room to put the bottles of medicine that had come from Denver on yesterday's stagecoach in the medicine cabinet, and headed for the office.

Susan Coulter was at her desk doing paperwork when Dr. Tim came from the back room, and he was about to tell her he was going into his private office to work on some patients' files when he saw Western Union agent Charlie Holmes come in.

Snow clung to Charlie's coat and hat as he handed Dr. Tim a yellow envelope and said, "This came from Dr. Thomas Watson in Glenwood Springs. He needs a reply, so I'll wait."

Dr. Tim nodded, took the telegram out of the envelope, and read it.

Susan saw the worried look on Dr. Tim's features. "What's wrong?" she asked.

At that moment, Mary came from the back room. "Dr. Braden, I was going to ask you where I should put the bottles of wood alcohol . . . but right now I want to know why you look so upset."

Dr. Tim met her gaze. "This is a telegram from Dr. Watson in Glenwood Springs. He says Dr. Logan hasn't shown up yet, and he wants to know if he was detained in his departure by the weather. He says it's snowing hard in Glenwood Springs.

"Charlie, wire Dr. Watson back and tell him that Dr. Logan left Central City early yesterday morning. Since the snowstorm hit later in the day, it must have detained him en route. Ask him to wire us back when Dr. Logan arrives there."

When Charlie was gone, Dr. Tim went to the wall pegs and took down his hat and coat. He said to Susan and Mary, "I'll be back shortly. I must let Tharyn know that Dr. Dane hasn't arrived as yet in Glenwood Springs. Oh, and Mary . . . the wood alcohol goes in that small cabinet next to the large one."

At the Logan home, Melinda Braden was helping Tharyn clean house, as was little Beth Ann.

It was a happy trio working together. At that moment, they were in the parlor. Beth Ann was singing at the top of her lungs a song she had learned in Sunday school. Tharyn and Melinda smiled at each other, enjoying the joyful sound of the little girl's voice.

Outside, the wind was howling around the eaves of the house, and the snow was piling up rapidly. Large drifts covered the yard, and the storm showed no signs of letting up.

A bright, cheery fire crackled in the parlor's fireplace, and sumptuous aromas of bread and cinnamon rolls baking in the kitchen permeated the house. It was a happy home, filled with love and the blessings of the Lord.

At one point, while Melinda was dusting the fireplace mantel, Tharyn carried her broom across the parlor to where Beth Ann was dusting an end table, and put an arm around her shoulders. She looked into the child's dark brown eyes and smiled. "Sweetheart, I love you so much. You are God's special gift to Daddy and me."

Beth Ann turned her face upward and puckered her lips. Tharyn bent down and received the kiss on her cheek from her little girl.

"I love you so much, Mommy. And I love Daddy so much, too."

A few minutes later, Melinda and Beth Ann went to one of the first-floor bedrooms to clean, leaving Tharyn to wash the big mirror on the parlor wall. She looked at her reflection and gave herself a private smile. A special feeling of contentment filled her heart. She whispered to her reflection, "Won't Dane be surprised when he gets home and I tell him? I have a strong feeling that this baby will be a boy!"

She closed her eyes. "Please, dear Lord, let this little one be born healthy and strong."

She opened her eyes, and a small stab of fear entered her mind. She quickly shook it away. "I can't go another seven months living in fear. I must trust my heavenly Father to see that this baby is all right."

She patted her tummy and sent her love to her unborn child.

There was a knock at the front door. Beth Ann hurried from the bedroom and darted down the hall to answer it.

In the parlor, Tharyn heard the rapid footsteps and the door open. "Mommy, it's Dr. Tim. He's here to see us!"

Melinda came down the hall from the

bedroom. She and Tharyn drew up together in the foyer.

As Dr. Tim stepped in and closed the door, he ran his gaze over the three faces and told them about Dr. Watson's telegram.

Fear threaded its way into Tharyn's heart.

Beth Ann saw that her mother was disturbed by the news, and she pressed against Tharyn's skirt.

Melinda spoke up quickly. "Well, I'm sure Dane didn't make it to Glenwood Springs because of the storm. He no doubt took shelter somewhere."

"I'm sure that's it, honey," Tim said. "But Tharyn, I knew you would want to know."

"Of course. Thank you, Tim."

Tim smiled. "Don't you worry now. He'll show up there, and when Dr. Watson's next telegram arrives with that good news, I'll send Charlie here to the house with it."

Suddenly there was a knock on the door.

Dr. Tim turned around and opened it. Charlie Holmes was standing there. He was invited in, and told them he had just learned that the telegraph lines were down in the mountains west of Central City. He could not send the return wire from Dr. Tim to Dr. Watson until service was restored by the Western Union linemen.

Dr. Tim and Charlie left together.

When Tharyn closed the door behind them, Beth Ann looked up at her mother with troubled eyes. "Mommy, Daddy is all right, isn't he?"

"Of course he is, sweetheart. It's just as Aunt Melinda said a few minutes ago. Your daddy no doubt took shelter somewhere between here and Glenwood Springs."

Melinda bent down and hugged the child. "Your daddy's fine, sweetie. God is taking good care of him."

In Glenwood Springs, Dr. Thomas Watson went to the hospital where his patient lay in a room on her bed, waiting for Dr. Dane Logan to arrive and do the hip replacement. He explained that Dr. Logan had not arrived yesterday as scheduled, and was not in town yet. Dr. Logan had no doubt taken shelter from the storm somewhere in the mountains.

On Friday morning, the storm was still in progress.

Tharyn and Beth Ann sat in the parlor looking out the front window, the child on her mother's lap. The fireplace gave off welcome heat. They both were hoping that Dane had turned back, and soon would be arriving home.

Beth Ann was talking about the big hug and kiss she would give her daddy when suddenly Tharyn peered through the falling snow and stood up. As she carried Beth Ann closer to the window, the little girl said, "What is it, Mommy?"

"It's a horse coming into the yard, honey. It looks like — it *is!* It's Pal! Look! Daddy's medical bag is tied to the saddle!"

"But where's Daddy? He isn't on Pal's back."

Tharyn eased Beth Ann's feet to the floor. "I'll be right back, honey."

Quickly, Tharyn put on her coat and darted out the door, slipping and sliding some in the snow. When Pal saw her, he stopped, whinnied, and bobbed his head.

Inside, Beth Ann watched her mother move up to Pal and take hold of the reins. She hurried to the hall closet, put on her coat and a scarf, and moved through the door, closing it behind her. By the time she was off the porch, her mother was leading Pal toward the small barn and corral behind the house.

Tears flowed down Beth Ann's cheeks as

she plodded through the snow behind her mother and Pal. Something had happened to her daddy.

Their next-door neighbor, Dale Yarbro, was shoveling snow from his back porch when he saw Tharyn leading the horse toward the barn, and little Beth Ann running behind her as best she could through the snow, sobbing.

Tharyn and Pal were passing through the gate of the small corral, when Tharyn looked back as the sound of Beth Ann's sobs met her ears.

Coming up behind the child was Dale Yarbro. He picked her up, said something to her, and hurried toward Tharyn.

As Dale rushed up, he said, "Tharyn, what's wrong?"

Tharyn asked him to come inside the barn. When they were inside, Dale placed Beth Ann in her mother's arms, and while he was removing the medical bag, saddle, and bridle from Pal, Tharyn told him the story.

Dale said, "I'll go to the clinic and tell Dr. Braden that Pal has come home with Dane's medical bag still tied to the saddle. Then I'll go tell Marshal Merrell."

Tharyn thanked him, and after feeding Pal and pumping water into the trough inside the barn, she took Beth Ann back to the house.

An hour later, Tharyn and Beth Ann saw Marshal Jake Merrell riding up to the house. They met him at the door, invited him in, and they sat down together in the parlor.

"Surely Dr. Dane has found shelter somewhere to wait out the storm," said the marshal. "He must've left the horse outside of wherever he was holed up, and something spooked him. He must've galloped away, and just decided to find his way home."

Tharyn sighed. "I hope that's the way it happened."

Merrell gave her an assuring smile. "I'll put together a band of townsmen to search for your husband, Mrs. Logan. We'll head out as soon as the storm is over. It wouldn't do any good to start out now."

"I appreciate that, Marshal."

"Dr. Dane would be wise enough to seek out some kind of shelter when that storm hit. He might have gone into a cave. There are plenty of those in these mountains."

Tharyn held Beth Ann close and blinked back the tears that threatened to spill from her eyes as she gave the marshal a tenuous smile. "I'm sure you're right, Marshal, but

441

I won't draw an easy breath until I see Dane walk into this house."

"We'll find him, ma'am. Try to rest easy. The Lord is taking care of him."

Beth Ann pointed out the parlor window and said, "Mommy, here comes Pastor Shane."

They met the pastor at the door, and as he stepped inside, he told them that Dr. Tim had come to the parsonage on his way to the office to tell him about Dr. Dane.

Tharyn told him about Pal returning home earlier with the medical bag tied to the saddle.

The pastor prayed with Tharyn, Beth Ann, and the marshal, asking God to bring Dr. Dane home safely.

Time passed.

The snowstorm in the Colorado Rockies was over by Sunday, October 1. On Monday, after eating supper with Dr. and Mrs. Bruce Stanton, the amnesic man spent some time with them in the parlor. Dr. Stanton was talking about an operation he had performed recently.

"Ether doesn't work like chloroform," Stanton said. "Ether was all right when it came into use in Europe and America in the middle of this century, but the recent advent of chloroform is such a blessing."

"Oh, no, Dr. Stanton," the amnesiac said. "Chloroform has been in use in Europe for several decades. Queen Victoria was given chloroform when she gave birth to Prince Leopold in 1853."

Dr. Stanton blinked. "How do you know this?"

Dane shook his head. "I can't tell you. It just came to me."

Dr. Stanton left his overstuffed chair, went to a large bookshelf, and took down an encyclopedia. Standing there, he flipped pages while his wife and the amnesic man looked on. It took only a moment to find what he was looking for. He read a section of the page, and looked back at his guest. "I'm amazed at this. You're right, my friend. Queen Victoria was administered chloroform when she gave birth to Prince Leopold in April 1853."

Mrs. Stanton said to their guest, "You must really know your history, or you have medical knowledge. Or both."

Dane shrugged. "Wish I knew. Well, folks, I'm getting pretty tired. If you'll excuse me, I'll go to my room and bed down for the night."

Later, lying in bed, Dane pondered his

knowledge of Prince Leopold's birth.

Is my memory coming back? How else would I have been able to comment correctly on Queen Victoria? But why would I know this?

He swallowed with difficulty. "Lord, please bring my memory back completely."

In the middle of the night, Dane dreamed restlessly and woke himself up, calling out, "Tharyn! Beth Ann!"

He sat up abruptly, putting splayed fingers to his head. "Tharyn. Beth Ann."

Then, like a flash of lightning, he was riding on a train. His beautiful redheaded wife was cuddling a little girl in her arms next to him. Tharyn said to the child, "So your name is Beth Martin."

"Mm-hmm," said the little girl. "My real name is Elizabeth Ann, but everybody calls me Beth."

Suddenly there was a tap on his bedroom door. By the moonlight that flowed through the bedroom windows, he looked toward the door. "Yes?"

"Friend, are you all right? I heard you shouting." It was Dr. Stanton's voice.

"I'm fine, but please come in."

Dr. Stanton stepped into the bedroom, a lighted lantern in his hand.

From where he sat on the bed, Stanton's

guest said with a lilt in his voice, "Dr. Stanton, my name is Dane Logan! *Doctor* Dane Logan! I own a clinic in Central City. I was on my way to Glenwood Springs to perform a hip replacement for a patient of Dr. Tomas Watson."

Stanton's eyes widened. "Dr. Dane Logan! Yes, I've heard of your expertise in hip replacements!"

Smiling happily, Dr. Dane said, "My wife's name is Tharyn, and we have a little five-year-old daughter. Her name is Elizabeth Ann. My pastor's name is Mark Shane. The mayor's name in Central City is Mike Anderson, and our marshal's name is Jake Merrell! My memory's back, Doctor!"

"Praise the Lord!"

Dr. Dane's hand went to his forehead. "I've got to send a wire to Dr. Watson."

"You won't be able to do that right away. The telegraph wires have been down since late Thursday afternoon."

Dr. Dane blinked. "And this is Monday, right?"

"Yes."

"Well, I'll go on home, then, and wire Dr. Thomas as soon as the wires are back up. I . . . I don't have my wallet, Dr. Stanton. Could you lend me the money to buy a horse and tack? I'll send you the money as soon as I get home."

Dr. Stanton smiled. "I'll buy you a horse and tack as soon as the stable down the street opens. It will be my pleasure."

Dr. Dane shook his head. "I appreciate that, dear brother, but I *will* send you the money when I get home."

"Well, if you insist. I'll let my pastor know that your memory came back and that you've left Vail on your new horse."

In Central City late on Tuesday afternoon, Tharyn and Beth Ann were sitting in the parlor talking about Marshal Jake Merrell coming to see them yesterday morning to let them know he and some townsmen were about to ride out to look for Dr. Dane.

Holding the secret of her coming child inside, Tharyn pulled Beth Ann close to her and prayed in her heart, *Dear Lord, what will I do if they never find Dane? What if he's dead? I'll have two children to raise and support. I — I know I'm borrowing trouble, but it's so hard not to think the worst. Please, Lord, help me to trust You as I should, and let Your peace rule in my heart.*

Beth Ann had been listless most of the

446

day, and had clung close to her mother's side. Looking up at her mother with tears brimming in her eyes, she said with quivering lips, "Mommy, I miss my daddy. He's the only daddy I've ever had. Can't Jesus bring him home to us?"

Tharyn squeezed the precious child tightly. "Oh, baby, of course Jesus can bring Daddy home. Sweetheart, Jesus knows exactly where Daddy is, and He also knows what is best for each of us. We have to trust Him to do what is right in our lives. Let's you and me pray right now that Jesus will take care of all three of us, and especially Daddy."

Beth Ann wiped her tears on the sleeves of her dress and sniffed. "You pray out loud, Mommy. I know Jesus hears all of your prayers. You prayed for a little girl like me, and here I am."

Her childlike faith touched a deep spot in Tharyn's heart. She took Beth Ann onto her lap, held her tight, and prayed.

When she finished praying, Tharyn placed Beth Ann back on the sofa where she had been sitting earlier, and said, "Honey, I've got to go check on the roast in the oven. You stay here. I'll be back in a few minutes."

Beth Ann had one of her dolls beside her

on the sofa. She picked the doll up and walked to the parlor window.

The sun was shining, and the snow on the ground was melting.

Suddenly Beth Ann saw a rider come down the street and turn his horse into the yard.

From the kitchen, Tharyn heard Beth Ann calling, "Mommy! Mommy! It's Daddy! Daddy's home!"

Tharyn ran down the hall, shedding tears, and whispered, "Thank You, Lord! Oh, thank You!"

When she reached the door, Beth Ann had it already open.

Tharyn dashed past her onto the porch as Dane was coming up the steps, limping slightly. Beth Ann was quickly on her heels.

"Dane! Oh, Dane, darling!" Tharyn cried.

"Daddy! Daddy!"

Dr. Dane Logan blinked at his own tears and gathered them both in his arms.